C000081567

SPECTRUM

SHORT STORIES OF SCIENCE FICTION, THE UNUSUAL AND THE UNPREDICTABLE

MICHAEL DUDA

MICHAEL\DUDA

SPECTRUM

For humanity. For in our hearts, we truly are unusual and unpredictable.

CONTENTS

EDGE OF TWILIGHT

PAPERS CLUTTERED the small table space allotted to Dr. Kelvin Gardwin. Kelvin shifted in his seat, trying not to accidentally push anything off onto the floor. It had taken hours to put the paperwork together and the effort seemed pointless. Perhaps he should be grateful that the security team even offered him the small amount of table real estate allotted to him. They didn't consider him key personnel and this did not surprise the technobiologist.

But if they were honest with themselves, they would do away with the language used to couch their fears—protocols for perimeter defenses, evacuation procedures and vapor pump activation sequencing. All of it boiled down to fear. If the Harvesters were capable of ingesting entire terraformed planets in days, perhaps they were the superior species. It would be a biological inevitability.

He cleared his throat and now waited. Dr. Loraine Jasmer continued to remain silent. The only other member from the biotech lab, she had offered no support during the discussions. This bothered Kelvin in more than one way.

"Does the programmed Erinnyes virus match Colony Six results?" Drexx Belford, the security team lead, asked.

"We don't know exactly what Dr. Marloy had produced. I have guesses but I refuse to speculate on paper," Kelvin replied.

"Your report doesn't describe your lab results."

"I exercised prudence. During the last several tests, the rats turned on each other. They became cannibals. Programming an intelligent virus is still relatively new ground for us. No point in raising alarms."

But his statement had already raised alarm. The engineers' wide eyes indicated that the point made had hit the mark—raw fear much like he had seen in the lab rats' eyes.

Security members at the table remained stone-faced. Colony Five's security team populated the chairs at the other end, surrounding their leader like a protective wall. Hands folded and closed in front, they looked on at Drexx Belford as a stone wall might fawn over a bricklayer. Drexx tapped a pen on an empty notepad as he reread the lab's conclusion.

Drexx looked over at Loraine. "And what about the bio-toxin?"

"It will be ready by the time the Harvester troopship arrives. Colony Six had used it with some success before they were completely ingested. But the Bleeders may have adapted. We estimate that it will only have a 30 percent success rate this time."

The Bleeders were the Harvesters shock troopers. During the meeting, security had dismissed the small stack of the alien's dissection images as being too complicated to be useful. Kelvin was of the opinion that if security couldn't shoot something, the subject held no interest for them. The response was unsurprising. But when Engineering found no value in the ingestion mechanics papers, there had been several heated arguments.

Drexx placed Kelvin's report back onto the table. The Andales system's sunlight streamed through the meeting room's windows. It highlighted a fresh coffee ring on the top page of the report. At least he had read it which is more than Kelvin could say for the rest of the security team. Then he stood up and clasped his hands behind his back. Shoulders slightly hunched, he looked like a man carrying an unbearable weight. Perhaps it was theater for the other team members. Kelvin watched him walk over to a window and stare out.

Outside the building, it was an amazing scientific and technological achievement. Colony Five's processing and administration buildings bustled with life. Further out, agriculture sectors actively worked at nurturing crops. And even further beyond, the artificial ocean Annyox fed life to the terraformed planet. In only a matter of days, a Harvester invasion force could consume it all.

"Dr. Gardwin, does anything else have meaning to you other than your science?"

"What exactly are you suggesting?" The question caught Kelvin off-guard. It felt personal, a place where he was not comfortable going to. It seemed best to answer a question with a question. "We know the Harvesters' end goal. Don't you think that Dr. Mablin Marloy did too?"

"Perhaps, but there's still hundreds of years before they reach Colony Four. Generations of study. At least we can buy them time."

"Dr. Marloy practiced good science."

Drexx slammed his hand on the table. "Seven stars, Gardwin. Colony Seven was overrun in weeks. Colony Six, in days. Her great failure was hesitation."

Loraine interrupted. "The lab cultures show that the new Erinnyes virus trigger is stable. The results could be different this time."

Kelvin struggled between his personal feelings for Loraine and a healthy need for scientific skepticism. But he had to stop this rashness before it got out of hand. "The cultures are untested. You'll be making a—"

Drexx cut him off with a wave of his hand.

"Dr. Gardwin, you are being reassigned. Dr. Jasmer will advise me from command center. You, instead, will oversee the Erinnyes virus operation near Annyox."

"Wonderful. I'll be doubly ineffective. On the front lines, only a few klicks out from the Bleeders' landing point, and operating a vapor pump that may dismantle your own defensive plan. I'm so glad you've thought this through."

"Dr. Gardwin, all of Colony Five *is* the new front lines for Earth."

Only his purely scientific interest in the Harvesters held him back from a retort. Kelvin could also play this game of tit-for-tat. If security hadn't downplayed the Harvester threat back on Earth, this situation could have been prevented years ago. He understood the games that had been played to ensure that funding for the colony projects continued without interruptions and the generous allotment given to security forces.

Hundreds of years of scientific advancement and it all culminated into a single emergency meeting. Perhaps he should have phrased everything in terms a space-aged gunslinger could understand. Humanity was the stakes at a galactic card game of survival. The only card Drexx Belford's security team wanted to play was a better weapon and, unfortunately, Kelvin hadn't been able to produce the results that they needed. He wasn't even sure if he actually ever could. At least they hadn't relegated him to sitting at some figurative version of a children's table while the important colonists did the real decision making.

He stared at Loraine but she didn't seem to notice. Last night they had fallen asleep in each other's arms as the air ventilation system brushed over their naked bodies. Now, the distance between them felt like kilometers. She nodded at Drexx, standing up to conclude the meeting in a professional manner. She packed away her notebook and walked out of the meeting room without saying a word.

Instructive 201.A: All blood type O-negatives will be designated No-Un. They shall have no name.

No-Un struggled to recall a memory that eluded her. She knew that it was important but she couldn't formulate why it was, exactly. She could barely turn her head inside the lychtosis chamber and the restraints made thinking difficult. Both purpose and fear divided her mind. It was an internal conflict, a struggle to recall a memory and a loathing for the alien monstrosity, the Bleeder, that slept next to her.

Bleeders perverted what it meant to be alive. Its ceramic-smooth face slept away the light years required to reach the next human colony for another invasion by Harvester troopship. No-Un imagined that its closed eyes dreamed of white sand beaches and lapping waves. Maybe it dreamed of a planet with water where it could bathe away its protective outer layer and flex strange, new muscle.

There would be no aging for the alien monstrosity as they travelled through space. They were biologically linked together. While the alien rested, transfusion tubes slithered out from its demanding veins. The tubes slowly fed off her body for that coming moment so that the Bleeder might rise and be strong. These privileged kings of conquered worlds could only take from others as they were biogenetically engineered to do. They sucked blood-nutrient from No-Un's withering body. Eventually she would replace the Bleeder as an exhausted husk inside the alien's someday coffin and ejected out to a dark void of vacuum.

Instructive 201.B: No-Uns should not speak. Their sole purpose is to conserve biological energies until needed.

No-Un worked her thinning lips. She had tried this before and failed each time. Her tongue twisted inside her mouth. What would she say? The restraints of the lychtosis chamber did not affect her speech. They only held her in place, ensuring that only her minimal physical needs were met. She had a source of protein and an expedient method to eliminate waste. Sensors regulated air oxygen levels and other machines monitored her blood nutrient. Somehow the chamber had kept her living on just like the Bleeder, if that's what this could be called. Yet it was the unseen force of constant motionlessness in space that had weakened her to the point of muscular atrophy.

"Erinnyes," croaked from her throat, more a whisper than a word.

The spoken word suddenly revolted her. She had set in motion a string of memories that spanned farther back than her now pathetic state of existence. Time was a planet, full of life and color, that appeared in her mind—blue and green and too bright a spectacle to imagine for long in her weakened condition.

Instructive 201.C: No-Uns shall be restrained. Their sole purpose is to conserve biological energies until needed.

An alarm triggered inside the lychtosis chamber. An

indicator softly blinked in muted color. Her failing eyes could just make out a mechanical shape approaching the chamber's membrane wall. She felt relief as a droid opened the door and crawled over. She distanced herself from the lingering memory of the blue and green planet, forcing her imagination to orbit above its gravitational pull as her function monitors were checked. To go any closer to the memory would mean pain. Then the droid administered a drug. Her mental state turned into twilight, someplace between a dull grey and an emotional horizon.

Sinking into the early stages of the drugged state, she lost the desire to care about the Bleeder's instructives. Instead, a desire for some other purpose returned to her, unhampered, a feeling that she hadn't experienced since... since when? And what purpose? How long had she merely existed inside this imprisoning chamber? She had lost track of time in any meaningful way.

The droid performed last checks on her. It emitted a synthetic smell, a lubricant, from its busy mechanical joints. No-Un had smelled the lubricant before and not just here. She had smelled it on that blue and green planet in her memory. She wanted to swallow the odor and let it live inside her body. Maybe that memory of the planet could grow and grow. And maybe she would soon remember something more.

There was a scrap of memory that persisted in her mind. Something. The administered drug inside her body resisted the memory. It offered sleep and forgetfulness. It offered pain if she resisted. It felt like hundreds of needles ran down her arms, causing her hands to twitch. Twilight turned to darkness and her vision narrowed. She didn't see the droid leave. A blissful state of mindless feeding waited if she would just give in to the drug. But the droid's scent lingered, real or imagined. And perhaps the fist she now clenched was imagined too.

———

Instructive 201.D: No-Uns shall minimize mental activity. Their sole purpose is to conserve biological energies until needed.

How long had she slept for?

This time, No-Un forced herself to visit the planet in her memory. She squinted through the effort. Pain continued down her restrained arms and legs, horrible needles that filled her body with fear. Somehow the Bleeder manipulated her nervous system through the feeder tubes. The pain radiated toward her mind where the memory of the blue and green sphere pulled her down, its gravity was irresistible now. She imagined herself spinning downward— out of control, nauseous and laughing to herself. How long *had* she fed the Bleeder since she last slept? She couldn't think of it now. An undefined regret, stronger than anything else, drove her to let go of any restraints holding her back.

No-Un was in a laboratory on the blue and green planet. The droid who had serviced her suddenly surfaced in her memory, its synthetic smell filling her nose. The busy machine crawled toward her where she stood inside a laboratory. Metal arms carried several small glass dishes with biological samples growing in them. It held one out for her. A nearby computer displayed, *Trigger Sample 1205: Final Complete?* But this was not what she wanted to see here. She must find something else inside this room so crammed full of biotechnology before the Bleeder called her back.

Outside a window, an apocalyptic scene raged—the Harvester invasion had begun. Men and women exploded into fleshy bits, ingested by hungry Bleeders as the invading kings absorbed their peon victims into their jig-sawed bodies. Some victims were captured whole. But No-Un remained calm. This past event could not compare to the ongoing horror she lived now. She must find something here in this memory. It would reveal what was taken from her when the Harvesters invaded this planet.

Instructive 201.E: Bleeders may administer new instructive when necessary.

The Bleeder interrupted her thoughts temporarily. She forced herself back into the memory. The droid patiently waited for her. She spotted something on its mechanical body and quickly approached it.

A shock of pain worse than before snapped her back into the reality of the lychtosis chamber. Her arms and legs violently shook, a new physical pain pushed beyond mere needles. Her head convulsed.

My lover needs me, sweet king of my lifeless dreams. No-Un laughed to herself bitterly. It was a gurgling throaty sound. She wondered if ice cream tasted like soured coffee and then realized that she had retched.

But not even her suffering gave the alien pause. More feeder tubes wriggled from its body. They crawled out from the Bleeder's ceramic shell, absorbing any fluids ejected onto the floor. Strangely, she admired the biological warrior's ability to adapt. It utilized every last bit of her nutrient no matter what form it took.

The Bleeder's response must have triggered the alarm again inside the lychtosis chamber. The droid returned, its synthetic smell filling the cramped space. No-Un welcomed this familiar presence, a diversion from the pain she was suffering. It busied itself with any final cleanup. And while the machine did so, the Bleeder eased off. She again felt the need to latch onto any bits of her memory. Pain and fear could never stop her desire to feel whole, to reclaim the memory that eluded her.

The droid then turned to inspect the Bleeder once more as he lay inside her someday coffin. Her eyes managed to study the back of the droid. The image was still a slight blur but No-Un could read a label. She realized that this was part of the memory she pursued all along.

Property of Colony Six, Biotechnology Department. Warning: Biohazardous. Contact Dr. Mablin Marloy immediately.

Dr. Mablin Marloy—that was her. She had a name!

A sense of being alive teased her, a small fragment of what she once was. The Harvesters hadn't devoured her identity. She had a sudden feeling of hope and it would free her mind from a nearly meaningless existence.

I am Dr. Mablin Marloy.

More Bleeder tubes moved toward her, a response too late to stop what had been set in motion. She wrestled with her mind again and another memory returned. An Erinnyes virus solution had been discovered in her lab. The solution had been incomplete but it was at least part of a solution to stopping the Harvesters' invasion.

Dr. Marloy had a sudden realization. It hadn't truly been regret that kept her hanging on for all these years in alien preservation. She had needed to complete what she had started so many years ago. Inside the cells of her body, and unknown to the Harvesters, was a key to halting future invasions. Her sacrifice would be a small thing when compared to the number of lives saved.

The computer terminal patiently waited: *Trigger Sample 3102: Destruction Begin?*

Ah, the so-called spectrum of human emotion. Kelvin hated himself for doubting himself like this in such a theological way. He was brooding over matters of right and wrong at his lab workstation. Teleology was of no interest to the scientist.

Entering the destruction code into the computer had become a game between mind and heart, an unfortunate and unnecessary position to be in. He should just enter the sample destruction code of Loraine's virus trigger sample and settle the issue. What did it matter if Drexx had him incarcerated? If anyone cared to discuss morals afterward, he could argue that he had ensured humanity's survival. Loraine's programmed virus could actually do as much harm or more as the Bleeders themselves, turning everyone into cannibals like the lab rats. Scientifically speaking, destroying the trigger sample was the right thing to do.

But he just stared at the terminal's blinking prompt. Through a window, an Andales moon cast shadows over the workstation. Minutes passed and still he sat motionless. He couldn't act. His personal connection with Loraine held him back. They enjoyed an intimacy together for the past few months that went beyond work. By destroying the code, he would break the bonds of trust between them. With Loraine, those bonds of trust had come together so easily. Destroying her work would put an end to it.

The door behind him opened. Kelvin didn't need to turn around to know who approached.

"I told Drexx that an escort wouldn't be necessary." Loraine sat down next to him on another high-backed stool, only inches away. It felt like a distance of klicks.

"Is the better side of restraint somewhere in the pages of

a security training manual? Impressive. I've needed a light read to help me sleep."

"Look, I don't much care for him either. But under the circumstances, maybe you misunderstand his intentions."

"I've seen the way he looks at you now—me at the front lines and you between his sheets. Too bad he won't live long enough to fully exploit this situation."

Kelvin suddenly regretted saying that. Sometimes he expressed his thoughts with too much precision.

Loraine didn't react with anger. She just looked at him, her calm grey eyes steady. "Why don't you give me some credit. This was my decision, not his. What I want is for you to trust my research."

She continued to look at him, demonstrating a firm resolve. Perhaps this was what he had found so attractive in her to begin with. But it still puzzled him that another scientist had sided with security. And despite her firm belief in her work, there were questions of test results that were still left unanswered.

"Loraine, I need to see results. I see nothing to convince me."

"You know who's work my research is based on."

"Dr. Marloy injected herself with a virus she programmed and still the Bleeders are coming for us."

She took his hand in hers, the touch warm and soft. He gladly returned her touch but it still wasn't enough to fully defrost the circumstance. "Dr. Marloy developed what she believed to be a solution. She believed that her Erinnyes trigger would work but it would take time. Or that it needed a second programmed strain."

"She panicked when the Harvesters attacked. She was desperate," Kelvin said.

"She had good data. I've studied her last transmissions over and over."

"I've never been able to makes sense of it. Her final message was cryptic."

"It could be a clue."

"*At the edge of twilight, I stand between two worlds unknown.* That's an epitaph, not science."

"I choose to follow her path where you do not. She believed in something."

Kelvin nearly coughed out a laugh. "Believe? We know that genomes reached their informational content millions of years ago. It's merely substituting new complexity for old. The Bleeders just somehow seem to manage the substitution faster than we understand. It takes time to realize that kind of knowledge and Colony Five doesn't have it."

Loraine let go of his hand. Kelvin suddenly ached for her touch.

"Kelvin, it means taking chances, advancing with risk. Maybe, even, hope."

"I prefer to trust in science."

"And what if there was more at stake than just science?" Loraine dropped her steady gaze and suddenly blushed. It was uncharacteristic of her. "What if there was someone else who was at stake?"

The memory of the last several intimate weeks together brought Kelvin a realization. "You're...you're pregnant."

"We're pregnant. I wasn't even sure I would keep it."

"Drexx knew?"

"I only told him first because of the circumstances. He's just trying to protect me. Old fashioned chivalry, I know, but he can't help his security training instincts."

Kelvin couldn't find the right words to say. Loraine moved his hand to her belly.

"Touch your child," she said.

He felt the slight curvature of Loraine and imagined a heartbeat that was too soon to be actually detected. At the palm of his hand was a contradiction. This new life desperately wanted to come into the world even if it would be destroyed. It would need protection and care. And yet it could someday continue the human race. This someday child embodied the definition of growing hope.

Kelvin experienced joy and sorrow at the same time. He collected himself. "This complicates things. You know that."

"Kelvin, sometimes there is more to life than just science."

She got up. His eyes followed her to the door. He felt alone.

"Since you two are such good friends now, did Drexx say anything to you about the Earth troopship?" Kelvin said.

"Ha, ha. But it's no joke. It can't get here in time. Earth forces have decided to establish a base at Colony Four."

"Funny how they had assured everyone on Earth that there was no threat. Now they come late to our ingestion party."

"Then I'll tell Drexx you won't destroy the sample?"

"Maybe you should question your own beliefs."

Loraine smiled. Kelvin hadn't really intended his last comment to be a joke, either, but he at least felt reconnected with her as she left the lab.

His mind turned to Dr. Mablin Marloy. It was presumed that she had been destroyed so many years ago when the Harvesters invaded Colony Six. By injecting herself, had she really accomplished anything? It didn't seem possible. He had ignored her work, choosing to study new viral triggers.

And how could Loraine's new programmed Erinnyes strain be another piece of the Dr. Marloy's puzzle? Sure, Loraine had put in the time and research into studying the new trigger. He'd seen her dedication in the lab, sometimes late into the night. It could just be another fated result no better than Dr. Marloy's. Or maybe it was something worse.

Destruction Begin? The computer terminal still waited for his response.

━━━

Dr. Mablin Marloy readied herself for ingestion. It was due her.

She had traveled light years inside a lychtosis chamber, kept alive by a mostly parasitic relationship. The Harvester invasion would begin tomorrow. The Bleeder communicated this final instructive, perhaps meant to torment her for disobeying so many times. Then there would be her death and she would be turned into more organic material that made up the alien's composite body.

She smiled to herself, the gesture weak but satisfying. *I stand between two worlds unknown.*

She carried inside herself humanity, vivid and alive, like sunrises over Colony Six. They were the men and women that had worked each day to provide better futures for those back on Earth. Each one their own microcosm and all part of something greater. And then came the Bleeder attack, a sunset that had swallowed them all.

Yet still they lived on through her. Their voices would be heard.

The Erinnyes virus also thrived inside her, triggered by her own body. There never would be a laboratory-created solution that could stop the Bleeders. She had discovered this in her work but she never had time to fully test the results.

A natural virus was an infectious agent that attacked its host. An artificially created one could potentially act differently. When programmed with a trigger, it was instructed to only replicate within cells of alien origin. In essence, it protected humans from invading life forms at a microscopic level. But her lab manufactured triggers had never properly activated the Erinnyes virus. Too late, she knew that she had to inject herself and become an organic laboratory. Morally questionable, perhaps, but two artificial biologicals did not make a right.

The real test was now.

Now her experiment would continue beyond her own mortality. She shared her fluids with the Bleeder. This meant that she also shared the virus. It was now as much a part of the alien lifeform as it was her. Perhaps it was also the reason she had been able to resist its total control for so long. But that time had come to an end.

Whatever biological components made up the Bleeder, the human side infecting the alien still did not dominate. Alien tubes writhed and grasped at her dying body. A hard suction pulled at internals.

Take me, conquering king, for I have a gift that shall pierce your armor.

Something faintly lingered as Dr. Marloy faded away. One last emotion burned, a cinder of dark light. Would her Errinyes strain actually work? Was this sunrise? Or sunset?

At the very edge of her own sunset, the scientist had crossed an unknown biological frontier. She knew that she would never learn of the results.

A tower stood half in shadow.

The Bleeder understood this to be a dream state. It had had many, a way to occupy one of its cognitive clusters while travelling the long years by troopship. During lychtosis sleep, the ongoing desire to feel "whole" manifested itself in the form of solving puzzles. It was a sort of game. Genetic codes appeared in the biological construct's sleep as imagined shapes. The results were then uploaded to the Harvester database for further analysis. It manipulated codes until a possible solution formed, a DNA sequence that would finally satisfy a never-ending craving to evolve beyond its current incomplete state of being.

But the brick tower looming just ahead displayed no puzzles on its cylindrical surface. The mental construct could not be altered or entered. It stood at least six meters high—unmovable and impenetrable. A heavy wood door strapped together by iron bands barred entrance. The Bleeder could see a keyhole but it had no key to gain entry. The archaic structure, itself, was a puzzle to be solved.

The Bleeder extended feeders to detect the origins of the building. Organic materials were sensed around the locking mechanism—human. The animal cells and other ingested lifeforms that partially made up the Bleeder's body retreated from the construct. These other fleshy components refused to further investigate what might be inside.

Human biological integrations urged the Bleeder to act. *Find the key. Inside is what you finally seek.* The small voice seemed to be slowly growing.

The Bleeder contemplated the lock but took no further action. It would wait by the door. It was time to wake and there would be more biological materials to ingest for its puzzle quest. Even so, a part of its thought process would remain in this particular cognitive cluster, working at a solution.

The small human voice cried out to be listened to. The Bleeder listened and then refuted it, probing the door once more with its feeders. The key was near.

━━━

A beautiful sun rose high above the golden shore of Annyox. If it wasn't for a large security force, hundreds of projectile rifles at the ready and Kelvin being stationed behind erected barricades, this might be a perfect Saturday morning.

As the Bleeders dropped into the terraformed ocean, he could hear a distant splash. Hundreds, maybe thousands, of the aliens plummeted down from the Harvester's troopship that hovered in the sky above. The large space vehicle moved to partially block out the sun.

The sight evoked both awe and fear in the security team and they grew silent. Shards of light gleamed off the invaders black ceramic shells. Somehow they managed to fall feet first through atmosphere and submerge into the cooling blue waters below. With a gravitational acceleration of just something slightly less than Earth's, the scientist admired the aliens' bold landing technique.

After the last alien made its drop, nothing happened for several minutes.

Security officer Dennis Allstot nervously peered northeast through a pair of digital binoculars, constantly adjusting focus. Kelvin noted that his large hands trembled slightly. He must have missed the training on how to remain confident before a genocide.

"Doc, they say the bio-toxin doesn't work," Allstot said.

"Dr. Jasmer adjusted the formula."

"Yeah, well, we're out here and up close. Too close. It better work."

"Detect anything?"

"The sensors still solid on the beach-side dispensers. Nothing activated yet."

While submerged, the Bleeders would break out of their protective shells. It was the early stages of adapting to their surroundings. They collected water over their softer internal biology to form something like a plasma membrane. Filaments gathered calcium and other materials to create a skin-like shell as they worked their way to surface. The invaders almost seemed fragile and helpless, a deception that Colony Five could not afford to believe.

"I see them! I see them!" Allstot pointed ahead.

Kelvin raised his own binoculars to his eyes. Dozens of the seven foot aliens propelled themselves onto the white sandy beach. Bits of organic matter filled out their hands and legs, all wrapped in bundles of chorded neural fibers. From what dissection reports had revealed, multiple cognition clusters controlled these extremities independently. The Bleeders were a fleshy jigsaw puzzle of various life forms ingested over the years. Grotesque, certainly, but Doctor Frankenstein of old would have been proud of the beauty of their fluid motions.

The Bleeders began collecting weapons from crates that were dropping from above. Several bio-toxin sensors blinked and then a cloud of gas covered the wave of invaders. Bleeders fell, twitched and stopped moving. Others slowed down and looked confused. The security team cheered, an unfounded optimism. If they had bothered to fully read the reports, they'd know that it was only a matter of time before the aliens adapted.

A second wave of aliens appeared from the ocean. Tentacle feeders extended from their core bodies and began ingesting the Bleeders that fell victim to the bio-toxin. Those that had been stunned were cut up while still alive. Then the new Bleeder formation advanced, now immune to the continuing stream of bio-toxin.

Allstot yelled at his team members to check their guns.

"The second line of dispensers has a second adjustment to the toxin. We were expecting this," Kelvin said.

"Yeah, well, they've got some sort of handheld microwave gun. Close enough and they cook us from the inside."

There was a grand irony at play here. Kelvin might soon be turned into a Bleeder's hamburger patty. His stomach turned and he felt sick. His mood only slightly less soured knowing that he may give the aliens a bad case of indigestion.

But he did have an alternative.

He held in his pocket an injector tube containing Loraine's programmed virus. All Kelvin had to do was insert the cylinder into the nearby vapor pump and activate the machine at the right time. The pump would fill the air and cover both the assaulting Bleeders *and* the security team. They stood tensed behind their barricades, hands gripping projectile rifles and ready to fire at a commanding word. Kelvin still wrestled with the science of it all. He wondered how long before they turned those large guns on each other.

At least Loraine was temporarily safe some 30 klicks back at the command compound. While she observed the front lines from remote displays, Kelvin may soon perform a live experiment in the testing of one's faith in blind scientific application. Not that he wasn't glad that she was away from danger. He was. But at the pace the Bleeders adapted to a second round of bio-toxin attacks, both himself and Loraine would soon become ingested and part of the invading force.

The nearby vapor pump blinked, ready for the newly programmed Erinnyes strain. The scientist considered other ways he might stop the Bleeders. Nothing came to mind.

"Dammit, the altered bio-tox didn't stop any of the second wave," Allstot said.

"I have more good news. A third wave has emerged."

"Why didn't we shoot them on the beach? They were weakest there."

"Colony Six tried that. They just split like amoebas. Made things even worse. The bio-toxin is still our best bet."

Allstot pointed at the vapor pump. "That's going to be our best bet. Use that injector tube now before we're overrun."

"Don't count your microbes before they ferment. I don't tell you how to do your job."

Allstot shot him a sharp look and said nothing. He left to check on some nearby team members.

At the edge of twilight, I stand between two worlds unknown. Dr. Marloy's final words were strange and haunting and somehow more poignant now.

Perhaps the scientist's sanity had splintered at the last minute, a nuclear fission inside the thermal chamber of an overheated mind. That kind of math didn't add up. Even at her final transmission, she appeared calm and rational. Maybe Loraine was right—the deceased scientist have given them a clue. If so, what was it? Perhaps—

Allstot came huffing back. "Doc, get that vapor pump going. They'll fry us. Those things actually run."

What the security leader missed was that the Bleeders had adapted again. They spread out, charging the barricades. A few projectile guns fired, most likely started by a nervous security team member. The shots had little effect. One alien lost a limb but continued on. This triggered a response from the other Bleeders. They held out archaic looking boxes that Allstot had guessed were a microwave weapon.

But the weapon could do more.

Globs of yellow mass shot out with a chunking thud. It lobbed over some of the barricades and splattered onto several grey-suited men and women. Their body armor had been designed for projectiles and some beam weapons, not chemical attacks. Kelvin could smell a cloying odor similar to rat poison. The aliens had turned the colony's bio-toxin onto the defenders. Security team members dropped and twitched. Some stood paralyzed, wearing wide-eyed expressions of something like a terrified animal trapped in a corner. The humans had become rodents scheduled for extermination.

I am at the edge of twilight.

Kelvin toyed with injector tube in his pocket and watched the world fall apart around him in slow motion. Could twilight stand between this world and the next, whatever that may be. Or was it inside a vapor pump? Dr. Marloy had injected herself for a reason.

It could be safer. Teeny, tiny worlds. Teeny, tiny babies. Big, big problems. Big.

He decided that he wasn't making much sense. He struggled to move his hands. Allstot shouted a command. Projectile guns thundered. Kelvin had to act now.

Kelvin didn't feel regret for not having destroyed Loraine's trigger sample that night in the lab. It was just the frustration of now not seeing this work come to some kind of satisfying conclusion.

Dr. Loraine Jasmer watched the video transmissions coming in on overhead displays. The Annyox perimeter was chaos. Drexx announced that the Bleeders breached the barricades at left flank but the brave men and women at the front still held the line. A grey-suited radio operator shot him a disbelieving side glance but said nothing. Like her, Drexx's morale booster seemed to have had little effect. If everything was under control, why were all personnel in the Command Center wearing body armor including herself?

Drexx stood erect and looked calm. She had to wonder what was going on underneath his veneer of bravado. To her knowledge, he had never actually managed a full-out combat scenario. His secretary broke confidentiality, once, and told her that years ago that he had failed to qualify for Earth military command school. Now he had become Captain of Company Disaster.

She wrestled with her doubts. Under the circumstances, it was difficult to be optimistic. Some of the displays showed men and women stunned and vomiting on themselves. Drexx didn't seem to notice any of that. Others were cut up and ingested by feeder tubes extending from the Bleeders' bodies. Loraine couldn't watch the microwaved victims without turning queasy.

More reports came in. The right flank had fallen and the team was at risk of being pinched—not good news.

"Dr. Jasmer, where's my telemetry report?" Drexx said.

She checked her display. Kelvin hadn't activated the vapor pump yet. "I'm not sure what's going on at the moment. The pump is operational but still waiting for the injector tube."

"I had hoped that seeing the Bleeders up close would

alter his perspective about them. I was wrong. He's suicidal."

Suicidal was definitely the wrong word choice. Over the last few months, she had gotten to know who Kelvin really was. He demonstrated an aptitude for viral programming and the Erinnyes project that hadn't been witnessed since Dr. Mablin Marloy. And his dedication to the lab work seem unflinching. These qualities initially attracted her.

But there was something distant about him. He could easily put aside any emotional dilemmas for the pure pursuit of research. If it meant choosing between caring for another's well-being or advancing scientific pursuits, she felt sure that the scientist would consider a human being nothing more than another biological sample grown inside a petri dish. Maybe she was wrong. She hoped so. But Dr. Kelvin Gardwin was, in a strange way, almost inhuman himself. Over time his alien-like personality had made her feel cold toward him. If it hadn't been for the pregnancy, she would have broken off the relationship.

She had to believe in him now. He had, after all, chosen not to destroy her trigger sample and that gave her hope that maybe there was something more to Kelvin than she first thought.

"I know he's narrow-minded at times, but he'll come through." Loraine managed to keep calm and steady.

"I've never understood what you see in him."

"You know that he's concerned about the possible side effects of the trigger sample."

"Oh? Maybe you're not so confident in your own lab results."

"I'm not going to use the red-button option, if that's what you mean. I won't activate the third bio-toxin formula."

"Dr. Jasmer, you are forgetting your role."

Perhaps he had been jealous, but Kelvin had been partially right about Drexx. He pursued her several times and she had always turned him down. The age difference was too much. She was 32 and he was going on retirement. But that had never stopped Drexx from taking pokes at Kelvin behind his back, saying, "He couldn't spot a nebulon star unless it existed under an electron microscope." Perhaps that was true except that she had gone too far in her relationship with Kelvin to turn her back on him now.

"A third formulation of bio-toxin will kill everything in the area. It's scorched earth."

Drexx marched over and pulled her aside.

"I can't afford a panic here. I'm responsible for the life of thousands of people. If those invaders make it to Earth, millions."

"And there's no guarantee the Bleeders still won't adapt to it."

"I can override you. I'm just doing you a courtesy. And him,"Drexx said pointing back at the displays.

"He's got a first name. It's Kelvin."

Drexx tightened his grip on her arm. "He may already be dead. More is at stake here than your emotions."

"Take a look at the displays. Does that look like you have anything under control?"

Drexx gave her a hard stare and released her arm.

"Officer Blant, replace Dr. Jasmer at her post. Engage emergency counter measures at my command."

The younger man gave Loraine a sheepish smile as if to apologize. Loraine wanted to tell him to jet off. But she couldn't blame the officer for doing his job. She stepped aside and calculated sabotage options. Nothing came to mind that wouldn't cause an outbreak of violence to restrain her.

On the displays, the Bleeders had pushed in toward the center of the defensive perimeter. Some of the security team engaged in hand combat. They were being overwhelmed. Suddenly, Kelvin came into view. He was grinning as if he didn't have a care in the world. The unexpected expression startled her, and in a strange way, made her see another side of him. She could also see the still unused injector tube in his right hand. One of the Bleeders approached him, its feeder tubes extending out.

"He's injecting himself with the viral trigger. What in seven stars does he think he's doing?" Drexx was shouting at her.

"Officer Blant, don't do it. Please wait," Loraine pleaded.

"They're getting wiped out!" someone else yelled.

Officer Blant looked over at Drexx. Drexx slammed his fist down on the center console. Blant looked confused and unsure of what to do. He raised his hand over the bio-toxin remote dispenser controls.

He's going to activate the red-button option, Loraine thought. She considered making a grab for his holstered handgun.

⸻

The key is here.

In one of the Bleeder's cognitive clusters, it watched a shadow continue to grow over the archaic tower. The darkness wrapped across the lighter half of the structure as if to blanket it. Then the blackness spread out to some part beyond the alien's contemplation and questioning. The shadow covered all of what the cluster could see.

Inside is what you seek, what you need, the small human voice spoke.

The Bleeder watched an etching take shape with an illuminated glow around the keyhole. It was in the form of a human man. He seemed to hold his arms out in a welcoming gesture.

Take the key.

Ahead, one of the Bleeder's other clusters identified something on the battlefield. Its vision seemed to have narrowed, allowing it to see one thing only—a man just like the one etched on the tower's locking mechanism.

<hr>

"Dammit, Doc, you'll commit suicide."

Kelvin ignored Allstot. Dr. Mablin Marloy's final words crowded out his thoughts again—*At the edge of twilight, I stand between two worlds unknown.*

Arms held open, he now stood before the Bleeder as it approached. He had experienced an epiphany that could only be realized under extreme duress. And what could be more frightful than facing your own death? What Dr. Marloy had realized so many years ago when she had injected herself with her own lab work was that *she* had become a triggered virus. For the programmed virus to replicate itself within non-human cells, it must first identify the genetic material of what was truly human. Only then could it infect other biological forms.

But her efforts hadn't been enough to stop the invasions. Whatever Dr. Marloy had infected the Bleeders with, it only partly altered the invader that stood before him. It would require a second dosage, an infectious agent that would attack the human parts that already swam around inside the alien. Dr. Marloy's human-like virus would appear to be virion to what had now been injected into Kelvin's body. It was one human-like virus attacking another to complete the destructive process, two wrongs somehow making a right. He could already feel his own injection acting on his body. Loraine's programmed strain was aggressive and fast, faster than the Bleeder's ability to adapt. Granted, he was nauseous and his vision blurred. A pain hammered in his head. But injecting himself had been the only solution.

Kelvin stumbled forward toward the Bleeder. Behind him, Allstot cursed and fired his handgun at it.

The loud sound made Kelvin's ears ring, the headache vanishing temporarily. The Bleeder raised its arm and returned fire with its box-like weapon. A warm splatter covered Kelvin. He could hear a gurgling sound. He thought of the fountain in front of the admin building. It was a beautiful blue. What covered him was not.

"You'll soon discover that our species has a terrible time of agreeing on anything. I think I'll miss them." It was all Kelvin could think to say to the Bleeder as it loomed over him.

The two stood, face to alien. There was much to admire about the towering Bleeder. Human and animal eyes covered its face in all directions, embedded at 360 degrees around the fleshy pink surface. It could never be taken by surprise by an exterior force. The eyes studied him, rapidly scanning up and down as if *he* was the experiment. Kelvin didn't doubt that what stood before him was intelligent. But in its jig-sawed form, a creation of so many different biological parts and organisms, it also looked somehow incomplete.

Kelvin's body trembled. The nausea was worse and his headache returned. But thoughts of Loraine's calm grey eyes overcame any physical pain. If he was right in what he was about to do, she could bring up her child in safety. This was the least he could do for her.

Or did he actually do this for science? That would be a selfish act, really. So hard to say. Well, it was too late now.

━━

On a Command Center display, Loraine watched the Bleeder ingest Kelvin into its body. It happened so quickly that all she could say was, "Oh."

The young Officer Blant excitedly pointed at the displays. "The Bleeders have stopped moving! Moons and garnet! They've stopped attacking!" He pulled his hand away from the remote dispenser controls, obviously relieved.

Other invading aliens had gathered around what had become of Kelvin. Their feeder tubes wrapped around him as if to caress a long lost relative. The remainders of the front-line security team gawked at the bizarre spectacle, their projectile guns lowered.

Kelvin had become half human and half...half monster.

Everyone in the command center cheered because the invasion had just ended. They shouted praises for Kelvin. Because of all the noise, they couldn't hear Loraine scream.

━━

The Harvester troopship had cleared the sky, the invaders deciding they had lost the battle. Loraine's security transport hovered up to what remained of the front line's perimeter. The bright sun fully reflected off the steel barricades. Many had been twisted or pushed aside like cardboard boxes. There were a large number of human casualties and a few Bleeders among the body count. Despite the pungent smell of ozone and the reek of cooked flesh, the battle really was over. The remainder of the Bleeders stood still, docile and seeming to wait for something.

Loraine got out and spotted the thing that had once been Kelvin. Drexx cautioned her but she sensed no threat from the hybrid alien lifeform. Slowly, she approached.

Kelvin was encased in a clear gel-like substance that served as an outer skin. Still appearing to be preserved as a whole, his five feet and ten inch frame didn't completely fill out the Bleeder's larger structure. Other organic matter flowed around him and the outer skin expanded and contracted in a steady breathing motion. As the Bleeder-Kelvin's body expanded like the mechanical actions of a lung, Kelvin's body pulled apart only to be pieced together again by internal nerve bundles at contraction. Kelvin's eyes scanned over her with cold calculation. They never blinked and indicated no personal connection to her.

"We are Some-Un," Kelvin said.

The word had been pronounced as *someone*, a peculiar choice to describe itself. A child may steal another's toy and call it, "mine," and this impressed upon Loraine in the same way. Something like a mouth formed at the surface of the Bleeder's head. Loraine waited and hoped to at least hear her name. When it finally spoke again, the words vibrated out in a rasping tenor, nothing like the voice she had once known so well.

"Do you recognize me?" she asked.

Bleeder-Kelvin extended several feeder tubes. Drexx cried out in alarm and tried to pull her back. But she sensed no danger.

Loraine held out her hand to Drexx to show him that she was okay.

"He's having trouble communicating."

Loraine wasn't completely sure that this was true but she had to risk it. If part of Kelvin was still inside the Bleeder, she may learn more about the Harvesters than anyone else had ever discovered. A single feeder tube moved to her arm and she rolled up her lab coat's sleeve, offering her bare skin to it. The tube felt soft and warm and it seemed to touch her with familiarity.

"Kelvin, do you remember Dr. Marloy's final words—*At the edge of twilight, I stand between two worlds unknown?*"

The feeder tube responded, tightening its fleshy mass around her wrist like a rope. It held her arm locked in place. A fine, sharp tip formed and pushed into her brachial artery, stinging temporarily. Drexx started shouting. Again, Loraine held up her other hand to show that she was okay.

She could feel her blood passing back and forth between the alien and herself. But it was more than that. There was an ebb and flow of language that went beyond the need for vibrating an air medium as with speech. Through the rapid movements of their shared fluids, she communicated a logic and understanding through a more intimate contact.

I am many things. I am one, the Bleeder-Kelvin said.

The voice pulsed inside her. Kelvin's own voice, the one she immediately recognized, was deep and soft. His voice trailed off with the echoes of many others that she didn't recognize.

"Kelvin, tell me why you did this to yourself. I need to know."

There was a pause. It felt like an eternity.

We are children of No-Un, yet not.

Images of an undiscovered solar system appeared in her mind. Loraine witnessed its creation during the gravitational collapse of a molecular cloud. A sun formed and planets orbited. One planet in particular moved in a path similar to Earth's.

There were differences, however. Due to a thicker atmosphere, the temperature was about 120 degrees Celcius. Many volcanoes erupted, churning gas and interrupting nutrients needed to form proteins and carbohydrates. Yet, she sensed that somehow an unseen intelligent life form existed here. It had survived and adapted to the harsher environment. She also sensed a great hunger. Not one that could be satisfied by consumption of food, but of one that could only be fulfilled through evolution. It was this unseen life form that she knew to be the Harvesters, the greatest of all adapters capable of even altering human technologies to their needs.

For thousands of years, our creators left us incomplete. No-Un searched for answers. Then No-Un became Some-Un and we have solved our puzzle. It replicates within, killing off what is unfinished and uniting that which is whole. It is the final adaptation. Those of us now on your Colony planet have the answer we seek. We will finally sleep. But know this, No-Un, you have been given something.

And then Loraine saw one final image. It was not an image of something that existed on the unknown planet she had seen just seconds ago. It was an image of humanity's future. The feeder tube released its hold of her arm. Bleeder-Kelvin opened his mouth. Loraine thought she could hear him gasp. Then he collapsed and so did all the other Bleeders.

Loraine watched the fluid shell around Kelvin's body break down and ooze into the soil. The alien life-support system that allowed for their last few minutes together was no more. He died with the Bleeder decomposing around him.

She began to sob.

Drexx came over but he maintained a slight distance from her. "Seven stars, Loraine, are you okay?" His voice was tense and low.

Loraine looked up and wiped at tears. As she did so, she something in Drexx's eyes—fear. Fear of what she couldn't quite say but she could guess at it. The Bleeders repre-sented an alteration in the human existence he had grown comfortable with and had nearly died for.

Kelvin's final image had shown her that humanity's future still remained uncertain. She couldn't tell Drexx what she had seen just before Kelvin died. She knew how he'd respond. She'd be quarantined for weeks, maybe even months or even years. He'd lock her away to make sure that another alien menace didn't somehow return.

Kelvin had given her a final gift. Inside her body now flowed an inactive virus. It was a new strain and it would replicate within her unborn child, altering it in ways she could not know yet. It would be undetectable until the final moments at birth. And when the child finally walked and breathed and spoke, only then would humanity begin to discover a new hybrid lifeform.

Some-Un had shown her the future. Yes, the Harvester menace would eventually return and only Loraine's child could understand how to truly stop the Harvester's final advance. This would be a new form of survival in the face of a potential extinction, even for the those who would be unwilling to accept it.

"I'm fine, Drexx." It was all she could say to him.

Drexx looked her over. "You sure? Anything feel different?"

Again, his fear flashed in his eyes. Loraine sensed something primal and ancient about it. The emotion was maybe as old as when *Acanthostega,* an extinct amphibian, first cautiously came onto land.

She paused for a moment. Instinctively, her hand touched her belly.

"No, nothing has changed at all."

STARS IN THE WINTER SKY

GINA HALF-HEARTEDLY SIPPED at her Saturday morning coffee and looked out of Anna's kitchen window. The January sky was grey and it painted snow-covered Lodgepole pines in a dull light.

"Fee, fi, fo, glum, I see the possibility of sleet in this winter humdrum," Gina said with another sip of her coffee.

"You're so gloomy. What about making snowmen?" Anna said.

Her new friend set a plate of warm, petite cinnamon rolls on the table before sitting down. Gina had just started a diet but now her stomach protested with a hungry growl. Eating low carb wasn't much fun. But her breakup with Todd hadn't been fun, either. She willed herself to stay strong.

Gina eyed the tasty looking rolls a second time, argued with herself, and then looked away. "Too cold to make snowmen. I'm hot blooded by nature."

Anna said nothing but Gina knew she hadn't convinced her.

Ever since Todd broke off the engagement, her fiery

spirit had dampened. During Anna's sizzling bacon and egg breakfast, Gina insisted that she was over that cheating jerk. She kept staring in her coffee cup while she had said it. Her bacon had turned cold and greasy, the egg yolk sticky.

Anna sighed and cleaned up the plates without another word. Then she returned to the table. "Well, Bah Humbug. What do you want to do today? We can't stare at this plate of rolls all day."

Anna snatched a roll off the plate and took a large bite, washing it down with a gulp of black coffee. She looked pleased with herself as she wiped away a few crumbs. Gina didn't know how she kept such a great figure. It was probably all the hiking she did in her backyard—if it could be called that. The woods spanned for 150 acres, butting up against the Colorado side of the Rocky Mountains.

"How about a nice fireplace and some scary stories instead? I've got one about how Todd forgets to brush his teeth."

Anna snorted out a laugh. "Cute. But you've got to quit thinking about him."

"I can't help it. It's not the same at night. When he would fall asleep, his breathing was slow and steady like an ocean wave. It always comforted me."

Gina had moved from Clearwater, Florida. There, she had the love and friendship of her two sisters and her mother. Whenever Gina felt a little down, the four of them would take a trip to the beach. While under a warm sun and sitting on golden sand, she could share any problem she had with her family and, in turn, she would receive encouragement and support.

Then Todd, her now ex-fiancé, graduated from medical school. The small ski-town of Spring's Peak, Colorado needed a doctor. So Gina followed, all alone except for

Todd in a cold-winter tourist trap. She made future plans for a wedding at the Justice of the Peace to keep herself from missing the beach trips. She saved money and planned to fly her sisters and mother up at a later date for a small reception—Todd had a lot of student loans and they took priority over the cost of airline tickets and catered events. Sacrifices had to be made or so Todd would always remind her. She never had the reception or flew her family up for a visit. Apparently sacrifices only had to be made on one side of the relationship—her side. Young doctors and rich, older snow bunnies had no problem living it up at her winter home.

Anna snapped her fingers loudly. Gina jerked up in her seat, startled by the sudden noise.

Anna smiled having gotten some attention. "My grandfather did tell me a story once. It's about the woods behind my house," Anna said.

"And?"

"It's kind of spooky. Are you sure you want to hear it?"

Gina considered the delicious looking cinnamon rolls again. "Sure. Anything to keep me away from those belly bombs."

Anna's voice dropped into a low register. "Okay, then listen up." Gina found herself leaning in to better hear. "In the early 20th century, there were a group of people who called themselves *Winter Revelers*. Every January they came out to these woods to celebrate all things snow and ice. Supposedly they would build elaborate ice sculptures and host nightly celebrations. This would go on for a week."

Gina swallowed a gulp of her coffee. "That's not so spooky."

Anna dropped her voice even lower, just above a whisper. "One winter they never came back out of the woods.

None of the Revelers except for an old man and a young girl."

"You're making this up." Now Gina was nearly whispering.

"No. Their headstones are at the Spring's Peak historical cemetery park."

"I don't believe it. A mother wouldn't let her child go off with the Revelers for a whole week in the woods."

"That's just it. Her mother *was* a Reveler. They somehow got separated."

"Okay. So why didn't the old man tell anyone what happened?"

"The people in the town tried to find out. The old man died soon after he returned. And the young girl was so traumatized that she wouldn't speak. Two years later, she also died. As silent as a grave."

Anna put an emphasis on the word *grave,* almost croaking out the word.

A shiver ran down Gina's back. "That is spooky."

Anna grinned. The toothy smile was so wide and bright, the kitchen suddenly felt warm again. Then her friend jumped up. She spread her arms out as if to embrace the cabin's pine ceiling. A smidge of icing was on her cheek.

"This day gets even better. We're going to carve a new trail out back. We're going to look for the Winter Revelers."

Gina should have guessed that Anna's story was leading up to something. She appreciated her friend's gesture to keep her thoughts away from Todd. But the idea of tracking through two inches of cold and damp powder wasn't exactly the way she wanted to spend a late morning. And looking for dead people in the woods creeped her out.

"Such fun!" Gina said it with a mocking tone.

Anna finished off the rest of her roll. She yummed it

down with one bite. "Such glorious adventure awaits. Let's get our gear. 'No,' is not an option."

Gina made one weak protest. Then she gave up and followed Anna.

Anna kept a closet of hiking gear. She made a quick inventory of what was inside—insulated boots of various sizes, hats (both fleece and wool), gloves, puffy jackets and waterproofed pants. There were even snowshoes and backpacks. It was an arsenal at the ready to tackle the worst of any winter assault.

"You're prepared. This is unfortunate," Gina said.

"Take that blue jacket. It should fit you."

Before Gina could put it on, Anna insisted that she wear a moisture wicking shirt as a base layer. Damp clothes in winter was to be avoided.

"What's in the backpacks?" Gina asked.

"Stuff like water bottles and a compass. Oh, and no cell phones allowed. This is an adventure."

Gina opened her backpack and pulled out a sealed pouch of air-activated hand warmers. "And I thought you were so rugged."

"Okay, I cheat a little. But if we always keep moving out there, we shouldn't need them."

By the time they stepped outside, Gina was covered from head to toe in rugged winter clothing. And her backpack was filled with day gear. Anna made a quick assessment and guessed that the pack weighed about fourteen pounds—roughly ten percent of Gina's body weight.

"I am dieting, you know. Maybe you estimated wrong."

Anna only grinned and pointed at an opening in the trees. Despite the overcast sky, visibility was good. The woods behind the cabin opened up at several places. 'Xs' in various spray paint colors had been marked on some tree trunks that led further in.

"Every time I work a new trail, I mark it with a slash. On my return, I cross the slash to know I've completed that part of the path," Anna said.

"Does the paint hurt the trees?"

"You really don't get out much, do you?" Anna grinned again.

The two women made their way over to a pine. A single slash mark was painted yellow on its scaly brown trunk.

"I've only gone about a quarter mile in so I didn't X it out. Let's see if we can make it to Blackbird Creek. That would have been a source of water for the Winter Revelers," Anna said.

"This is a little weird, you know. I mean, looking for dead people in the woods."

Anna nudged her. "Tick, tock. Tick, tock."

"The mouse ran up the clock. Except I'm not a mouse."

"And I'm not your ex-fiancé. Let's get going. We've got to get back here before sunset."

Anna talked about details of the hike. They would walk east at a pace of about two miles-per-hour. It was 11:30 am, and if they kept it up, they would reach Blackbird Creek by two. She didn't seem to be concerned.

"We'll be back here for hot cocoa before the sunset."

"Which is what time?"

"Probably five thirty. No earlier than five."

That was another thing Gina still had trouble getting used to—the shorter days. Winter sunsets in Florida were almost always seven-thirty pm or later. And winters were never this cold. It was twenty degrees. Her breath came out in smoky puffs.

"We're not going to get lost, are we? I don't want to be stuck out here."

"Just follow me and the yellow markers. You'll be fine."

Anna headed out. She looked rather silly in her beanie. It was topped off with a fuzzy yellow ball made to look like a smiley face. The cheerful reminder kept bouncing up and down as if playing in the crisp air without a care in the world. Gina decided that it summed up her friend perfectly —an endless optimist who enjoyed herself no matter if her new Florida friend might be turned into a hiking popsicle. But perhaps Anna's unwavering optimism was why she liked her so much.

They hiked for half an hour, Gina always following Anna and her bobbing beanie. From all the walking and the protection of the layered clothes, Gina was surprised by how warm she actually was. Maybe a little too warm.

"Can we take a break."

Anna paused to mark another tree trunk with a yellow slash. She nodded in satisfaction. The smiling fuzzy ball nodded too.

"We still have a ways to go."

"I need to cool down. Let me catch my breath."

Gina disregarded any more protesting from Anna and settled down on a nearby bumpy tree trunk. The top of the tree most likely fell over because of the weight of snow that had clung to its branches. She took a swallow from her bottle, the water cold and refreshing.

Anna advised her not to drink too much. Then she looked at Gina's jacket pocket.

"You didn't?"

Gina reached into the left pocket and pulled out a napkin wrapped around a two petite cinnamon rolls. She hesitated after unwrapping the tasty treats. Anna wore a look of disapproval.

"You shouldn't have brought that," Anna said.

"Maybe you're right. I'll save if for later. I could feed it to an animal."

"That's what I mean. It's bad for wildlife. And you never know how an animal might react to you carrying food on you."

"What? Is a squirrel going to throw acorns at me for trying to give it a delicious cinnamon roll?"

Anna shrugged her shoulders. "Just don't feed the wildlife. Let's get going."

"I just sat down."

"Tick, tock. Tick, tock."

Gina grumbled. "I told you, I'm not a mouse."

Anna playfully kicked snow at Gina. "We've got five hours of sun. The forest boogeyman doesn't come out until dark."

"Ha, ha. Can you imagine living back in the days of the Winter Revelers? No cell phones. No GPS."

"Amazing, wasn't it?" Anna grinned. And then she began walking again.

Gina grudgingly got off the tree stump. Her legs were a little stiff and her body temperature had started to cool. She knew her feet would be pretty sore by the time they returned. If they didn't die of frost bite or something first.

"Yeah, just amazing."

But Anna and her smiley-faced beanie were already farther ahead than Gina liked. She picked up her pace so as not to fall behind. They hiked on for another hour, saying little. Anna continued marking yellow slashes every twenty feet or so. Gina looked around.

If she were at home, she'd probably have spent the day

pining over old pics of Todd that she hadn't had the willpower to take down from her favorite social media site. Maybe she would even have worked up the nerve to write a poem on one of Todd's recent posts, arm-in-arm with that blond bimbo. *Tons of bleach on her head, She wears ugly shoes, Her fake tan is fading, But she's still screwing you.* It was like a meaner version of "Roses are Red." Then she would draw a big 'X' over his face. That would be a pathetic waste of a day.

Maybe there was something to be said for being away from the distractions of modern technology. On social media, nature was just another jpeg alongside thousands of others that were posted daily. You clicked a *Like* out of obligation to a friend's list and then quickly moved on to the next pic—nature's majesty reduced to ordinary routine. But Gina was inside nature's jpeg. It was alive and it did more than stimulate her eyes for a brief glance. She could smell the earth and decaying leaves as she kicked up snow. The smell lingered as a nearby branch groaned. And she could almost feel the nearby trees press in like a blanket, hiding her from the rest of the world. This was what lay deeper in the jpeg, below its 2D surface. Deeper down was a living presence and a simple mouse click couldn't do it justice. The woods might even share secrets with Gina as long as she was willing to use all her senses. There was almost something supernatural about it. Perhaps that was why the Winter Revelers had come out here years ago. Maybe they came out here to experience something that the ordinary couldn't reveal.

Anna stopped in her tracks.

"What is—" Gina tried to finish but Anna shushed her.

"Quiet. And don't move."

A loud snort sounded just to her right. She looked over

to see a deer. Dark eyes stared at her as steam puffed from its black nostrils. Ribs showed through the animal's panting sides indicating that it may have been searching for food. But despite the deer's hungry appearance, it still was large. A two-hundred pound body finished at black-tipped tail. If the animal had been a dog, Gina could have expected its tail to wag to show her that it was friendly and ready to be fed. The black-tipped tail didn't wag.

"It's a Mule Deer. A buck. It hasn't shed its antlers," Anna said.

Gina didn't know if this was a good thing or bad. The buck's antlers forked out into several directions and ended in sharp points. If Anna had implied that the antlers might somehow be fragile, they certainly didn't look it.

The buck just continued staring and snorting.

"Maybe it's hungry." Gina offered, hoping to ease the tension.

"No. We've startled it."

Gina disregarded her. She pulled out the cinnamon roll from her jacket pocket.

"Gina, stop. What did I say about feeding wild animals?" Anna hissed.

"How about something sweet and tasty, Mr. Deer?" She held the roll out for the deer.

The deer snorted again and stamped at the ground. It dropped its antlers. They didn't look fragile. They looked ready to—

"Gina, run! It's going to charge us."

If Gina hadn't jumped out of the way in time, the buck's antlers probably would have impaled her. The animal crashed into a nearby tree. A loud cracking sound filled the air. Pieces of bark splintered and sprayed outward. The buck looked slightly dazed.

This was her opportunity to make her escape. Gina started running.

"This way! This way!" Anna was huffing it through a thicker patch of pines. It should slow the angry deer down.

Gina didn't give it a second thought as she picked up her own pace. She could hear the deer snorting again. Thumping hooves grew closer. She almost ran into a tree. Gina stumbled, then regained her legs.

Anna pointed at a drop-off they were quickly approaching. "Down there. It won't follow us."

The snowy ravine's slope was steeper than Gina had anticipated. Her booted feet slipped. Anna tried to grab her. Both women went tumbling down to the bottom, twisting up into something like a human pretzel. When Gina finally stopped moving, it took the two women a few minutes before they could get untangled and pick themselves back up out the deeper snow that had settled at the bottom.

Above, the deer stopped just at the edge of the ravine. It looked down, made one last snort and turned away. It seemed satisfied enough with their misfortune.

"Anna, do you think it gave up?"

"I don't know. But we're not going back up there to find out."

Gina brushed herself off. When she patted powder off her jacket, that's when she realized her backpack was missing.

"I've lost my backpack. Help me find it."

The two searched around. There was no sign of it anywhere in the three feet of cold snow. Gina looked up and toward the top of the ravine. There was no sign of the buck.

"Maybe I dropped it when we started running."

"Maybe. But we can't go back up there with that buck

still hanging around. Don't worry, I've still got mine. It has a map and a compass. We'll find our way out of here and be back on track."

"On track to what?" Gina checked her watch. "It's already one-thirty and we could still be miles off from Blackbird Creek."

Her legs had started to ache from the hiking and the tumble. The boots already felt too tight. And snow had gotten under her layered clothing during the tumble. It was now melted and wet in uncomfortable places. Turning back seemed like a much better idea.

Anna wasn't having it. She held the map and compass in her gloved hands, consulting the compass as she marched onward. Then she pointed down the ravine. The ravine had not tapered off. On both sides, the steep banks still climbed up.

"We continue in this direction. There should be an outlet somewhere just ahead. I'd say we won't be too far off from Blackbird Creek when we climb out."

"Anna, what happens if it gets dark before we get there?"

"It won't."

Cell phones suddenly seemed a more attractive option than all this picturesque, rugged outdoors. At least you couldn't get lost and freeze or starve in a jpeg pic. But if Gina had brought hers, would she have been able to call for help? She doubted it. The phone probably wouldn't have been able to get a signal under all this tree canopy. And the trail—if it could be called that at this point—was pretty far outside of Spring's Peak.

"But what if it does get dark?"

Anna paused for a moment and then smiled. "You are such a worry wart."

Gina didn't feel any better.

They shared Anna's water bottle as they worked their way through the ravine. They were conservative with their sips. This also worried Gina. Why was Anna being careful with the water? Gina was starting to build up her thoughts into something like a mild panic when Anna yelled out, "Hooray!"

She pointed ahead. There was a break on the right side of the ravine where it tapered off. Gina could see a carved path that led up and out.

"See. I told you," Anna said.

The climb out was exerting. Gina grabbed at exposed tree roots, struggling to pull herself up. Hand over hand, she was panting and her arms burned as she worked up the incline. She was out of shape. The last time she had done anything requiring this much exercise was at the Spring's Creek slopes. Being from Florida, she didn't know the first thing about skiing. Todd told her that it would be a good way for her to lose weight. He had skied many times in his teens. Gina couldn't figure out how to strap the two plank-like pieces of fiberglass to her feet. But Todd was too busy assisting the older snow bunny who he had just met. She kept commenting on how his strong hands worked her straps. The memory somehow gave Gina the strength as she grabbed at the final root and pulled herself over the top and back out into the woods.

The pines clustered together tighter here than at the beginning of the trail. Fortunately there was no sign of an angry deer that may decide to charge when offered a petite cinnamon roll.

Gina labored to catch her breath. "Let's go back to the cabin."

Anna looked at her wristwatch. "It's only two-thirty.

We've got plenty of time." She didn't sound winded from the climb up at all.

"You said we would reach Blackbird Creek by two-thirty. Won't it get dark by five?"

"I said no earlier than five. Sunset will probably be later, like six or six-thirty. I've hiked these woods most of my life and never had a problem getting back."

"Anna, look around you. Do you see any of your yellow marks on the trees?"

Anna shook the map in her hand. "I got us out of that ravine, didn't I?"

Gina said nothing.

"Look, you're my friend. I won't let anything happen to us," Anna said.

And to prove it, she walked over to an old, gnarled pine tree and marked it with a yellow slash. Its twisted trunk looked almost human. The similarity was so striking that Gina imagined that one of the Winter Revelers had been cursed and petrified to serve as a warning to other hikers who dared to venture this far in. Gina wasn't exactly encouraged by her friend's assurances but Anna obviously wasn't backing down.

"Tick, tock," Anna said.

"Say that again and I'll throw a snowball at you."

Anna beat her to it. Light powder covered Gina's face. Gina picked up a handful of snow and returned fire. Then they both giggled like two middle-school girls and called a truce.

"When we get back, I'll make us a double hot cocoa," Anna said.

"I want three marshmallows in mine."

Anna jumped up with excitement. Gina marveled at her friend's endless amount of energy and enthusiasm. She had to admit to herself that it was somewhat reinvigorating.

"Blackbird Creek shouldn't be too far ahead. Let's go.

Feeling a little better now, Gina followed. She still wasn't quite sure why she had agreed to this hike. Maybe she was a natural-born follower. She had followed Todd to Spring's Peak and look where that got her--dumped her for a snow bunny. Now she was following Anna on some goose-chase to find missing dead people. Hadn't she learned her lesson once already? And if she were honest with herself, she'd admit that despite Anna's new friendship she still felt alone without Todd. That bothered her most of all.

"Something's wrong. We should be at the Creek by now," Anna said, interrupting Gina's thoughts.

Her friend looked puzzled and stopped to consult her map. Gina looked around and gasped.

"Gina, what is—" Then Anna saw it too. Behind Anna was the creepy gnarled pine tree that looked human. On its trunk was the yellow slash. They must have walked in a circle for half-an-hour. "It's impossible. I followed the map."

"Anna, let's go back to the cabin."

Anna looked at her watch. "Well, it's three now. Maybe you're right."

"I know I'm right." Finally, some common sense was returning to her friend. Getting back to Anna's cabin wouldn't be soon enough. Only now that they seemed to be lost. "So, which way?"

Anna's face scrunched up. She seemed to struggle for an answer. "The compass is pointing magnetic North."

"Is that bad?" Gina was trying not to let panic creep into her voice.

Anna just scratched her head and puzzled over the map. She checked the compass several times. She muttered something about shifting magnetic poles. Even the beanie's smiley face seemed to frown.

Peering over her shoulder, Gina could see that West on the compass was to their left. Anna had said they had been hiking East toward Blackbird Creek. If her math was right, it seemed simple enough that all they had to do was follow the compass in the opposite direction. For once, maybe Gina didn't have to be the follower.

"Gina, stop. You're heading West. We'll just walk in another circle."

Gina looked back. "I saw the compass. I'm going back. No more of searching for Winter Revelers." She began to walk away.

"No, stop. You're not reading the compass right. It's a mountaineering compass. You have to turn the dial to get the proper bearings." Anna waved her back. "I'll show you before you *really* get lost."

Gina had no idea what a *mountaineering compass* actually was. She remembered that her mother once had dash-mounted compass in her beater 1985 Ford Thunderbird. The device seemed pretty straightforward—whichever direction you were headed was marked by an obvious red line. But Anna's flapping arms indicated a nervousness that Gina had never seen. She looked almost panicked and Gina had to stop herself and admit that maybe a hike in dense woods wasn't as simple as a trip to the beach.

Gina sighed and turned back. Relief passed over Anna's face.

"The best thing to do is not panic, Gina."

"How can you say that? We could get stuck out here. And it will be dark soon."

"I'll show you how the compass works." Anna held it out for her to see. "You have to—"

Gina could see the compass needle start to rotate clock-wise. At first it ticked like the second hand on a watch. Slowly it travelled to markings North, then East and then South. Then its speed increased—like really fast. In seconds, it spun so quickly that it became a blur.

"Have you ever seen it do that before?" Gina said.

Anna tapped at the compass housing. "It could be magnetic interference."

"Or it could be that we're lost."

Anna shot her an annoyed look. "And I already told you that I'd get us out of here."

She began to walk off in what might have been the direction W on the compass. Five feet, ten feet, fifteen and tapping at the compass as she walked on. At twenty feet, Gina lost sight of her as she disappeared behind a tree.

"Anna?"

No answer.

"Tick, tock?"

Still no answer. It was very quiet. The silent pine trees continued to press in. A light snow fell, the flakes softly drifting down around their trunks without a sound. No branches groaned.

Gina swallowed down a lump of fear. She dashed over to where she last spotted her friend. No Anna.

"Anna. Where are you?"

Behind another tree about 30 feet away, a smiley-faced beanie poked out. Anna grinned back at her. Then she motioned her over.

Ahead, a clearing opened up in the woods. It was in the shape of a perfect square about thirty feet on each side. There appeared to be stones planted in the ground like markers. Gina counted eighteen total. They lined up in neat rows of six each.

"That's something we haven't seen before," Gina said.

Anna was already investigating. She walked around several of the stones, studying the ground. "I think it's a grave site."

"I wonder if it's the missing Winter Revelers."

"That elderly man and the young girl could have done this. No wonder she was so traumatized," Anna said.

"But why go to this much trouble?"

"Animals, maybe. The elderly man didn't want the bodies in the open. They could have been chewed at."

"You don't think he killed the other Revelers, do you?"

"Seriously? He barely made it out of the woods before he died. No way he could have overpowered the rest of them. Besides, the girl probably wouldn't have trusted him to lead her out of these woods."

"And I can't believe he could find the strength to bury everyone."

Anna shrugged. "Maybe the girl helped. Doesn't really matter. At least we're not walking in circles."

That was true. But the clearing creeped her out. She walked toward the other end of the grave site. The stone markers were of various sizes and mostly oval in shape. Streaks of pink and brown marbling ran through the stones, giving them an almost fleshy look. About every four or five feet another one sat at the head of a rectangular depression of soil and snow. Strangely, no snow fell on the depressions. The sooner they could leave this place, the better. She was going to ask Anna if they should head out and over an incline to her left when a light wind picked up. She heard a faint sound.

"What is it?"

Gina shuddered. "I thought I heard singing."

"That's great! Maybe someone's camping out here. We

can get a ride back. I'll ask them later why they were tres-passing."

Gina walked slowly behind. The air changed, stinging tendrils of cold that slowly crept underneath her jacket and gloves. When she reached the top of the incline, the singing stopped.

Just below her was a shallow valley. The skeletons of four make-shift cabins stood abandoned in falling snow. The roofs of two of them had collapsed. All of them had charring that indicated a fire broke out and had gutted them. Gina could see the remains of a few empty bunks through some collapsed wood in one of the walls.

Seeing the lifeless buildings was perhaps the most unsettling thing yet. At least at a grave site you knew that the dead were in the ground. But here lingered the ashes of the living.

"It's getting really cold. My hands are starting to hurt."

Anna reached back and pulled out the pack of hand warmers. She opened it and shook the two pouches inside. Then she handed one to Gina.

"Just tuck it into one of your gloves. Careful not to burn yourself. If it gets too hot, move it to the other glove."

"One's enough?"

"Trust me. That thing can make you sweat like a pig invited to a barbecue."

Gina was about to laugh except Anna's face indicated a look of seriousness. Her friend was right, though—the pouch was already working as she placed it into her left glove. The welcomed heat quickly travelled up her arm and began to warm her all over. But now they had a new prob-lem. The sun was starting to set in the winter sky.

"At least we have shelter."

Gina's mouth dropped. "I thought you knew these woods. Camping here in the cold is the best you can do?"

"We have to make the best of it. The compass is still acting weird." Anna held it out to show her. It was still spinning. "I can build us a campfire here," Anna said.

This didn't comfort Gina. The sky was growing dark fast, the first stars beginning to show. They had no idea where they were. And trying to read a map at night would have been nearly impossible even with a flashlight. She imagined becoming another Spring's Creek legend where someday two more women would stumble onto her frozen body.

"I can't do this. I'll freak out."

"We have to make the best of this. I'll collect some firewood."

"Where? Look around. Everything is covered in snow. I thought firewood had to be cured before it could be burned. At least I know that much."

Anna shrugged her shoulders. "I think there's enough from the cabins to salvage." And to prove her point, she walked down into the shallow valley.

There were enough pieces of wood scattered about in the wreckage. This included wood shavings for tinder and some smaller pieces that could serve as kindling. For having been exposed for so long in the open, Anna said that it was amazing that what they collected was so dry.

Gina was eager for any bit of hope at this point. They got to work, clearing out a campfire site under the partial cover of a gutted cabin. Following Anna's instructions, Gina made a tinder bundle into a kind of teepee. Anna finished the campfire by adding selected fuel wood above it.

"Is this safe? I mean, after what happened here," Gina said.

Anna shrugged again. "We still have water in my bottle. It's not much, but it should be enough to at least sprinkle on the embers."

When the fire's blaze rose up, it was greeted by cheers. Gina got as close as she could tolerate. The light kept the darkness that now surrounded them at bay. She felt a little better.

"Can you imagine being eight or nine and seeing your mother burned alive in a fire?" Anna said.

Gina didn't feel so great now. "Thanks for reminding me."

"I mean it. If that's what actually happened to them."

"So you're saying the case of the missing Winter Revelers is finally solved? That's comforting."

Gina's legs ached so she dropped next to the fire and tucked them up into her arms. She realized that she was hungry and pulled the two cinnamon rolls out of her jacket pocket. Anna eyed the pastries and this time seemed glad to see them. Gina hesitated then offered one to her hungry friend. Anna plopped down next to her and smiled.

"Thanks. That buck sure doesn't know what he's missing, huh?"

Gina managed to smile despite being lost, the fatigue and surrounding cold. "Anna, how do you own all this property?"

"It's been in my family for generations. We used to own more. A lot of it was donated to a national park."

"Seems kind of...I don't know...lonely."

"Look up above. They keep me company."

Above the fire's crackling flames, the stars began to come out. Gina hadn't been able to see stars in Florida. Or she hadn't payed much attention in those days. Perhaps this was something she could enjoy. Hundreds of tiny white dots twinkled like jewels in the sky. They seemed to be looking down on her.

"Maybe they're watching us now," Gina suddenly said.

"Who?"

"The Winter Revelers. Who else?"

"I hope not."

"I mean in the sky. Amongst the stars."

"That's poetic. Tick, tock."

Gina yawned. "The mouse ran up the clock."

She was too tired to protest about being compared to a small and furry rodent even if the gesture was meant to lighten the mood.

But maybe her friend was right about one thing—maybe she was acting like a timid mouse. Was Todd really worth all the self-inflicted depression that she had put herself through for the last several weeks? It was true that she wasn't as coordinated as some middle-aged snow bunny on the ski slopes. But today she had managed to escape a charging deer, get lost in the woods and yet still find it in herself to help make a campfire. And maybe tomorrow morning, they would find themselves back at Anna's cabin. Sure, she was cold and hungry. But she was surviving an adventure. There was an inner strength in her that she didn't even know she possessed. And if she gave herself another chance, that hidden strength would also rekindle her own inner fire.

Anna said something else. Gina thought she heard her say that they would be safely back to their cabin by tomorrow morning. Her voice sounded far away. Then near. Then far away again, muffled like it came from being underwater. Gina couldn't be sure if she was dreaming. The hundreds of stars above were moving. They swirled clockwise faster and faster, like the compass's needle. They paused. Then blinked in unison. Then they grew larger as if approaching her.

"This is too weird," Anna said. She must have seen the moving stars too.

A loud crack sounded nearby. Then another. There was a shock that shook the ground. Gina was startled out of her trance. She looked behind her.

"Anna, we've got to go." Her breath came out with quick, short bursts.

Icicles quickly grew along the roofline of the burned-out cabins. They glinted starlight. They would have been beautiful if they hadn't formed into long daggers of very sharp ice. One broke off and fell onto the ground. It shattered into tiny pieces and the scattered shards started to grow up and out of the ground like pointed knives. More icicles dropped and shattered. The deadly pieces steadily crept toward them.

Gina thought of the buck that charged her earlier that day. She was not going to sit still and wait for icicles to impale her. She jumped up. Anna didn't say a word. She quickly did the same.

"Oh, geez. Oh, geez." Gina was practically panting from fear.

"You can do this, Gina. I believe in you." But Anna's voice also came out in puffy bursts.

They both ran toward a patch of woods. North, south, east or west? It didn't matter which direction. They just wanted to get away from the ice daggers. When Gina glanced back, the campfire was buried in impaling stalagmites that glinted starlight. And the ice daggers kept coming. The women moved as quickly as they dared in the dark.

She could hear the pursuing ice splinter and crack just

behind her. The air turned even colder. Their breaths chugged in white clouds of panicked steam. The only safe passage was a dark path that ran ahead through a dense patch of trees. Gina didn't hesitate. She almost stumbled on an exposed root before regaining her balance. She dashed inside.

And suddenly, the splintering sounds stopped. The ice daggers halted at the entrance to the patch of woods.

The two women caught their breath. For several minutes, they said nothing but panted in the dark. Finally, Anna broke their silence.

"I don't have my backpack. My compass and map were in it." Her voice trembled. All the confidence Anna exhibited earlier in the day had been frozen out of her by the supernatural events of the night.

"The compass wasn't working anyway. We'll find those trees you marked."

That was all that Gina would say as she began to move through the dark patch of woods. This time, she led the way. She felt a spirit of determination spring up inside and she almost laughed to herself at the pun she made. She was already lost—what difference did it make which direction they walked. They were cold and hungry and so missing out on sleep didn't really make anything worse. Beside, the woods had to end somewhere, didn't it?

It didn't take long to get through the patch of woods. After groping at a few tree trunks and one stumble over a thick root later, Gina could see more starlight just ahead. Cautiously, she stepped out into another clearing.

Unlike the first clearing dotted with planted grave-stones, life-like statues of ice gathered together here in a circle. She counted them—sixteen, seventeen, eighteen. Eighteen statues, the same number as gravestones. Men and women of various ages stood facing inward to form a large circle. They wore long coats trimmed by frozen fur collars that glinted white. Many of the men wore Stetsons and bowler hats. The women's hair was pinned back under wide brims. In all of the statues hands, they held unlit torches.

They looked so real. Gina expected them to move. But they didn't move...they sang. Softly at first, their voices slowly rose until their harmonious music seemed to fill the sky itself. Gina listened to the song. She knew that the voices came from the statues themselves. They sang a merry harmony of the winter solstice. It was a world that gently slept. A world of snow painted all in white. And a waiting sun would one day soon blanket all in comforting green.

And then the tempo and mood changed—slower, the voices grew softer and sadder. They sang of the stars above.

As each of us gaze upon them,
If only for just a moment,
The stars look back down upon us,
Forever.

And our own lights will someday fade,
Yet the stars themselves will always burn,
They are eternally bright,
Forever.

Then the voices hushed. Gina perked up her ears. In the center of the circle stood a lone ice statue. The woman stood tall and proud, her slender body covered in icy silk and frosty lace, head tilted back to gaze at the heavens. Small dots of twinkling lights hovered around her forehead like a crown. And her lips, full and round, opened to the stars as if in a forever song.

"Do you hear her, Anna? It's beautiful."

"Hear what?"

Gina said nothing, the ice woman's voice enchanting her. It sang a simple melody. Her lone voice rose high and sweet in a song about a winter dove now lost and all alone.

> To where has this little bird now flown?
> Away from me, your hearth, your home.
> Don't be afraid, little bird,
> For soon we will be together.

When the icy woman finally stopped singing, Gina realized that she had tears in her eyes.

"She wants me to help her," Gina said.

Anna looked around. Her brow was furrowed. "Who? Who wants you to help?"

"The ice woman."

Anna looked suspiciously at her. "What ice woman? Maybe you really are freaked out."

Gina ignored the rebuff. She shared an understanding with the ice woman. The woman had been a Winter Reveler who died in these woods years ago. Her daughter had escaped the woods with the old man to Spring's Creek.

Gina walked over to her. In the icy woman's slender hand hung a locket. Gina took it and put it in her jacket pocket. The small dots of twinkling light that hovered around now swirled around Gina. They lightly brushed and tickled her. They meant no harm. She felt a warm love and caring radiate from them. Then they flitted over to the trees ahead and transformed into glowing icicles. Dozens or more of frozen lanterns shone out in a ghostly white.

"Follow the glowing icicles," Gina said.

Anna shook her head. "You really are freaked out."

Gina started walking again, confident in where the glowing icicles were taking her. Anna's mouth gaped open but she followed anyway. Perhaps her friend decided that if the two would die out here, at least they wouldn't be alone.

Gina didn't feel cold or scared anymore. She should have been. Neither she nor Anna had backpacks. They were lost. And who knew where the glowing icicles were really taking them. But somehow she knew that the ice woman cared enough to see her safely back to Anna's cabin. Perhaps she felt some maternal instinct for Gina. Or perhaps regret and love for her own missing daughter guided them to an eventual reunion.

She walked for at least two hours, probably more. The glowing icicles continued to take them over inclines and through the woods. If Gina hadn't become so sleepy, she would have probably taken the time to look around. Instead, she just managed to keep her weary eyes on the lights that guided her.

"Look! It's one of my trail marks!" Anna yelled out. Gina saw dots of light swirl around a tree trunk marked with a yellow slash. "And I see more ahead. It shouldn't be much longer," Anna continued.

As more yellow slashes appeared, the glowing icicles slowly disappeared. The twinkling lights began to fade as the dawn sun slowly rose above the tree tops. Gina felt like she was losing a friend. Anna recognized the path and said it wouldn't be long before they saw the cabin's porch lights.

"How did you know how to find the way back?" Anna said.

"The ice woman showed me."

"Well, did she tell you to put something in your jacket pocket? I saw you do that back in the second clearing."

Gina pulled the locket out and opened it. Inside was a

faded picture of the beautiful woman holding a young girl's hand. Tomorrow, she would take the locket into Spring's Peak. She would visit the historical cemetery and place it at the grave of the young girl.

"It looks like an antique," Anna said.

"It belongs to someone special."

"Well, we can talk about it after we get some sleep. The cabin is just ahead," Anna said in a mock scolding voice. "Let's get going. Tick, tock. Tick, tock."

But Gina didn't reply. The ice woman's song still haunted her.

> To where has this little bird now flown?
> Away from me, your hearth, your home.
> Don't be afraid, little bird,
> For soon we will be together.

Gina looked up at the stars above. There were hundreds of them fading away in the new dawn sky. On the large canvas of a space above, two stars managed to stand out. They stood close together, their white light still strong and beautiful. They were glittering jewels in the cold, winter sky. She didn't feel sad about Todd or middle-aged snow bunnies anymore. As long as Gina could always see the two stars, she would never feel alone.

She smiled.

NEVER TRUST A CAN OPENER

I'VE NEVER TRUSTED our can opener. This week I avoided it by scraping by with pantry remains, serving family meals of peanut butter sandwiches, a wilting salad littered with olives from a suspicious jar at the back of the refrigerator and Raman noodles floating in a neon colored broth. These meals have driven my husband, Bob, to open his wallet. Pak-N-Save ran a special on tuna in the Sunday *Toledo Daily* and Bob gave me the *meets-our-budget* nod of approval. No glossy, resealable foil packets with those benign plastic zips. No modern EZ-Open! pull tabs that leave behind smooth aluminum lips. Just eight-to-a-package-so-you-save-more, raggedy-edged cans.

Once, I tried out a cooking class at the community center. The other stay-at-home mothers covered their perfect print blouses with starched aprons and they handled kitchen utensils like a master mechanic worked a wrench. Wearing bohemian hip-huggers and an exposed belly ring, I destroyed an egg with a whisk.

It was best to accept my shopping mission by first studying the enemy. I pulled out the contraption with a bulky hand crank from the kitchen utility drawer. It has cold steel wheels, one with serrated teeth for grabbing and a sharper one for cutting. A bleeding finger was in my future and Bob and our two children, Dillon and Terri, will weep and toss flower petals over my shriveling, tetanus-filled body.

My Mother never had this problem.

Bob looks up from his novel. Now he's reading me.

"I'm sure you don't want me to help." He clears his throat. "Let's skip lunch. We'll save money."

I love my husband, but his sympathy only makes me think of that brand, "Chicken of the Sea." And maybe Bob and I could do without, but the kids do need to eat.

"I can do this," I say.

I try staring the device down. The can opener lays on the counter, its black-handled maw gaping, promising a mechanized death by unsubstantiated fear. *I'm waiting, Shelia*. I once read a free article online in the *New York Times* about Norman Borlaug, a 20th century scientist who defeated worldwide famines through plant breeding. I battle something named *KitchenAid*.

I raise the trash bin lid but Bob stops me just in time.

So this is how my week goes after shopping for the tuna: Monday, I place a tuna can next to a loaf of bread, a squeeze mayo and a jar of sliced pickles and prepare to make Bob's work lunch and something for the kids' school day. I just stare again. Bob comes to my rescue and opens the tuna can. One damsel in distress saved. *Poor little me!*

Tuesday, I cut into a can followed by a vacuum-sealed *Hisssss*. Sounds like a venomous snake. Or any snake. I drop both the can and the opener. Tuna juice all over. In a past life, was I Cleopatra and I now carry a fear that spans thousands of reincarnations? I recognize something. Progress?

Wednesday, I pinch my finger when I pick up the can opener. Panicking, I wash my hands repeatedly. No blood but no lunches. I tell Bob that I'm a bad mother. He hugs me; More sympathy.

Thursday, Bob says I can sleep in. He makes lunches. I consider Sylvia Plath'ing myself. But I'm sure that I'll end up wedging my hands in a broiler rack, my pinkie fingers spread out in a distorted version of a Trekkie's Spock, a very unpoetic way to go. And the appliance is electric. I wake up at 10am and settle on cups of coffee and over-caffeinating myself.

It's Friday. It's either me or the can opener.

On Main Street and Fourth, a big retail store sells the latest kitchen tech solutions. It's the kind of place that the perfect moms test out prototype nuclear egg cookers and then return home with coffee makers that they will reprogram in several computer languages. Their eyes will judge me as I pass by the cookware aisle, accusing me of spending too many hours with poetry and other impractical time-wasters in high school. It's the kind of place Mother would have shopped at.

But I'm desperate. Fortunately, the place is empty and only one sales associate walks the floor this afternoon. I confess to my problem and Tiffany shows me the electric openers.

I spot the hazardous power cable and the sticker price and jerk my hand away from a fire engine red model.

"They're too expensive. Do you have any manual ones with a mom safety feature?" I say.

Tiffany's brow furrows. Then she smiles, pointing at a bargain bin.

Jumbled inside are several cut-resistant kitchen mitts. I

pick one up and try it on, the bulky thing more padded than a linebacker's uniform.

Something bubbles, a moment that must have been submerged in a pool of murky Mother memories. I was ten. Mother ridiculed my stubby fingers as I struggled to open a can of pie filling. But then she yelled out, "Dammit!" and shattered her Betty Crocker image of superiority. On the back of her naked hand was a magnificent purple blister on toasted flesh. My only triumph ever, I said to her, "Mommy, you should have worn the mitts." She slammed the oven door closed and didn't speak to me for the rest of the day.

The bargain mitts fit my adult hands. A left-hander sporting playful kittens partner a right one with yellow tulips, a perfect seventy-five-percent-off combination for my can opener problem.

I surprise Bob on Saturday afternoon with lunch. He watches as I slowly open some albacore and feeling like a clumsy crustacean. But I don't drop anything.

I must have been beaming because Bob grabs me and kisses me. I pinch his nose with the right mitt. He doesn't even notice my claw-like hands. The kids are grinning as if they're watching a cheesy movie. I can imagine the trailer: *Lobster Mom defeats can opener and saves lunch.*

MORTAL IMAGE

LIFE MATERIALIZED in the Heavenly Plane. She'd been told to meet Death here but the training seemed pointless. She already performed her job as a Harbinger well, exceeding all expectations. Elijah, her supervisor, had said so.

"He told me I was his best employee. He meant that, right?" she asked herself out loud. Life stood alone outside the Mortal Plane and so, of course, no supervising archangel offered her an encouraging response.

Well, it was a job after all. She would have to do her best and follow orders.

When Life had just passed on from Mortal existence, Elijah had told her that she was a perfect fit for the role as the Harbinger, Life—she would be a work success story. And she had been or so she believed. Sure, she had doubts. Her still elusive memories of her past life caused her doubts. Whatever her previous experiences as a Mortal had been like, she didn't think that they had been good ones. Would they somehow affect her on the job now? She hoped not.

She took in a deep breath and exhaled slowly. "The past

is the past, right? I'm happy, right?" Why should she be so worried? She was being silly.

Life looked around and saw a gap into the Mortal Plane —unusual, because she hadn't opened the gateway. And no other Heavenly Entities were nearby including Elijah. Perhaps he had willed the gateway opened from his main office. If so, the archangel exercised more power than she imagined.

Inside the gateway, the Harbinger could see an outline of a room. It revealed no details, a milky ethereal substance covering the furnishings in cloudy particles. They floated around what looked to be a bed, a chair, and two human forms. One was lying down while another sat. Whatever was inside the Mortal Plane *did* worry her—had Elijah told her everything? She had asked about a hundred questions about this meeting with Death before she left. And she got no answers. Well, if Elijah's dead-eyed stare and a "His will be done" was an answer, his seemingly indifference to her concerns offered little comfort.

She wasn't being punished, was she? Life tried to recall any mistakes that she might have made recently. There was that time she applied too much Bread of Manna. A family of squirrels nested in an old oak and Life tried to help them. She only meant to revive the rotting tree trunk before it fell over. Too many crumbs caused the tree's leaves and branches to violently grow. The explosive nature scared the fuzzy animals away.

No, that couldn't have been it, Life consoled herself. And she doubted that Elijah would put her into harm's way. The Harbinger tried to remain positive despite her doubts. She pushed through the ethereal boundary, a substance as soft and light as down feathers, and entered the room inside the Mortal Plane.

The room was a hovel. A small desk lamp splashed dirty yellow light across stained and scraped walls. Magazines littered the molding carpet. A rusty cot that should have been a junkyard dog's bed violated a quarter of the space.

An old man lay on the bed. He looked worse than the room. His spotted hand gripped a bottle of gin, as if coveting any remaining alcohol that might evaporate from inside it. A stained and tattered T-shirt exposed a swollen belly covered in red spots. The old man sucked in air through vomit-and-blood-crusted lips. Life looked inside his body and saw fluid creeping through withered veins and arteries. Sores and malignant tissue covered his various diseased internal organs.

Life brushed at her green gown and then smoothed out her clean hair, disturbed by the decrepit things she witnessed now. "Who is this old man?" she demanded. This time she got an answer.

"Cirrhosis of the liver, pancreatic cancer, and respiratory complications. I believe there is cancer developing in his neck, as well."

Another figure rose out of the chair. His eyes glittered like clean silver coins when he looked at her. He must be the Harbinger Death, she thought. Death was a haphazard mix of Mortal fashion. Knotted strings of black hair poured out from and down his head, brushing the collar of a black 1980's Members Only jacket. A pair of dark baggy pants and stark-white Converse tennis shoes completed his outfit. Death looked over at the old man and shook his head.

Life found his verbal bluntness crude and his choice of wardrobe off-putting. She would have to make the best of this meeting because she expected little from her counterpart Harbinger. A cheerful disposition always lightened the mood.

"Hi, Death. I'm Life. Employee ID zero-one-one-two-three-five. Elijah told me I was to report to you."

"You're an uptight one."

Death burped and grinned at Life. The smell of rotten meat filled her nostrils. He held out his hand to greet her. She saw dirt crusted under his yellowed fingernails. She didn't return the handshake.

Death pulled at the bottom of his shirt and wiped his fingers on the cloth hems. "Sorry, I just looked after a mass killing. A messy affair."

"You could also use some help with your appearance," Life said.

Death looked down at his jacket and baggy pants. Then he looked back at her. "What? You don't like the retro look?"

"The eighties went out with the nineties. And we're in the next century if you hadn't noticed. Looking at you, I doubt that you have," Life said.

"I got so tired of carrying that scythe around. Besides, I think it scared the Mortals. Not like they really have a choice. But, you know, client consideration and all that."

She rolled her eyes and hoped to keep this meeting as short as possible. "I was told to meet you here. For exactly *what* is beyond me. I'm not in trouble for the squirrels, am I?"

Death's brows knitted. "What squirrels?"

She glared. "Then tell me—why am I here?"

"Oh, yeah, that business. I guided you from Mortal Existence. So you do know that, right?"

Of course she knew that! That was one of the first things taught in training. All recent ex-Mortals were given the job title junior-level Deceased before assignment. After passing away, Death handed each a new employee package which included the standard *Congratulations! You've been selected to enter Heaven!* letter and an employee handbook. He acted like an HR department head. And the whole process seemed to go along smoothly. The funny thing was, no one seemed to lament leaving the Mortal Plane. Or demand that they resolve some unfinished business. Or at least, that part of the new-hire process was never discussed in her training.

"I get the feeling that you're not telling me everything."

Death coughed and cleared his throat. "Well, I kind of blocked your memories when you passed on from Mortal Existence. Standard procedure, you know. Sometimes they just don't want to go. Want to cling to the past and all that."

Life didn't understand how her memories could be blocked as if locked inside a chest and hidden away from her. She crossed her arms. "And how will you return them? Probe my mind?"

"It's more like a tickle," Death said.

She imagined his dirt-crusted hands squishing around in her head. That seemed even worse than having the memories taken—at least she couldn't recall that. "I'll pass."

"I'm under orders. Elijah said it would help the old man. We both don't have a choice." Life snorted at hearing this. "You don't remember the car accident? The burning wreckage?" Death said.

Something tickled Life's mind. She seemed to float.

"Your long-gone relative takes your hand, guides you toward the light... ." Death made a dramatic hand gesture as if walking a child toward a carousel.

In a blink, mental images snapped into her thoughts. A distorted movie film seemed to play out in frames of rapid sequence. The people in her mind's eye were blurry, dark and grainy. A face came into focus. She saw the face of a woman. "My...grandmother! I remember."

Death bowed.

"No more tickling," she told him. "I'll leave."

"Sorry, I enter minds so frequently it's become a habit. I should have warned—."

Someone banged on the room's door. "Hey old man. You got to leave."

The door flew open and a squat, stocky man entered the room. His dark matted hair and greasy mustache accompanied a yellowed undershirt. A furry canopy of body hairs covered both his arms and shoulders. If the stocky man was the landlord, he matched the cesspool décor in what attempted to pass as a weekly rental. He should be paying his tenants just to tolerate his body odor.

The old man on the bed did not respond. He only continued to wheeze for breath.

"Hey, wake up. You didn't pay your rent. You sick or something?" The stocky man shook his tenant but got no answer. The bottle of gin rolled under the bed and out of sight. "Damn. I'm gonna' call the hospital but you'll have to pay extra for my phone minutes."

As he turned to leave, he passed through Death. Mortals couldn't see the two Harbingers but it didn't prevent him from sensing them. The man shuddered and made the sign of the cross before closing the door behind him.

"So, shall we get on with this? It will only take a few moments," Death said.

"Why here? Why tickle me with your dirty telepathic tentacles in this dirty room? I won't do it."

Death took a deep breath through his nose. "Guess I'll just have to do it the hard way."

He unzipped and removed his jacket. Then he began to unbutton the unfortunately matching black shirt underneath. Life immediately turned away. She was afraid that Death would also take down his pants and perform some kind of retro, memory-returning Macarena while totally naked. It was too much to bear. Elijah might reprimand her for leaving the jobsite too soon but she was sure that she could eventually reason with the archangel.

"I'm done here." Life swept her hands out, the motion pushing away the air in front of her. The Heavenly Plane took form.

As Life took a step forward, Death reached out and grabbed her arm. Sharp, bony fingers hooked into her skin. She looked at his face. His silver eyes were embedded in a grinning skull.

"The old man's time in the Mortal Plane is almost at an end. You must be here when he dies," Death said.

Life tried to pull away. Green shoots sprouted from her arm and wrapped themselves around Death's claw. The shoots withered into dust. More immediately grew out to replace them. Death would not let go. Life and Death were entwined in a supernatural battle which could only end in a draw.

She suddenly remembered the Bread of Manna. With her free hand, Life reached into a small bag tied to her belt and pulled out a handful of bread crumbs. She cast them into Death's face. The crumbs struck his cheek bones and forehead, instantly igniting into small flames.

Death let go of Life's arm and brushed away the crumbs. Life rushed to a corner of the room. She turned to see small particles fall like tiny stars from his face. Each one vaporized into a strobe of green, red, silver, or yellow as it collided with the carpet.

"You are making this difficult," Death muttered. The flesh returned to his face but tiny scars dotted where the skin had burned.

"I'm calling the main office," Life said.

Death scratched his butt. "Who are you—"

"Shh." She held up a hand as she flipped open her phone. Life struck several keys on the number pad. After each button press, a small white glow haloed out and a harp's chord resonated. She turned on the speakerphone and looked at Death but he seemed indifferent. After a few seconds, someone on the other end picked up. Life asked if she could speak with Elijah.

"This is Gabriel. How can I assist you?"

The archangel's voice boomed out like a blaring orchestra, striking the air with the impact of an audio hammer. Trumpets and the sound of crackling flames rose and fell after each syllable.

"This is Life. I'm asking permission to leave the jobsite."

"She just won't cooperate," Death said over her shoulder.

Gabriel sighed and the sound pushed air around the room. Some of the magazines that littered the room's floor flipped open. "I'll put you on hold while I look into the matter. Please wait."

Soft voices spoke in cryptic languages over the speakerphone as Life and Death waited. She pursed her lips and adjusted her hair. She wondered how many cabinets resided in the main office's filing system. The squirrels would have found a new home. Death just paced his side of the room, hands tucked inside the baggy pants.

The voices vanished and Gabriel came back on the phone. He apologized for the delay. "Life, I've reviewed your file. It states that you must complete this assignment per Death's instructions."

"Oh my God! Death just attacked me."

"All I can tell you is that this is God's will and it must be done," Gabriel said. "And please do not use His name in vain."

"His will. His will. That's all you angels ever say!" Life wasn't surprised so many Mortals became agnostic. "So I'm just expected to let Death have his way with me?"

"I'm suggesting that you two work out your differences and complete this assignment," Gabriel said.

Life stomped her foot. She told Gabriel thanks for nothing and snapped closed her phone. She was between a rock and a dead place—she could leave the job site and get into who knew what kind of trouble or she could suffer through...through this.

Death grinned at her. The scars hadn't improved.

"What? Want to administer your tickle now?" Life looked at Death's dirty fingernails again and felt sick. "Bet you'll love that. Maybe I should just lie down and die a second time."

"Help the old man leave the Mortal Plane," Death said calmly.

"No probing?" Death crossed his heart. Life still wasn't convinced. "So how do I help him leave the Mortal Plane?"

"Don't freak out, okay?"

"Oh, G—" and Life quickly corrected herself. "Geez. You're not going to get naked are you?"

Death ignored her. He finished unbuttoning his black shirt. When he removed it, he exposed taught dry skin pulled over a bony ribcage. Underneath his skeletal mass, Life could see a glowing heart that beat with a slow rhythm. Thud, thud. Thud, thud.

But what disturbed her even more was the filthy shirt he held in his right hand. He snapped the shirt once, then twice and it transformed into a thin black veil. The fabric looked like a mortician's mess rag—what might have once been a soft silk surface was now covered with blood, phlegm, and other human particulate.

"Gross. What is that?"

He held it out to Life. "It's the thin veil between this world and the next."

"Seriously? I thought that was just a metaphor."

"There's often truth to such things."

"I hope you're not expecting me to touch that thing."

"You'll need to place the veil over the old man. I'll guide you."

Life frowned. "Gross."

"There's something beautiful here if you look carefully." Death shook the veil and hues of blues and purples rippled up and down the material and underneath the encrusted filth. His eyes shimmered again. "Take it."

She considered leaving the jobsite again. She hesitated before snatching the veil from him. As soon as she did, a sudden cold shocked her fingers and ran up her hand.

"What is this thing?"

"You'll be OK. That's the Taking. The veil draws in life. It reacts stronger to you."

A force rushed through her body and Life's hands were forced together. They rose above her head, both sets of fingers stretching out the veil at shoulder height. A thin blue light streamed across its edges, corner to corner, stretching the material further so that it grew wider in her hands. She tried to drop the veil but it clung to her unwilling fingers. Her arms spread further apart.

"Please, make it stop!" Life said.

Only Life's mind and eyes remained under her control as her feet began to act on their own. They stepped closer to the old man who still lay dying on the bed. She willed them to stop but the effort did nothing. When she got within arm's reach of the old man, his bloodshot eyes sprang open. His body jerked up like a macabre marionette and a bubble of spittle pushed out from his toothless mouth. He beckoned Life forward. She couldn't turn her head from the grotesque display.

The old man's breath rattled in Life's face. It became a steamy mist that curled and snaked from his nose and mouth. Life's hands grew warmer. Pale heat bled out from her fingertips and snaked down into the center of the material, blending together with the old man's breath. The veil's black threads slithered around like snakes eager to devour the remnants of Mortal existence. They squirmed and writhed and took shape. Body fluid splatters spread out and changed colors to create shades of blond hair, pale skin, green eyes and red lips. Life watched as her own face appeared in the center of the veil.

And that's when the old man stopped breathing. Drool dripped down his chin as he reached for the veil. He coughed and a ghostly body crept out from his open mouth. A hissing voice escaped from somewhere deep inside his throat.

"Leanna, *deus exsisto vobis parvulus.*"

Leanna. She remembered that name.

The stocky landlord came back and banged on the door. Somehow, it had locked itself. "Hey, old man, what are you doing in there? I called the hospital."

The doorknob rattled but the door refused to open. The stocky man's noisemaking grew distant, as if the walls pushed the world away from the room.

"And now, the Submission," Death said. His voice faded to a whisper.

Life tensed. The old man wrapped his arms around her. His body pressed against her like a child showing affection to a parent.

"What do you want from me?" Life said.

A small boy's voice cried out inside her mind. The old man smiled and his eyes changed colors. She looked into a deep ocean blue. As she continued to gaze, the color seemed to continue on with no horizon. Their minds locked and they became one being.

Tired I've grown and in dirt I will lie.

As the hoarse voice crept into Life's mind, a sadness touched her. Yet she sensed something more—a timeless void surrounded the two. For this very moment, the old man's body could not change and could not decay.

Life repeated her question in thought. *What do you want from me?*

A story I've lived and one you have known.

Tears trickled from the old man's eyes as more emotions rushed into Life. A lifetime of neglect, despair and regrets seemed to flood out from the old man's soul and into her heart.

How do I know you?

I was the seed that planted you and the sun that grew into your heart.

The movie frames popped back into Life's mind just like the first time Death had tried to probe her mind. Only this time, they didn't stop. She watched the old man push a little girl on a swing. He became younger, the creases melting from his face. The girl giggled and begged to swing higher. The scene smeared and faded.

Who is that little girl?

Through my ways and through your eyes, you withered from my touch.

A new movie played. The man and a woman were yelling at each other. The woman pointed at a liquor bottle. She picked up the little girl and stormed out of the room. Everything faded.

Why are you showing me this?

The anger that spilled was the anger that fed you.

Colors mixed and shapes took form. Life saw the man knock on an apartment door. Lines formed around his mouth and eyes. He was middle-aged now. A teenage girl opened the door and Life recognized herself when she was Mortal.

"Leanna," the older man said, "I've come to apologize." Then Leanna opened the door and the man stepped inside.

You're...my father?

Dust you became before dust I must go.

The middle-aged man crawled from the wreckage of a burning car. His bloodshot eyes wept. He looked back and reached out his hand. "My daughter," he moaned. "Leanna, forgive me."

"You drove the car that killed me?" Life said.

She got no response. The movies stopped and waves of silence crashed over her. Life had only her own thoughts to console her as the old man's body died in her arms.

She heard banging again, the sound muffled behind the closed door. Life laid the old man's body on the bed and dropped the veil. Only the old man's ghost remained standing. The ghost gazed at her in silence.

Life looked at the veil. It had returned to its previous form as a black shirt. Only, she could sense a part of the old man's Mortal remains now part of the cloth material. Death walked over and she handed it back to him. He quickly put it back on and buttoned it back up.

"Why show me all this now?" Life asked.

"Your father was part of your memories. Part of you. Can you forgive him?" Death said.

Life didn't really know what to say. The old man had seemed remorseful, even sad and filled with true regret. But a twinge of anger suddenly stirred within in her. Perhaps it would take time.

Life looked at the ghost but didn't know what to say.

"Doesn't our need for love change us? Move us in new directions?" Death said.

"I don't know what I feel right now."

"You will."

A starry light splintered through the wall where the bed pushed against it. Beyond the wall, a tunnel stretched out to some unknown end. A burst of warmth and a feeling of caring surrounded her. The ghost held out his hand like a child and waited for Life to guide him.

"Show him the way," Death said. He smiled.

This time, Life smiled back. "To his new life or mine?"

Death shrugged.

She cautiously reached out her hand; the ghost's fingers were light as mist. "Are you ready, Dad?"

The ghost said nothing, only pointing toward the starry light.

LAST OF LASTS

DAVID GRAYSON STOOD outside the Focus Chamber. One of three test subjects—himself, Jan, and Little Jack— David waited for Doctor Stern. Doctor Stern would soon arrive in the Threading Experimental Control Center, or TECC.

Jan had already entered the chamber. Her thin arms were in front of her as she gripped the bio-electric transfer rail. She maintained focus on the polycarbonate walls.

David watched her. The drum of Jan's heartbeat was already climbing. He could hear it pulsing on a nearby monitoring station. Condensation of her breath was building against the thick plastic interior of the chamber's wall. Thanks to the booster injection, Jan would soon reach a state of hyper-anxiety. David always disliked this part of the experiment.

"Ready, David?"

David turned to see Doctor Stern approach. His white lab coat covered his lanky body and gave him the appearance of a walking stork. Little Jack limped alongside the doctor.

"Let's do this," David said.

Little Jack said nothing. He rolled up his sleeve to indicate that he was ready for the mind-altering booster. The bruised tissue marks from repeated jet injections were evident on his upper arm. Doctor Stern's long, thin fingers gripped the jet injector. There was a hiss of air and Little Jack grimaced.

After the Doctor nodded, Little Jack rolled down his sleeve and hobbled over to the Chamber.

David, Jan, and Little Jack had volunteered to endure this type of ongoing testing. It was called Threading. David did it because he needed the money. He was out of work and his college loans were behind on payment. Jan was in a similar situation. Little Jack had been homeless, so any paycheck was a good paycheck.

But the payments came at a cost. They soon discovered that all three of them were now no better than lab rats. Every morning they were given a booster to enhance the experiment. And what was unusual about the injection was that it induced a type of temporary mental condition. It lasted through the Threading. And sometimes beyond.

Sometimes the effects suddenly returned in the evening, long after the booster had worn off. The effects only lasted for a few seconds. But they were occurring more and more. David was growing concerned that even if he quit the Threading program, the booster effects would return again and again. Even without the boosters. He worried that his mind might eventually erode into some kind of broken state. What that mental state was, exactly, he couldn't be sure of.

"David, have you talked with Jan? I want to know before I give you the booster," Doctor Stern said.

David shook his head.

"I know you care for her David. I do."

David studied Doctor Stern. It was always difficult to read anything in the man's grey eyes.

"Maybe you could try new projected images," David said.

Doctor Stern had once explained that the thick plastic walls of the polycarbonate chamber acted as an impact resistance lens. The light beams contained visual information. When directed at the chamber's walls, the light would come to focus on Jan's eyes. It formed multiple images that only she would see during the Threading.

As she entered a boosted state of hyper-anxiety, her thoughts splintered. They fractured into a series of present projected images and future imagined possibilities. Jan formed a story of the projected images that played out in her mind like a thread. It was like rolling it out of a spool of string until it finally reached some conclusion.

Simultaneously, her thoughts made tangential jumps. They formed new stories, new threads. The more jumps Jan made, the faster an energy counter would climb. Theoretically, she should eventually exhaust all tangential possibilities and the joule counter would hit full capacity. She would reach the final thread.

"She won't make her mind go there," David said.

After each failed Threading, Jan shared her private thoughts with him. She was afraid that if she jumped to the final thread, she wouldn't be able to piece her mind back together.

It was a dark place where Jan was afraid to go. No threads seemed to fully form there. It was the final tangential possibility.

She called this final thread the Last of Lasts.

Several members of the science team were busily working at their stations. They studied Jan's brainwave telemetry. David peered over the back of a lab assistant's white coat. A joule counter slowly ticked up, a device that converted her mental activity into an electrical signal.

The lateral images of Jan's mind displayed orange highlights. This was where her brain was responsible for dealing with her boosted anxiety. When Threading fully began, the lateral images highlights would turn bright red and spread across the screen as if her mind was on fire.

"I have high hopes, David. But I expect you to be more cooperative in the future."

David got ready for his booster. He was nervous. He rubbed at a metal token he kept in his pocket. He could feel the outline of a palm tree stamped on one side.

Before leaving college, he had found the token under his dorm room bed while cleaning. It was silly trinket, but for some reason he had held onto it. Maybe it continued to offer him hope. One day soon, he would find a job and pay off his college debts. Then he would have enough money to visit a tropical island, far away from the Massachusetts cold.

"David, I won't ask you to push yourself beyond your capacitive limits. That's why we've done something different with the projections today."

"Look, I don't want anyone getting hurt."

Doctor Stern made a quiet laugh. "Have you ever heard of an infinity mirror?"

"Yeah. A kind of mirror that that when you look into it, it looks like it continues on forever in the background."

"Yes. A 19th century novelty, perhaps. It's an illusion that has even been reproduced through computer simulation. But this is the year 2000. We will recreate one today through projection of light."

"I don't see how this is going to help."

The doctor tapped at David's head. David didn't like the patronizing gesture, but he said nothing.

"There are aspects of our personality that we don't even know exist. Imagine being able to explore yourself. To discover who you really are. And who you will finally be in a single moment of time," Doctor Stern said.

"So you will project an infinite image of Jan to herself. Then when she Threads, her mind will be tricked into exploring everything. Even that final place she's afraid to go. What she calls the Last of Lasts."

"Tricks are for magicians. This is science."

Trick or science, David still worried. Jan had said that if she unspooled the final thread, something bad could happen to her.

"Her mental energy conversion. What happens when the joule counter hits full capacity?"

Doctor Stern smiled as if he was speaking to a child.

"Then with the boosters, all of you could become a conduit of great power. Your minds could move mountains. Perhaps literally. Imagine the possibilities."

"And what if something else happens? What if it's not what you expect?"

Doctor Stern patted David on the shoulder. "This is science after all. We learn something new every day."

He gave David the jet injection of booster.

The chemical booster immediately made its way up David's arm like worms that crawled under his skin.

The boosted effects were different for David. He didn't suffer hyper-anxiety, like Jan. Or hallucinate, like Little Jack. Instead, David felt like he was more open to the sensations of his surroundings. Eventually his muscles would stiffen and he lost control of decision making. He also lost all sense of time.

When boosted, all David could do was *feel*. He could actually sense the mental energies of both Jan and Little Jack within his mind's eyes. It was through this concentrated brain activity that Doctor Stern hoped to convert David's mental activity to some form of physical energy.

David slowly made his way over to the Focus Chamber to join Jan and Little Jack. The booster continued to work on him.

The chamber door made a soft click behind David as an electromagnet locked him in. Vents above whispered circulated air so that the three of them could breath.

David prepared himself. He wrapped a wireless telemetry band around his forehead and wrists. Then he gripped the bio-electric transfer rail with both hands. The rail spanned the length of the chamber. It was made of highly conductive copper, a good material for the transfer of energy between the three Threaders. David could sense that it was already warmed by Jan and Little Jack's mental activity.

He faced out to watch Doctor Stern talk with someone working one of the control stations. The procedure would begin soon.

"Are you ready, David?" Doctor Stern mouthed the words from outside the chamber.

David couldn't hear the words, but he understood the meaning and nodded.

To his right, Little Jack had already slipped into a hallucinogenic and catatonic state. His hairy knuckles were locked around the bio-electric rail. Drool hung from his open mouth. He stared at the floor. David could smell the man's sweat. But the mental energy radiating from Little Jack was immediately felt across the bio-electric rail.

For experimental purposes, Little Jack was like a bobbin that a spool rested on. He served as a grounding point during the Threading. Little Jack's mind had latched onto some bit of selective memory while in his catatonic state. His mental energy felt focused and small, like a dot no bigger than the size of a pin's head. As long as David remembered this sensation, he could eventually retreat back to it to complete the experiment.

David would then communicate this sensation back to Jan. It's how he always managed to bring her back from her Threading. She would slowly wind back the threads. Then she would piece her mind back together from a splintered state. Thanks to Little Jack, David always felt a relief to know Jan would be okay.

The booster was really kicking in now.

David's mind was becoming an open conductor while Jan's breathing rapidly increased. He sensed her energy feeding into him. It entered his hands, crawled up his arm, and along his neck. He fed off of Jan's mind, absorbing her mental energy. In a way, his experimental relationship with her was parasitic. This was probably why he most disliked Threading.

The theory was that when Jan's joule counter hit full capacity, the peak energy she produced would supercharge a portion of David's brain. His brain would then be permanently altered. All thanks to Jan.

Doctor Stern couldn't actually say what the full result would be. There was speculation that David could become a walking energy detector without the need for boosters. Or he would develop the ability of rapid computation and extreme intelligence. Who knew? Doctor Stern believed that David was a vessel, ready to receive the gift of becoming something more than human. But was David ready for such a change? Was the world? And at what cost to Jan?

Beams of light were directed at the polycarbonate walls. They focused on Jan. David could only watch them through the see-through walls.

Jan's breathing accelerated even more. In-out-in-out. The condensation of her breath spread across the plastic interior wall. It partially obscured the view of the joule counter on the nearby workstation. David could just make out the joule counter climbing.

His muscles stiffened. His hands shook. The ability to make decisions dulled. Time was losing meaning. All he could do now was *feel*. David felt the bio-electric rail grow warmer, almost hot to the touch.

Mental energy was flowing in. Little Jack's focused dot was no bigger than the size of the head of a pin. At the same time, Jan's energy came at him in steady pulses. The two energies commingled as Little Jack's moved around inside it like the nucleus of an atom. As long as Little Jack's mental energy didn't overwhelm David, Jan would be okay.

The projected light beams changed.

They split into an array of colors that formed a square shape in the air. Then a smaller array appeared within the first. It repeated the same color pattern while a third shape began. It was a square within a square within a square.

The spectacle dazzled David's eyes. This patterned shape continued while forming new squares within more new squares. David lost himself, hypnotized by the barrage of shapes that seemed to go on forever.

He could feel his mind changing. It was as if the beams of lights formed a door that waited to be opened. And when it did, a multi-colored aura of energy would embrace him. It would become one with him. It wanted him to forget everything else. To forget Little Jack. To forget Jan. Just feel the door open. Feel the door. *Open it, David. Open—*

Jan whimpered. The sound broke the light's hypnotic spell over David.

He suddenly realized that Little Jack's dot of energy was disappearing from his mind. David was losing it. Its sense of existence vanished and reappeared before vanishing again.

If he didn't do something fast, David would lose it altogether and Jan's mind would be lost.

Doctor Stern pointed at the joule counter and grinned at the lab assistant.

David's thoughts raced but he couldn't act. Was this what the Doctor had wanted all along? That to get through the final boundary, Jan's Last of Lasts, he must sacrifice her mind?

In David's hypnotic state, he had forgotten about Little Jack's dot of energy altogether. He would have allowed Jan to have continued threading to infinity. And with no sanctuary to return to, Jan's mind would never return from her splintered state.

Little Jack's dot faded again. Jan's whimper turned into intermittent gasping.

With no sense of time, David couldn't tell for how long this was all going on for. His own boosted state held David back. His hands shook. His stiffened muscles would not release the transfer rail. He struggled to concentrate, to make his feet move, to try and grab Jan and snap her out of her state of mind. But he couldn't get himself to act.

And even if he could shake Jan back to consciousness,

would the sudden interruption permanently shatter her mind?

All David could do was *feel*. And what he felt was anger. The emotion grew within that area of his mind where Little Jack's sanctuary and Jan's splintered energy commingled.

He thought of Jan. Of how scared she must be right now. Of how Doctor Stern considered her nothing more than disposable. David's anger grew more and it overwhelmed all his thoughts.

The anger burst out. David could feel the emotional disruption leave his hands and flow outward along the transfer rail. Jan gasped and David heard her collapse to the chamber's floor.

David somehow must have forced Jan to spool back her mind.

Outside the chamber, Doctor Stern pointed at David. His brow was furrowed and his mouth turned down in anger. The joule counter was dropping. The projected lights shut down. A lab assistant rushed over and unlocked the Focus Chamber door.

David's booster effect began to wear off. His hands relaxed even though they felt somewhat heavy and stiff. This was unusual, because it usually took hours for the booster to fully work its way out of his body. He was able to release the rail and turn his head. Jan lay shaking.

Doctor Stern stood in the doorframe of the focus chamber. His face was taut. A vein stood raised on his forehead. His mouth was twisted in a look of both frustration and disgust.

"You are on the brink of greatness, David," Doctor Stern said.

David glared back. "You would have destroyed her mind."

"You short-sighted—"

David found the strength to ball his shaking hands into painful fists. He stepped forward. The doctor stood only several inches from him in the small chamber. Then he punched Doctor Stern in the nose.

Blood sprayed as the doctor stumbled back. Both hands covered his wounded face. Drops of blood fell on the floor.

The lab assistant grabbed David. He held him back from punching the doctor a second time. David was too weak to resist.

"We'll do the experiment again tomorrow. No more weeklong breaks before another Threading," Doctor Stern said. He looked over at Jan who shivered as if she were freezing cold. "I don't care if she's ready or not."

David could do nothing but watch Doctor Stern leave the experiment's control center. The lab assistant would not release him so that he could help Jan. He was forced outside the chamber as more assistants came in. They carried her out like a limp rag doll.

Little Jack still gripped the transfer rail, locked in a catatonic state. David felt just as helpless.

That night, David knocked at Jan's dormitory door. She didn't answer so he let himself in.

The room was dark except for one light near her bed. Clothes she had worn earlier were tossed on the floor in a crumpled pile. A discarded book lay open on the floor. David made his way over to her.

"You weren't at dinner. I brought you a piece of cake," David said.

Jan said nothing. She lay on her side in bed wearing a t-shirt and pair of shorts. Her dyed black hair was disheveled. Her back was to him and it rose and fell in slow breaths.

David could tell that the booster had worn off her. He put the small plate of cake next to the lamp that rested on a nightstand.

"Jan, are you okay?"

There was silence for a moment. "You shouldn't have stopped me today."

"What do you mean?"

"The booster's symptoms. I had more tonight. I can't take this anymore," Jan said.

"Maybe you should drop out of the program. Doctor Stern can find someone else no problem."

Jan turned over to look at him. In the pale yellow light, he could see her mascara more clearly. Dried tears had streaked her face.

She shook her head. "I don't think the side effects can be reversed. I can't live like this anymore."

David sat on the bed. "You don't mean that."

"I want to splinter my mind. Forever."

"But you were so scared in the chamber."

"I...I don't remember. Maybe I was. But I've thought about it. I want to go to the Last of Lasts and never come back."

David reached into his pocket. He pulled out the metal token with the palm tree and placed it in her hand.

"I found this just before I left college. When I start to give up hope, I rub this between my thumb and forefinger. It reminds me that there are better places in this world. This token gives me hope."

Jan's lips trembled. "I want to forget all this. Forget everything."

"There's more for you Jan. There's more outside of this lab."

Jan made a weak smile. She briefly held the metal token up to the light. The stamped palm tree glinted. She gave it back to David.

"That's sweet. But I don't think there's hope for me."

"Jan, the Last of Lasts. There's some places we probably shouldn't explore. Don't let yourself go there tomorrow."

"David?" Jan's brown eyes were wide.

"Yes?"

"Will you hold me?"

David lay beside Jan and wrapped her in his arms. She felt small and frail. She shook slightly as she cried into his chest.

"I wish I had your hope. I do," Jan said.

"Maybe together we can do something. Maybe we can cross the Last of Lasts together."

"How?"

That was the million dollar question.

Tomorrow, Doctor Stern would devise some way to ensure that David would not interrupt the experiment again. And if that happened, Jan would never stop threading. Her mind lost forever in a splintered state. And David wouldn't be there for her.

The only solution David could think of was that he should try to focus again on his anger. Somehow it had helped him to overcome his boosted state during today's experiment. The emotion had enough energy to interrupt Jan's threading.

Could he produce that kind of anger again?

Jan's breathing had quieted as she drifted off to sleep.

As David lay there, he concentrated on the image of Doctor Stern's bloodied face. He imagined himself squeezing the image into such a tight space within his mind that it pressed together like a pill capsule under compression.

The image burst out and escape. David tried again. Over and over he worked on this until he became mentally exhausted.

He wasn't sure if the effort was useful. Hopefully, he had conditioned himself so that he would still remember where the anger resided. What else could he do? Doctor Stern had scientific training, a support staff, and advanced technology. All David had was his feelings.

David felt like an ant among giants.

The next morning, someone banged on David's dormitory door. When he opened it, three stone-face security guards in black uniforms walked in.

The men were abrupt. They told David to quickly change because the experiment would begin soon. They answered no questions and refused him the option of breakfast.

After he was dressed, they cuffed his hands behind his back. This was obviously a precaution to ensure that David didn't cause any more problems for Doctor Stern.

When David arrived at the TECC, Doctor Stern was already there talking with a lab assistant. His nose had stopped bleeding but a large bruise and some swelling served as a reminder of yesterday's altercation.

David smiled to himself. It was a small bit of satisfaction

which made up for the uncomfortable steel handcuffs that restrained him now.

The guards ushered him over to where Little Jack stood waiting. The short man raised his hands as if to say, "Why?" David motioned with his eyes over at Doctor Stern. Little Jack made a vulgar gesture with his middle finger at the doctor's back and then grinned. David returned the grin.

The guards must have also come for Jan. She was already in the focus chamber prepping. She had changed out of her shorts and t-shirt from the night before. But her hair was still disheveled. She hadn't cleaned off the streaked mascara from her face. And her eyes looked tired and confused.

Her breathing was accelerating as condensation built on the polycarbonate interior.

David had no way to speak to Jan. He could only hope that their time together last night had changed her mind about the Last of Lasts.

"It's good to see you cooperating, David," Doctor Stern said.

"I'm handcuffed. Do I have a choice?"

David thought again of the anger that he tried to encapsulate in his mind last night. Just like a pill capsule. Seeing Doctor Stern in the lab now only made the emotion more intense and more difficult to compress.

The Doctor picked up a needle syringe and pointed it at David. The syringe was something new.

The lab assistant nodded. Together, Doctor Stern and the assistant walked over. Doctor Stern made a smile that was probably intended to be mocking. David thought the act to be comical. A bulbous swell had spread across both the Doctor's upper lip and nose that resembled something like a purple onion.

"I don't blame you for yesterday. You were boosted. And your little act of—" The Doctor's face grew dark and red for a moment. "Your act of enthusiasm was most likely due to the temporary symptoms of dementia."

"Take these cuffs off. Let's prove your scientific theory."

Little Jack grunted a laugh and slapped at his knee.

The lab assistant used a jet injector on Little Jack's exposed arm. Little Jack grew quiet. A guard assisted him as he hobbled over to the focus chamber.

"You've had your fun, David. Now I have mine."

Doctor Stern leaned close. His breath came at David's face in hot puffs. It smelled faintly of breath mints, something the Doctor probably used to cover up the stale odor of morning coffee.

The Doctor held up the same syringe he had shown the lab assistant a minute ago. Inside it was an opaque yellow solution.

"It contains Scopolamine. Some call it truth serum. My intent is different. We'll be doing a narcosynthesis on you as a controlled intravenous hypnosis. It will enhance your booster."

The long needle burned as it entered David's arm. A few seconds later, the Doctor finished and patted him on the shoulder.

"Wouldn't want you to harm yourself during the threading, David."

"You don't care about us. Any of us. Just your results."

Doctor Stern said nothing.

A guard forced David over to the chamber. The uniformed man opened the door and unlocked the cuffs. David's body felt relaxed. He didn't resist. The syringe had already started working. When the guard told him to place his hands on the bio-electric rail, he complied without a second thought. Then the guard left the chamber and locked the door.

David felt weightless.

He looked over at Jan. Her breaths came in quick, short bursts. In-out-in-out-in-out. It was like a ticking clock. Then the sound turned into a humming bird's beating wings. David's mind jumped to the image of a butterfly as it hovered on soft breeze.

How wonderful this chamber felt. It was warm in here, embracing him like a blanket. Its protective walls kept away bad doctors and mean guards.

He wanted to say something to Jan. But he couldn't quite remember what.

"Butterfly. Okay. Little pill." That was all he could manage to say.

The little pill. Was that from last night? Was it curved and smooth and shiny? David wanted to taste it, a fragile thing upon his tongue. He envisioned bright colors swirling inside its tiny capsule. He wanted the colors to break free and fill his mouth with rainbow warmth. A pill full of rainbow colors seemed funny and this thought made David laugh.

But he grew quiet when the projected lights began. Multiple colors. Squares within squares. David watched them and thought they were beautiful.

From somewhere nearby, David could hear the sound of waves. They seemed to ebb and flow onto some distant shore. Back and forth. Back and forth.

Was that someone breathing? No. He was floating on water. Somewhere nearby there must be an island. He imagined palm trees rooted in white sand.

He remembered how much he liked palm trees. And the ocean. And islands. But he couldn't see them now because a fog spread before his eyes. He tried to reach out and wipe away the fog. His hands wouldn't cooperate.

What if he swallowed the pill? That pill full of colorful swirling lights. Would that light shine out and show him where the island was?

"I wouldn't want you to harm yourself, David." Doctor Stern's voice seemed to loom nearby. But that was impossible. David was floating in the ocean.

David imagined picking up the pill and putting it into his mouth. His arms grew warmer. Then, almost hot. Then his tongue grew hot. The heat crawled up his neck.

"You've had your fun, David."

But David wanted to bite into the pill. To taste the swirling colors as they broke free. He wanted to see the island.

The pill lay hot on his tongue. It made his brain hot. Fire hot. For a moment, he became afraid.

"David, you are just an ant. Ants cannot go to islands," Doctor Stern's voice said to him.

But ants could live on islands. It made no sense. David grew angry. Then furious.

"Wrong. Wrong, Doctor Stern."

David would prove what ants could do. He bit into the pill.

David's hypnotic spell was immediately broken.

It was like an explosion. Energy erupted from his brain. It traveled down his neck and out his hands. He couldn't stop it.

Again, another mental explosion. This time, the energy rushed out from all over his body. It was a convulsion of so much force that it caused the air to crackle and arc. The smell of plasma filled the chamber.

"Stop!" Jan screamed.

David turned his head. Jan was gripping the bio-electric rail as if she would fall from some great height.

David could see white, ethereal threads flow out and spread out from her eyes. They wavered in front of him. Then they wrapped themselves around his arms and upper body, touching him with their bristled feelers. They pulled tighter, and he knew that they could crush the life out of him.

David couldn't control his mind. The explosion happened again. His mind was on fire, a volcano that continued to erupt.

The threads responded by pulling tighter, feeding off his energy and hungry for more. They were parasites that would suck him dry.

"Release me," David said. He meant it as a command. It sounded like a plea for mercy.

The writhing threads hesitated, still hungry.

"If you don't release me, I will shut my mind off. You will starve." He wasn't actually sure he could do this but he had to try the bluff.

The threads obeyed. They pulled back and away. David began to collect his thoughts again as the threads retreated.

"David, I can't see. I'm blind," Jan said.

Jan's eyes were milky white. They were the same color as the ethereal threads that had erupted from them.

Little Jack had come out of his catatonic state. He gawked open-mouthed at something outside the chamber walls.

Doctor Stern, the lab assistants, and the uniformed guards stood in place. Doctor Stern was caught in a pose of excitedly grabbing a guards arm and pointing at the focus chamber. He appeared to be alive and frozen in time.

David's mind convulsed again. Little Jack radiated a

blue field that rippled out from his body. The field spread out and covered everyone outside the focus chamber. The field must have acted as a time distortion field.

David realized that he must be like a battery for both Jan and Little Jack. He had stored and now sourced mental energy for their new abilities. Jan could emit the ethereal threads similar to what she had done during the experimental procedures. Little Jack seemed to be able to stop time or force people into a catatonic state of sorts.

But David also realized he might be able to control them to some extent.

He focused his thoughts on the chamber walls. The ethereal threads responded. They spread out in a complex pattern over its hard surface. David sensed that they weren't willing to expend any more of the precious, mental energy he supplied them. It would take someone else to force them to act into their full capacity.

"Jan, listen to me. I want you to imagine that the chamber walls are broken into a million pieces. Can you do that?"

Jan still gripped the rail. She was blind and afraid. She did nothing. David touched one of her hands. Slowly, she let go of the rail. She put her hands in his and nodded in agreement. David felt convulsions of energy flow from him and into Jan. The threads glowed.

It should have been impossible. Doctor Stern had told David that the focus chamber's walls were impact resistant enough to take a bullet. The thick polycarbonate cracked. Lines spider-webbed under the ethereal threads grip. Seconds later, the walls splintered and dropped into thousands of small pieces of plastic.

They were free.

David's mind was rapidly cooling off. He most likely

spent all of his mental energy on the effort to destroy the chamber wall. The threads snaked their way back into Jan. David sensed that they waited to someday emerge and to be fed again.

He squeezed Jan's hands. She returned the squeeze. They had survived the Last of Lasts mentally intact.

"We're leaving this place," David said.

"What about Doctor Stern?" Jan said.

David looked around at the frozen men in the lab. The Doctor had never budged. Little Jack still pulsed a blue field, but it was growing dimmer.

"Little Jack's already taken care of him."

"I can't see anyone."

"I'll explain later. But we have to get going. Let's just hope that whatever Little Jack did will last until we're far away from this building."

All three of them made their way out. They stepped over pieces of broken plastic. David guided Jan as they worked their way around the time-frozen Doctor Stern and his scowling guards. The doors that lead out from TECC were only a few feet away.

The Doctor, the lab assistants and the guards never moved. David imagined Doctor Stern's frustration when he later discovered that his 'lab rats' had escaped. He grinned.

When the three of them made it out to the hallway, David could see the exit out of the building. No one tried to stop them.

"David, where are we going?" Jan said.

David reached into his pocket and fingered the metal token. He pulled it out and flipped it in the air. The token landed back in his hand. The palm tree glinted in the overhead light.

"Let's go find some hope."

Little Jack just slapped his knee and snorted a laugh. Another blue field rippled outward from him, much fainter than the previous ones. It was something like a hiccup and it gave him the appearance of a blinking Christmas light.

Minutes later, they were outside. The sun was shining on them like a warm day on a tropical island.

WINTER SLEEP

A STILL-GREEN LEAF clings but limbs of solid oak somehow stretch wide and tall. Piles of dead brown vegetation. Pungent dirt that slowly molds. A chilling wind sighs through empty Central Park benches. Greying cumulus now grow darker over shadow painted skyscrapers, fists of cauliflower vapor over four hundred and seventy square miles forced into a cold, dead dream.

Today, the single leaf wears a green coat with borders of summer squash yellow and orange pumpkin trim. Tomorrow and tomorrow, only sickening, scaly tree bark. And Winter's skin will cover Park and City in cracked ice and lumpy snow.

Further is where life returns to begin again. The leaf is only one of many to be plucked by the gathering storm, a miniature tempest of tumbling lobes. It's a desperate scraping of dry, bristle-tipped teeth against the gritty earth. And it will finally lay to rest and feed the sleeping acorns that wait for Spring.

Soon.

The leaf trembles as the cold wind stirs. The oak tree bends. The last scraps of sun fall below the skyline. Yet a thousand lights and many more shine out against the starless black.

AA FOR HAPPY THE MOUSE

THE 101 COFFEE Shop in Hollywood is a Monday night AA purgatory for Happy the Mouse. He shows up weekly to admit to another episode of his drunken shortcomings while C-listers and aspiring waitresses gaze wide-eyed at the ninety-year-old animation star. Besides his trademark ears, it's his four-fingered gloves that everyone in the coffee shop knows him for. When Sweetie had been there for him, the gloves where always a washed pearl white. Now they're yellow because he's let the laundry pile up, he eats too many greasy takeout dinners and he watches too much porn.

He doesn't look his age and he certainly doesn't act it: He raises a boyish grin when he says, "I am Happy, an alcoholic," and talks about how he chucked an emptied whisky bottle through one of his front windows. His gloved hands cover his mouth as he laughs out a *Ho, ho shucks* after admitting that he streaked down the Walk of Fame, waving his blue pants and screaming, "Sweetie!"

But Happy *feels* ninety.

There was a time when he felt twenty. Sweetie would *Yoo hoo* and the two would twirl each other around and he'd break into a playful hamburger dance. Silly the Dawg always stood by, slapping his knee and yucking out a couple of *Garshes*. That was all before the yachts, the mansions and the Porsche collection. That was before the long slide into late nights of two or more six packs. Before falling asleep by the Olympic-sized pool just to cool down the morning amphetamines that keep it all going. One evening, he came back from a voice session to discover an empty house. And Silly had picked up the slack.

Happy wraps up his confession to the AA group.

He looks over at an empty chair that he asked be placed next to him at this meeting. He wants to pick up his cell phone and call Sweetie. He'd ask her to come and listen to his apology. He'd show her a new side of him, one that's something more than just new bows and diamond studded sundresses. But he knows that Silly would only show up, too. Happy stares at his yellowed gloves—a stranger's hands. He envisions them wrapped around the backstabber's spaghetti throat. He decides not to make the call.

A new waitress is here tonight—legs that don't quit until Friday and she keeps eying him. She probably wants to screw some agent's contact information out of him. But hey, that's the price of fame. And there's always going to be another new waitress.

Still, he thinks about next week's meeting and how he'll ask again for that empty chair. Maybe then he'll finally make that phone call. Maybe.

WAKING FROM AN ETERNAL SLEEP

THE VILLAGERS of Dinnish Pa'kor stood on the shore of the Lake of Shadows. They gathered in small groups as they quietly spoke of Dabi's murder.

Shiran did not join the others. She knew that many of the villagers were intrigued by the recent events. The great yellow suns warmed their nearly naked bodies while they nervously talked amongst themselves. They spoke of secrets. Some stole glances at Dabi's covered body that lay by the Lake's poisonous waters.

Instead, Shiran stood near Abian.

She wanted to say many words to the shackled man. He kneeled in the sand, head cast down, rough steel collars wrapped around his raw-chaffed wrists and neck. Two guards stood behind him. They held thick-handled wood shafts tipped with spearheads. These weapons were meant to cause a painful death.

But Abian said nothing.

This angered Shiran. "It will go even worse for you when you are submerged in the Lake of Shadows. In there, your body will dissolve. You will not have an eternal sleep amongst the stars."

Abian looked up at her. His hazel eyes were dull from days of captivity and hunger. Somehow, he managed a smile.

"The Unmarked Ones have secrets. I have seen them with my own eyes."

"You are a liar. A liar would kill his own brother, my husband."

"Let me show you the proof of my truth. The power that the Unmarked Ones hold over all of us will come undone."

"Again, you lie. The Unmarked Ones were sent from the stars. They guide us to eternal sleep."

Shiran turned away from Abian. She no longer wanted to look at her husband's murderer. She could only think of her own secret. She had never revealed it to her husband Dabi before his death. It was her one regret and caused great sorrow within her heart.

She walked over to Dabi's body and she prayed to the Great Judge. She prayed that her secret would reach Dabi in the stars above. She also prayed that her husband should be found worthy of the sacrifice that he had made.

Before Dabi's murder, the Unmarked One named Saluman had brought wondrous news regarding a villager by the name of Jojing. The Great Judge had chosen Jojing to be taken to the stars for eternal sleep.

Both Dabi and Abian had volunteered to escort Jojing to his final rest. At first, Saluman protested. He said that this was unusual. But he consulted with the Great Judge. A large gift of food and wine had appeared near the village that night. The Great Judge must have looked favorably on Dabi and Abian's escort.

Shiran had relished in her final moments with her husband, Dabi. In the village, there was much celebrating. And Shiran had made love to her husband for the last time. Now he lay dead on the Lake's sandy shore.

The Unmarked One named Saluman approached her. Like all Unmarked Ones, he bore no black markings above his left brow. It was known that all Unmarked Ones were sent by the Great Judge as it had been for many hundreds of generations.

"Shiran, the Great Judge will soon deliver us a new gift. I have seen it in a dream. Let us look to the stars," Saluman said.

Saluman was a wise and fair man. His visions had always proved to come true. When crops had failed, he would ask the village to pray to the Great Judge. Then he would dream. Gifts would soon appear somewhere just outside the village.

Shiran ran to him and clutched at his hand.

"Abian has returned with my husband's mutilated body."

When Abian had returned, he dragged Dabi's body behind him like some dead tree stump. Dabi's face was so brutalized that she could no longer recognize the man who once had held her in his strong arms. Her heart had broken beyond what she thought was possible.

Abian had claimed someone else had done the wicked deed. But no other witness could confirm such a tale of twisted imagination.

"Your pain must be great. But how do you know that it was Abian that killed your husband?" Saluman said.

"Because he makes a false claim."

"And what is this claim?"

"He claims that men in black clothing murdered Dabi."

"Does he have a witness or proof?"

"He has none."

Saluman looked over at Abian who was still shackled and kneeling in the sand. He seemed to study the accused man. Some of the villagers gathered near. Finally, Saluman cleared his throat and spoke.

"We must always remember that the Great Judge would never wish harm to a villager. Condemning someone to the Lake of Shadows is a serious punishment. I must be fair. I will talk to Abian, the accused."

More villagers gathered around as Saluman made his way over to Abian. Abian did not look up.

"You claim to have seen other men murder Dabi," Saluman said.

"Yes. They wore black clothing and carried weapons I did not recognize."

"And did this happen near the end of the world where the stars and land meet?"

Abian looked up. He smirked.

"There are no stars. There is only a great wall which keeps us here. The black clothed men were sure to see to that. They grabbed Jojing and chased after Dabi and me. Only I escaped."

Some of the villagers murmured. Saluman looked around and raised his hand to quiet them.

"Abian, this is a strange story you tell. There are only the stars at the end of the world. It is known that no one lives further beyond the village."

Other villagers nodded their head in agreement.

"And how is it known, Saluman? No one else has seen where the stars will meet the land. Only you say this," Abian said.

Shiran became enraged at Abian's blasphemous words.

Her husband had died at the hands of that lying madman. She screamed and charged Abian so as to beat him with her fists.

Saluman and other villagers held her back. Shiran's arms were restrained. She could not wipe at the hot tears that streaked her face.

"Abian, the trouble you cause a grieving widow," Saluman said.

Abian's voice softened. "Shiran, I hid from the black clothed men. They spoke to each other as they searched for me. They knew your secret. The one that you had not revealed. Not even to Dabi before he died."

Shiran stood in shock. She was no longer struggling, no longer crying. How could it be that Abian knew that she carried a secret? It had never been revealed to anyone else.

"Do not try to worsen Shiran's state of mind," Saluman said.

"Shiran, I will tell you your secret. Then you can judge me for yourself. Will you listen?" Abian said.

Saluman turned red-faced. "Now you are being cruel to her. How can you do this?" Saluman said.

"Shiran, search your heart. You know I would never harm my brother. I have always loved him. That is why I went with him on escort. I wanted to protect him. The only thing I am guilty of is not saving his life."

"Perhaps you wished to have Shiran for yourself. In *your* heart, you believed that you could make Shiran your wife," Saluman said.

Saluman's face continued to grow redder as he yelled out the words. Shiran was surprised by the Unmarked One's anger. She had never seen him this way.

"And would I have brought my brother's body back for everyone in the village to see? Why not just hide it? I could claim that Dabi had also had walked off into the stars," Abian said.

The villagers agreed that this was reasonable.

Shiran also agreed even though this went against her feelings in her heart. She was curious. Did Abian really know her secret? This could be a test of truth to prove that proved that Abian lied. He should at least be allowed to reveal it before being tossed into the Lake of Shadows and dissolved into silence. Then Shiran's conscious would be cleared.

"I think I will pass my judgement now. It seems obvious that this man cannot be trusted," Saluman said.

Shiran held her hand up. "Wait. I want to hear what Abian will say. Tell me, Abian. What is my secret?"

Abian paused. "As the black-dressed men searched for me, they said that you were pregnant. They knew Dabi was the father. They could not allow you to give birth inside the village."

The other villagers stood silent. They looked at Shiran.

She stared at Abian. New tears streamed down her face. How could he know? Finally, she nodded.

"It is true," she said, "I am pregnant with Dabi's child."

When the crowd heard this, they yelled out that Abian had the visions of the Unmarked Ones. The Great Judge had spoken through him.

"This is madness. Impossible. He is not Unmarked. Quickly! Take Abian to the Lake of Shadows," Saluman demanded.

The villagers chanted, "Let Abian speak. Let Abian speak." They pressed in closer and surrounded Saluman. The guards looked nervously around.

Shiran walked over to Abian and touched his face.

Saluman attempted to grab Shiran and stop her. The villagers turned on him and held him back.

"If you are not the one, do you have any proof of my husband's murderer?" she said.

"My hands are shackled. Reach into my pants pocket. I have killed one of the black-dressed men and taken a trophy from him."

When Shiran pulled her hand out of Abian's pocket, she held a small, metal disk with a red jewel. The disk was cool to the touch. The red jewel pulsed. Strange symbols were etched across its golden surface.

The circular disk felt alien to her. Could it have come from the stars above? But if so, why did it cause a revulsion within her belly? This was an object that held its own secret. And this secret was greater than her own.

"The black-dressed man I killed wore that on his shirt," Abian said.

Shiran turned on Saluman. "Why would the Great Judge send others to harm Dabi? He was innocent." She spoke loudly so that all the villagers could hear her.

Abian interrupted. "Because Saluman has lied to all of us. I will take you to the black-dressed man's body. There, you will see one of the murderers."

Shiran held the metal disk up to the sunlight for the other villagers to see. It changed colors in the light, turning green and then blue and then back to a golden yellow. Some reached out to touch the alien object. Each time, their hand quickly retreated.

"Abian has shown me proof. Release him. I no longer seek an ill-gained justice," Shiran said.

The villagers agreed. The two guards removed Abian's shackles. He rubbed at his wrists and neck. Then he smiled.

"Your husband shall have his justice. I will take you to the proof."

Saluman shouted obscenities at the crowd. He told them that they were fools. That the Great Judge must have had a reason for killing Dabi. That Abian was just as guilty. And perhaps even Shiran conspired with them in a sinful way.

The two guards grabbed Saluman. They dragged him along as the villagers followed Abian and Shiran. The two of them walked side-by-side.

Shiran travelled west with Abian. They passed by the Lake of Shadows, through a woods and then into a clearing. The sun began to lower. Blue sky changed to streaks of orange and pale white of the late afternoon.

No one spoke as they walked except for Saluman. He frequently warned that the Great Judge would be angry at the villagers for treating an Unmarked One so poorly. Saluman behaved in such a way that he no longer appeared to be the wise man that Shiran had once believed him to be.

Near dusk, Abian pointed out a small cave. Its mouth was just barely visible in a large hill covered in thick, green grass.

Many of the villagers suddenly became nervous. They scratched at themselves or restrained one another. They seemed afraid that they were near the entrance to where the stars met land.

Even Shiran worried that they could violate a sacred space set aside by the Great Judge. But she did not see any stars or anything else unusual peeking out from the dark mouth of the cave. Still, she held back.

"Do not worry, Shiran. I will go into the cave. I will soon return with proof," Abian said.

Shiran watched him disappear inside. Her thoughts

turned to the alien disk Abian had showed her. How could a black-dressed man be so different from herself and the other villagers? How had recent events caused Abian to doubt the Great Judge and the eternal sleep in the stars?

"This will end badly for you all," Saluman said.

He glared at Shiran. Spittle had gathered around his mouth from yelling and constant complaining. She said nothing.

When Abian reappeared, the crowd stirred and craned their necks. Shiran stepped forward. Her curiosity overcame any fears that she might have.

Abian dragged behind him the body of what looked like a man. He wore a black shirt and pants. White stripes ran across the shoulders and down the legs. A wide belt wrapped around his waist. The belt held cylindrical shaped objects in leather loops. One object in particular puzzled Shiran. It was a long metal rod attached to a grip, a grip for a knife or a tool.

On closer inspection, she saw other things that made this black-dressed man different. He was taller than any villager by at least a full head. On top of his bloodied skull were many strands of fiber that looked like brown string. Like all the other villagers, Shiran's head was smooth and naked. When she touched the brown strings, their soft threads shifted and exposed two fleshy objects. They stuck out at both sides of the black-clothed man's head.

Shiran touched the sides of her own head. She only had two holes which were covered by a stiff, brown membrane.

"Shiran, look at his face," Abian said.

His eyes were blue like the sky above. They stared at nothing, vacant of life. *He is missing something. But what?* Then she realized that the black-clothed man had no markings above his left brow.

"He is unmarked like Saluman," Shiran said.

"These unmarked men live behind a wall north of here. They took Jojing there. But I do not know why."

"How did they kill my husband?"

Abian nodded at the long metal rod on the black-clothed man's belt. "One of them had pointed it at him. There was a loud sound like thunder. Then Dabi fell dead."

Furious, Shiran snatched the metal rod from the belt. It felt heavy and cold in her hands. The rod's grip was rough with a textured pattern. She marched over to Saluman and pointed the rod at him.

"Is this how I use it, Saluman? Do I name the person I wish to kill and point this? Tell me. Why are you unmarked? What secrets do you carry inside you?"

Saluman's eyes were wide with fear.

"Please, don't point the gun at me. If you put it down, I'll tell you what I know."

"This gun must have great power. If you do not tell me, you will be dead like Dabi."

Saluman flinched when Shiran moved her hand. But she gave the gun to Abian instead. Then she held up the metal disk.

"What is this object?"

"It's an identification badge. All uniformed security wear them."

"You know so much about the black-clothed men. Who are you really?"

"We're from a planet very far away from here. It's called Earth. It's beyond the stars you see. You call us men but we're not the same race. We are humans."

"Then why are you here?"

"To study you. Sometimes we perform experiments. That's why you've been tagged with the brow markings."

Shiran struggled to understand Saluman's words. She did not know what an *experiment* was. Or how villagers could live beyond the stars. She shook her head in confusion.

"Yet you look like us. Not like the black-dressed man. Your head is naked. Is this—"

"I was altered to look like you. For years, we have walked among you. We guide your primitive culture. We form your beliefs."

"And so the Great Judge has been planted in our heads like the food we grow? He is only a story that you and other humans have made up?"

Saluman nodded.

The other villagers were troubled by this. They asked questions amongst

themselves.

"We should kill him, Shiran. To punish Saluman for what he has done to Dabi and all of us," Abian said.

Shiran rubbed at her pregnant belly. The villagers now knew that they had been deceived. The humans would soon know, too. She feared that more humans in the stars would soon come for her child.

Even if the village were to take a stand, they would be no match against more human guns. They would all be massacred. Their best chance was to retreat, to hide, and to warn other villages.

It would not be easy to convince them. They must take the alien metal disk and the human gun with them as proof. It was their best chance. Perhaps there would come a day when the village of Dinnish Pa'kor and others united to push back the human invaders. And maybe her unborn child would lead them all to a day of freedom, a day of no experiments.

"Let Saluman go. He will send a message back to the other humans."

Abian protested. The other villagers looked shocked.

"We must be wise. There is no Great Judge that we can rely on to guide us with false words. If we kill Saluman, the humans will come for us that much sooner. We must unite with other villages and prepare. Only then will we be ready for them."

Abian walked over to Shiran to give her the gun.

"No, you must learn to use this. And we must teach others. You will become our first soldier."

Then Shiran turned to Saluman.

"I want you to take a message back to the humans."

The guards released Saluman's hands. He wiped at spittle from his mouth but he did not become aggressive.

"What would you have me say?"

"That we know about the humans. And soon all the other villages will too. If you do not leave our planet, we will someday hunt you down. And then we will come for you in the stars and hunt you at your very own Earth."

Saluman shook his head. "I will tell them. But you have too many generations to evolve for that."

"And today is the first day that we wake from our sleep in the stars."

Abian commanded Saluman to leave or there would be consequences. He pointed the gun at him. The other villagers watched the human shamble off, mumbling to himself.

Shiran turned to walk away. She waved at her people to follow. They followed.

Two moons had formed above in the darkening sky. Shiran tried to imagine life beyond the moons. What would it be like to visit places somewhere beyond the stars? A place where there were no secrets. They were not places where people told stories of Great Judges. They were places of new beginnings.

This would be a future that was made by her hands and the other villagers. No Great Judge. No Unmarked Ones. No secrets. This was a time that she had finally woken from a near-eternal sleep.

THE BIG CRASH

AFTER THE LAST of the steel weights were stacked on floor racks, the Iron Will's Trainers joked around. They balled their wipe-down rags into tight terry cloth wads and flexed their biceps at one another. Each man and woman grinned and teased as the front desk manager held out a grey bucket for them to toss in a Friday night's worth of collected bench sweat. But they quieted down when the last rag dropped into the now full bucket. The manager cleared her throat.

"You guys really are the best trainers ever," she said, her blond pony tail bobbing as she looked over each of them. "A new gym just opened a block away. But you keep our clients coming back for more." Then she curled her tanned and muscled arms into a show of strength. The trainers looked at one another. Hints of tense hope were in their eyes.

"There were days when corporate had doubts," the manager continued. And as if defying anyone to silence her, she stared at them in a momentary silence. Then she finally raised her strong chin and let out a howl of victory. Her blue eyes flashed. "So despite the rumors, we are not shutting our doors. Iron Will's will be the best gym in town!"

All the Trainers let out a cheer. Everyone palmed high-fives. After several suggestions, they agreed to a nearby bar that specialized in low-calorie cocktails. One round of drinks, more jokes and they called it quits at midnight because some of them had to lead a spinning group at six a.m. A few hooked up for an intimate evening.

The year was 2008 and one of the worst housing market crashes in Orlando Florida's history. Many local gymnasiums lost client memberships. These less service-friendly ones eventually closed their doors for good. Iron Will's lingered on because they did by example—their trainers had been selected for their superior physical attributes, enthusiasm and dedication. Mostly recruited through body building competitions, a few of the trainers were also discovered in local newspaper ads and online submissions. Each of them ate egg-white diets and journaled a scale's daily measurement. A two o'clock client training session meant two o'clock. They sweated through at least five sessions a week in tank tops and leggings. And they always said, "Thank you," to the client on their way out.

So there always seemed to be an incoming cliental based on reputation alone. But that never stopped the trainers from worrying after punching out. They often wondered if they could do anything else other than constant dumbbell presses and protein supplements. And they hid this fear of an outside world, a world away from Iron Will's and from one another.

"I've heard corporate's coming tomorrow," some of the trainers said.

"So goes the rumor," others said and then returned to their treadmills.

Corporate walked through the Iron Will's doors wearing rumpled ties and stiff-looking leather shoes. Trainers smiled. They whispered *safety audit* to one another as if the words held some kind of protective magic. But too many black suits spent too many hours behind closed doors with the front desk manager. That morning she had told them, "Expect great things." Now her promise evaporated from their minds like water in a distant oasis.

At closing, the trainers stacked weights. They waited. The silence felt heavier than the cast iron plates in their hands. It wasn't the manager that finally spoke to them—she had left the building hours ago.

He said his name was Bob. He wore a haircut too short on one side and combed back to cover a bald spot. Fat gathered around a buttoned-up collar and his belly pushed against a leather belt that creased at the buckle.

"It's nothing personal," Bob said. He coughed, then waited.

"I'm in a bodybuilding competition. How can I afford to pay the fees?" one Trainer said.

"I didn't expect this. I don't know where I'll go," a second Trainer said.

"Can we transfer to another gym?" But those locations already had full staffs.

Bob's baggy, seemingly endlessly tired eyes never rested on anyone for long. A few painful seconds of silence passed and the Trainers felt a mercy when he continued.

"It's the numbers. There will be severances for each of you."

The trainers single-filed out the front door with sealed envelopes in hand. A click was heard and a locked door behind them confirmed that Iron Will's had closed its doors forever. Each one wished each other good luck. Some said the gym a block away might be hiring. A few cried and hugged. Then the entrance lights went dark and the group broke up.

The trainers walked out to the parking lot one last time. Each searched for their cars in inky night air while loose gravel scattered under their shuffling feet.

GOOD-BYE, SWEET MERCURY

THERE WAS NEVER A BETTER place to be dead than at Aunt Jeanie's three-bedroom Chicago bungalow on Christmas. Early in the morning, disheveled and sleepy children bumped into unforgiving walls as they searched for a bathroom, a kitchen, and a spot closer to an oversized tree in the family room. By afternoon, exhausted parents grabbed any available bottles of wine. And when the evening stars cast tiny gems of light on a crisp outdoor snow, Tim's ghost watched old folks huddle around a roaring fireplace, toast to future never-will-bes, and sing about better times that happened many years ago.

Time moved slowly in the house, so there were always a few more seconds for Tim to say good-bye.

"Ticktock, ticktock," Maple said.

Tim waved her away. "She'll know I'm here."

He hovered over his sleeping daughter. She nestled deep under soft, warm blankets and dreamed of someone far away. Tim wanted to caress her hair and tell Rachel that everything would be all right. Vaporous hands passed through body and living soul. He spoke the girl's name, but she didn't move, oblivious to her deceased father's voice. He imagined that he smelled her hair and felt the tiny breath of life exhaled from her parted lips.

Maple mumbled something. Then the spirit guide grumbled about midnight being just around the corner. "This is never easy. But we have to go."

"It's not fair."

"Change. Can't stop it."

"I could have done more," Tim said.

"What? Done what?"

Tim stared out at the night sky. He watched a few dark clouds drift by, briefly hiding an unexplored space beyond the mortal atmosphere, and he imagined uninhabited celestial bodies somewhere far away, still waiting to be explored. Feeling lonely, he recalled the time he had named the planets of the solar system. Rachel had been so impressed.

"Mercury was her favorite," he said to Maple.

Maple laughed, a playful lilt. "It symbolizes childhood. Fitting."

"I'll name it after her. 'Heavenly Rachel.'"

"Beautiful. A wonderful gift."

He gazed once more. "I should stay."

"No one will ever know you're here."

He considered Maple's words. "And what else is there?"

Maple told him about space and time, that they were both finite and infinite in this house. Tim straddled a dichotomy: on one side, eternal darkness trapped a sentimental spirit. Like a never-ending cycle of theater, new life scenes began, and strangers acted out unfamiliar roles. When another curtain of mortality closed, a forgotten phantom remained the sole audience of another ambiguity. On the other side, he could embrace true life.

The spirit guide's voice softened. "Look once more at the night sky."

He did, and he had a vision.

The window opened wide—then wider—until the sun stood frozen and silent not more than few meters away. Much smaller than the actual size, it didn't burn him. But he sensed a fiery emotion inside the gaseous mass: an intelligence, a caring, or a love. Tim reached out to touch the life-giving star, and images of Rachel's birth flashed in his mind. Laughter and joy erupted from the father's mouth.

Seven clustered orbs, no larger than tennis balls, hovered nearby. But an eighth, gray planet stood apart. Tim thought of Rachel, his death, and an immeasurable distance that separated a parent and a child. He dropped his hands, and his smile wavered. A vast vacuum of space seemed to momentarily pull air from his lungs, and seven planets pressed in closer, waiting for something to happen.

When an orange flare burst out from the sun, Tim gasped.

The flame struck the eighth planet, helpless to escape the energetic plasma that quickly burned the rocky surface. Tim tried to pick up Rachel, cradle her in his arms, protect her, but his vaporous hands couldn't touch her. The colorless planet surface soon transformed to green growth. And deep inside his heart, Tim knew that Rachel would grow and thrive too.

On her sixth birthday, his daughter had told him she was a big girl now and not to be afraid. He struggled with the memory, as the small celestial body began to spin away from his view. He couldn't stop the travelling sphere. The father struggled to find some words that might matter. But there were none. And when the little planet faded into soft bands of milky light, Tim thought he saw the faces of Aunt Jeanie and others.

He closed his eyes for a moment. Distant night sky returned. And in his mind, a quiet peace grew. The father made a choice. "Good-bye, sweet child."

"We must go," Maple said.

He nodded.

The stars twinkled one last time in a black-and-silky sky covering Aunt Jeanie's Chicago bungalow. Sleep once again soothed old folks and parents. The last of the stubborn children surrendered to a dreamy bliss, anticipating another tomorrow. And somewhere far above, Mercury orbited a blazing sun.

COSMO'S TALE

EIGHTH GRADER ESTHER PRING browsed YouTube
Monday night. She giggled at Sid Vicious grabbing his
groin. She wondered how to stick a safety pin through her
nose without it hurting too much. Videos were so much
more fun than school.

Some of her Melton Middle School classmates were too
boring—like Janet Belorna boring. She wouldn't try to sneak
a switchblade into her school backpack. Well, it wasn't
really a switchblade—it was a butter knife. And its dull
serrated edge was too blunt to do any harm, anyway. It was
just for fun.

"Let's be ninja assassins. It's better than cat pics on your
phone," Esther had said as she revealed the butter knife to
Janet at third period.

"Are you crazy bringing that thing in here? I've got to
report that to Mrs. Wisa." Janet had said with a furrowed
brow.

"Oh, my God! What a goody-two-shoes. I'll toss it in the
garbage if you keep your mouth shut about it." It was no
wonder Esther didn't ask Janet to participate in the school

fundraiser. Esther wanted more exciting friends and she had a plan to make some.

She leaned back in her bedroom chair. The room was nice but boring. What if each of her glossy cat posters were rearranged so that they no longer were ordered by feline cuteness? A print of a sleeping Siamese was closest to her desk's hutch. The playful cat looked like her own pet, Cosmo. She loved her cat but he always did the same things everyday—play, eat, sleep. The cat was now curled up on her lap, an unmovable lump. Esther gave Cosmo a dutiful scratch and listened to his soft, rumbling purr. This used to delight her. But now his insistence on planting himself on her lap made her feel chained to her seat.

Esther looked over the fundraiser sign-up sheet that lay on her desktop. She tapped at the name *Trish Fernandez* carelessly scrawled in blue ink.

Trish had an edgy reputation. She always wore flip-flops mismatched with an anarchist T-shirt. She didn't seem to care what she wore or what others thought of her. Some people said that she often lied and stole things. She almost always skipped third period with Melody Dimbrowski, the two eventually showing up in fifth period smelling like a head shop. Esther tried several times to work up the nerve to talk to her. But when Esther passed Trish in the halls, Trish just eyed her with a sleepy gaze like a bored cat deciding what to do about a mouse that scurried by.

Some weeks Esther saw more of Trish's brother, Jamie Fernandez, at the Melton High baseball games. He looked straitlaced in his uniform—tall, dark-haired and enthusiastic. It was Dad's pro baseball stories as a shortstop that got her interested in the game from an early age. And watching Jamie Fernandez in his snug fitting uniform only made the game that much better.

So when Mrs. Wisa announced in second period the end-of-the-year fundraiser, Esther volunteered to do a kissing booth as long as Trish was assigned to her team. Mrs. Wisa hadn't liked the idea of a kissing booth. She had said that the girls were too young, being only in eighth grade and all the other usual concerned adult things that teachers always say. Esther remembered what her father told her about when he first signed as a pro player. "I wasn't the best player," he had told Esther. "But I tried hard. I took risks and got signed. You got to take chances if you want something bad enough." So Esther stuck to her guns and Mrs. Wisa had finally relented.

Taking some risks had paid off for Esther but Mrs. Wisa still laid down some rules. There was the usual stuff like all fundraiser teams must rent a booth and all teams must have at least four members. Fortunately, Esther was also able to recruit Cristee Gradings at the last minute. Mrs. Wisa also added rules just for Esther's newly formed team, the Glam Cats. The teacher insisted that Esther give out wax lips to do the actual kissing—no lip contact was allowed. And so was having to wear a teacher-approved team t-shirt and a two hundred dollar deposit on the booth to ensure that the girls followed through with the fundraiser. Mrs. Wisa wasn't taking any chances and Esther suspected it was for Trish's benefit.

Well, it was getting late.

Esther shut off her computer and climbed into bed with a groggy Cosmo. The cat circled around before settling on a nook between her upper arm and elbow. She looked out the window at the night sky. The stars were twinkling like little fairies that could make wishes come true. She smiled before drifting off to sleep. Her wish was coming true—the Glam Cats were about to do something interesting.

■ ■ ■

Slurping, snuffling and burping into their food, the other kids ate their school cafeteria lunches. Esther wondered how she tolerated it. Food wrappers and messy plates littered the tables. Sometimes the discarded food scraps didn't even make it onto a table, squished into the concrete flooring by a thoughtless sneaker. But she still wasn't sitting in the worst section of Melton Middle School's cafeteria. No, the worst section was the farthest corner of the cafeteria known as No-man's-land.

Esther could see Glenda there, sitting alone in a bookish mess. Several paperbacks, notebooks and pencils were scattered on her lonely table. She picked at a plate of limp spaghetti while holding an opened novel up to her face. Esther knew it was Glenda—aka Witch Girl—hidden behind the book because a crumpled black hat perched on top of the kid's head. A silver bow topped off the weird apparel.

The cafeteria was not a good place to hold a fundraiser meeting but it would have to do. While Esther waited for the other Glam Cats—Trish, Melody and Cristee—she wiped down her own table. It didn't have to be messy like everyone else's table, after all. Then she carefully unpacked items from a crisp, brown bag—a plastic spoon, a fork and some white paper napkins. Finally, her lunch was arranged in a reasonable order. Esther positioned a drink box to her left, smiling with some satisfaction. Then she patiently waited as she ate. To be honest, she was a little surprised when she finally did see Trish and the other two girls finally walking over, lunch trays in hand.

Esther waved them over.

"Glam Cats, who am I?" Esther said. She licked her arm

and rubbed at her left ear. Then she scratched at the table several times. "Cosmo, that's who."

Cristee, who carried a stuffed lion with her at all times, got into the fun. She used the toy like a pretend tail, prancing around and shaking her rear end. "I'm Kitty-Kitty, meow, meow." Her voice squeaked like in a cartoon.

Melody watched Cristee's playful antics and grunted out a laugh. She scratched at the air and made a low growl. "Tommie, that's who," she said.

Trish smiled but she did nothing. Her sleepy eyes just stared at Esther. "I forgot my name," she said.

Cristee wiggled over to Trish and waggled the stuffed lion at her. "Silly, you're Ragamuffin," she said.

"Oh, yeah—sure. Meow," Trish said. She scissored her fingers, making two whiskers before dropping her tray onto the table and flopping into her seat.

Cristee continued to play, wiggling her toy at some boys behind her. They cheered her on. But lunch time only lasted so long. Esther shook her head and Cristee took notice. She sat down like the rest of them, flopping the toy lion next to her.

"We have the two hundred dollar deposit for the booth," Esther said.

Trish shrugged. "I've never donated. I don't believe you."

Esther reached into her backpack and pulled out a white envelope that contained her Dad's contribution. Written in black marker was *The Glam Cats Fund*. She opened it and showed Trish the contents.

"My Dad gave me the money. Can you believe it?"

Trish munched on some potato chips while gazing at the green bills that Esther counted out. "You could do a lot of things with that money."

"We'll just need to raise a little more cash for our T-shirts and the wax lips."

"Swag can be expensive."

"I'll find everything online."

"Bet you haven't gotten a quote for anything."

Trish wasn't cooperating but Esther expected this. Esther had half expected her new friend to have skipped out on the fundraiser planning session altogether. She still smelled like a headshop.

Esther cleared her throat. "I'm making calls after school," she said.

Trish smiled, something she rarely did. "I know how to get a big discount on T-shirts,"

"Like how?" Esther said.

Trish continued gazing at the two hundred dollars. "My brother plays baseball. You know Jamie, over at Melton High. He can get lots of swag for cheap," Trish said.

"I couldn't impose on him."

Trish looked over at Melody and rolled her eyes. "No, wouldn't want to do that," Melody snorted.

Cristee seemed oblivious to what was being discussed. She turned and mewed at the boys behind her. They catcalled back, someone saying that they wanted to feel up some nice kitty. Mrs. Wisa yelled across the cafeteria for the boys to quiet down.

"Well, I've never actually met Jamie. OK. I bet you're brother could help." Esther said.

"Just give me the money you've got now. Then I'll give it to him. He'll buy everything."

Esther wrinkled her brow. If she gave Trish the deposit to buy swag, the Glam Cats wouldn't have money for the booth.

"Why don't we do a car wash to raise the swag money?" Esther said

Trish just sneered. "You don't trust me? I thought you wanted to be my friend."

Esther felt shock. She didn't mean to have offended her new friend. She vigorously shook her head. "I don't want to sound that way. It's just that—"

"I've got to go, Coz-*mo*." Trish said her pet's name with a strong emphasis on the *mo* part. Melody snorted again.

"But we haven't finished our fundraiser meeting," Esther protested weakly.

"Yeah, well, I've got more interesting things to do at the moment."

Trish and Melody got up and walked away. They left their half-finished food trays, not bothering to pick up after themselves. Esther felt her neck and face flush. Cristee hadn't noticed anything. She just kept waggling her toy lion at the boys. Everything was over before it really even began. It had been the first meeting of the Glams Cats and Esther already felt like she was on her own.

■ ■ ■

Despite three hours of after-school research—and what seemed like endless phone calls and pointless negotiations —Esther had accomplished nothing. Every vendor demanded a minimum order of twenty shirts. The best quote was given at a cheerful $175 plus shipping and that meant that Esther had no money for a kissing booth deposit. One vendor reluctantly agreed to a print-on-demand arrangement for ten dollars a shirt. But he expected Esther to pay an additional $300 fee for the graphic designer's time. That was more than the two hundred dollars that Esther had and she didn't even have wax lips yet.

She was not having any luck. She told Trish about it the next day in the cafeteria.

Trish just shrugged her shoulders. "Yeah, I told you."

Melody snorted.

"The car wash still isn't a bad idea. We could raise the swag money this Saturday," As usual, Cristee was of no help, waving her toy lion at them and making cat sounds.

"A fundraiser for a fundraiser. You know how ridiculous that sounds?" Trish said.

"Do you have a better idea?"

"I already told you how."

"Then we won't have any money for the booth deposit. Can't you chip in something?" Esther said.

"Look, I don't even want to do this. I just agreed to the fundraiser because my Mom thinks I'm doing something after school besides hanging out at the old shack."

Cristee stopped playing with the stuffed toy. Her eyes grew wide. "Ooo—in the woods behind the school?"

"Yeah, that shack," Trish said.

"If nobody chips in, the kissing booth fundraiser is scrapped," Esther said.

"So scrap it."

"Maybe this fundraiser could be more than just a school project." Esther hesitated and chewed at her lip before continuing. "I was... I was hoping that we could be friends."

Trish looked Esther up and down. "You want to be friends? Meet me after school at the old shack. Today. We can talk about the fundraiser there."

Esther looked over at Cristee. She was hugging the toy lion close and shaking her head. "The shack. No way. Unh-uh."

Trish was saying nothing, her face a blank slate. Her blond bangs hung down in her eyes but Esther could see her sleepy-eyes just staring at her. It was just like in the hallways. She looked like a cat playing with a mouse. Esther couldn't read anything into her facial expression. But how bad could an old shack be? There should be nothing to worry about. And she didn't want Trish leaving the lunch table again like the previous meeting.

"Why there?" Esther finally said.

"I go back there all the time, Scaredy-Coz-*mo*. So do you want me to get involved in this thing or not?"

"I guess. Is it hard to find?" Esther finally said.

"Just walk straight into the woods from the south parking lot. Follow the path."

"OK, fine. I'll meet you back at the shack after school."

Trish smiled a Cheshire cat of a grin. "See you there, buddy." Then she said nothing more and left the table. Melody scurried behind, snorting as she shadowed her.

■ ■ ■

The final bell jarred Esther out of her seat. Her bright blue Nikes echoed in the sickly yellow cinderblock hallway as she made her way to the unused southeast door. The exit sign above the door seemed to flicker a red warning to turn back. Fortunately the door didn't have an emergency alarm. She stuck her tongue out at the sign and stepped outside.

An overcast Florida sky hid a gloomy Thursday sun. Still, the hot and sticky asphalt grabbed at her shoes as she followed a chain link fence on her left. A few cars to her right hid parents faces who waited to pick up their children. She didn't think that anyone noticed just another fourteen-year-old in a school parking lot. But it didn't stop her from feeling nervous about heading out towards the woods. Esther thought of her father again. "I took risks and got signed. Got to take chances if you want something bad enough." Well, Esther really *was* taking some chances.

She reached the far southern end of the parking lot. She saw that the bottom section of the perimeter chain-link fence had been cut and forced up allowing anyone bold enough to squeeze under sharp points of rusting steel. No one called after her or tried to stop her as she wiggled under the opening.

On the other side, she looked around. To the east and through gnarled pine trees were low-lying palmetto. The prickly plants grudgingly gave way to a narrow path that dared her to go deeper into the woods. Judging by the crumpled cigarette packs and broken beer bottles, this path was only travelled by certain types of kids. Esther cautiously walked on, trying not to scratch her backpack on the old, scaled tree trunks that crowded her on both sides.

The woods were still and quiet. Her Nikes made almost no sound as she walked over dead pine needles that had begun to cover the sandy path. It was as if the trees, themselves, tried to hide the shack from her, hoping to stop invaders from trespassing deeper inside. Some of the closer Palmetto speared at her ankles. Esther kept her eyes glued to the path, still determined on taking risks.

It paid off when, a few hundred feet ahead, she heard some laughing. Two people were talking and the voices sounded like Trish and Melody. More broken beer bottles and a burned-out fire pit confirmed that she was close to her destination. When she stepped out into a clearing, she immediately spotted the shack—if it could be called that.

The shack was a barely standing toolshed. The walls leaned to one side; rust and mold crawled up the sides and around the doorframe. If there had ever been a door, it was now missing. And as if to improve the structure's appearance—or as a bad joke—a mailbox made from a breadbox had been nailed to a rotting stump growing out of a patch of dead grass to the right of the doorway. It was a testament to teenage incompetence and *I-don't-give-a-shit* spirit.

Trish must have heard Esther approach. She peeked out of the shack's entrance and waved Esther inside.

Melody lounged on one of three weathered, folding lawn chairs with Trish on one of her own. Esther tried to be casual as she sat on the third chair but the flimsy seat rocked forward when she sat down. She glanced around at the graffiti covered interior. *Hole in the Sk-Eye—C What U Want to C.* And above the lettering was a large bloodshot eye in dribbled red paint. It gazed upward at a literal hole where an aluminum roof may have once been.

Trish must have noticed Esther staring at what passed as a stoner's version of prophetic wisdom.

"I look up and see Nirvana," Trish said.

All Esther could see were tree branches, pine needles and a few dark clouds. "It might rain," Esther offered.

"There's an invisible ladder. You have to climb it to get to that special place."

"To where? I don't see anything."

"This is one of the rungs of the ladder," Trish pulled out a rolled ziplock bag from her backpack. She shook it at Melody.

"The mail is delivered," Melody said.

Melody grabbed the baggie and pulled out a rolled joint. Esther had only seen pictures. A police officer had held a school drug awareness presentation in seventh grade. Esther snickered during most of it despite all of the scary stories of people jumping off of tall buildings because they thought they could fly. Besides, the tallest building in her area was Melton Middle School and she had already seen Freddy Whitmere jump off the roof on a dare. Freddy suffered a sprained ankle and detention and nothing more.

Melody struck a lighter and sucked in. A foreign herbal smell invaded Esther's nose.

"This will take you to up that ladder," Melody said.

"Where's Cristee?" Esther said, trying to change the subject.

Melody snorted before taking a hit on the joint. "She thinks a ghost haunts the woods."

"That's weird," Esther said.

Melody exhaled cloying smoke and passed the joint to Trish.

"So is that stupid toy lion she now carries," Trish said.

"I wondered about that," Esther said.

"She won't say why," Trish said with an exhale. "Jamie said it's a good thing Cristee is so stacked or no one would talk to the little freak," Then she took another hit on the joint.

"Jamie knows Cristee?" she said.

"Yeah, he came out here once. I think he was looking for me," Trish said.

Melody snorted again. "Cristee used to come out here until the whole ghost thing." Her eyes were glassy and she seemed to be losing interest in the subject so Esther didn't ask any more questions.

Trish held the joint out to Esther. "You smoke?"

Esther studied it. There wasn't anything truly scary about the joint—it was just some dried plant rolled up in dingy paper. In fact, Trish hadn't even done such a great job of rolling the sticklike thing. It bulged at one end and tapered off too tight at the other. And it was slightly bent. It looked more like a deformed finger than some magical instrument promising to take her to a magical place. Whatever threat the police officer had warned her about at the drug awareness presentation--well, this comical thing wasn't what she had imagined. Besides, what tall building could she fall from?

"I can't wait all day," Trish said with growing impatience.

Esther took the joint, her hand shaking a little. She sipped at the tight end as if drinking through a thin straw and quickly blew out a white puff.

Trish laughed. "You're a virgin. You have to inhale and hold it in."

Esther tried it Trish's way. The smoke burned her lungs and she dropped the joint. She jumped up and coughed violently.

Trish and Melody started laughing. "The virgin broke her cherry-o," Trish said.

Esther struggled through watery eyes to see Melody pointing at her and slapping her knee. She tried to find her chair and missed the seat, falling on her butt. The other two girls laughed louder.

Trish leaned over and plucked the joint out of the sand. She held it out. "Try it, again."

After Esther managed to regain her vision, she sat down. She wasn't coughing anymore. And even though there had been the initial surprise from the hot smoke, the experience really hadn't been that awful. Or had it? She made a silly smile to herself but wasn't sure why. She took the joint again.

"Hold it in," Trish reminded her.

Esther managed not to cough so much the second time. She sputtered out a few smoky trails that curled out of the corners of her grinning mouth. She felt her eyes squint. They were still a little watery. She imagined herself looking like a cartoon dragon and laughed. She couldn't help it.

"This is good shit." She passed the joint to Trish, who took a hit.

"Pot's nothing. There's way better stuff than this. One day, I'm going to climb that ladder," Trish said.

For some reason, Esther thought that was the most amazing thing she had ever heard. "The ladder to Nirvana. See what you want."

Trish passed the joint off to Melody and then leaned forward. She gazed intensely at Esther. Something important was about to be said and Esther found herself in deep concentration.

"Jamie talked about you," Trish said.

Esther locked eyes with Trish. Trish's eyes displayed sincerity, caring and, most of all, acceptance. Esther had passed Trish's test. She felt a sudden and deep bond with her new friend that connected each other without the need for words. She had finally found a great friend. This was better than she could have ever imagined.

And then she thought of Trish's brother, Jaime Fernandez—tall, dark haired and enthusiastic. How that tight fitting uniform fit so--

"Really? What did he say about me? I mean...he doesn't even know me."

"Not like that. I mean like to help us buy the T-shirts and other swag."

Esther leaned in toward Trish. They were practically nose-to-nose. She almost tipped in her lawn chair as it seemed to float underneath her. "What did he say?"

"He thinks you're cute." Esther almost gasped. But she

said nothing as Trish continued. "He said he would help with the T-shirts,"

"Did you mention the wax lips?"

"Yeah, all of that stuff," Trish said.

Esther's brow knitted. "How does he know me?"

"Don't you go to his games?" Trish took a long drag on the joint. Esther didn't remember handing it off to her.

"I go to lots of high school games with my Dad. He used to be a pro player."

Trish exhaled smoke and smiled. Esther thought of a cat. "I bet that's where he saw you," Trish said.

"So I'm supposed to give him the money? What then?" Esther said.

"Don't you remember, buddy? You give me the money. I give it to Jamie."

That seemed to make sense. But there was still the matter of other costs. And the kissing booth deposit. Would Jamie visit the kissing booth? "How much are the shirts?" Esther said.

"I think he said fifty dollars."

Esther took the joint from Melody and inhaled again. Feeling hazy, she couldn't seem to add the math in her head but she knew that fifty was a great price. "OK. I'll give you one hundred. I've got the deposit money with me."

"It'd be easier if you give me all of it. You know, the wax lips and all that."

"But I need some of that money."

"I'll give you back the difference tomorrow. I'll give you back the rest tomorrow."

Trish was glowing now. Esther saw the color of friendship radiate in yellow and blue light. *C What U Want to C.* A white envelope marked *The Glam Cats Fund* appeared in her sweaty, clenched hand. She saw herself give it to her new friend. The deal had been made and Trish now had the deposit money. Something in Esther's gut ached. She wasn't sure why.

"Looks like third period tomorrow is dunzo," Melody said. "Dunzo."

The word *dunzo* made Esther laugh. She repeated it, changing it to *dungo* and then *dumbo*. She wasn't even sure what Melody had meant by *dunzo*. But it sounded funny.

Esther's head felt heavy. Her thoughts went blank for a short time, and for a moment, she forgot where she was. She almost panicked before she realized she hadn't moved from the shack. Her mind wandered several times. She struggled to stand as she grabbed for her backpack to leave.

"How about another Glam Cats meeting. See you at lunch tomorrow?"

Trish smiled and Esther's gut cramped.

"Yeah, sure buddy. Lunch tomorrow. Meow, Coz-*mo*," Trish said.

Esther somehow managed her way down the sandy trail and back through the woods. She didn't remember much of her trek out. She managed to stumble back under the chain link fence and onto the now empty school parking lot. The sun drooped down into the darkening sky. Or maybe that was what she imagined. And she didn't remember walking home. As she approached her front door, the only thing she could remember was that one word Melody had said back at the shack—*dunzo*. *Dunzo, dunzo*. It beat in her head like a drumbeat that wouldn't stop.

■ ■ ■

Esther soon found out what Melody meant by *dunzo*.
Trish had skipped Friday's third period class and lunch.

Esther spent more time chewing her lip instead of her own plate of meatloaf. Cristee played with her food and hummed, oblivious to anything else. It was pointless to complain to her about Trish. Once, Esther snapped, "Shut up." Cristee stopped humming and scowled. Esther said nothing more. She never saw Trish all that day.

When she trudged into the gut of a tightly packed Melton Middle School bus at the end of the day, Esther could only think of the deposit money she had so carelessly given away all the way back home. The weekend hadn't been any better. Esther debated with herself—should she go back out to the old shack and see if Trish was hanging out? After her last experience, the place unnerved her in a weird way. She had lost control of her faculties while smoking the joint and she didn't like it. She tried Trish's phone several time but only got her voice mail. And again on both Monday and Tuesday, she never saw Trish or Melody in both the school halls or in the cafeteria.

On Wednesday, Esther decided to walk to school in the morning. Dark clouds above reflected her mood. Rings burned around her sleepless eyes. She arrived at school, her nerves a twitching storm of emotions. When the lunch bell rang, Esther nearly flew to the cafeteria.

She was first to the table. She quickly wiped it down and hastily laid out her lunch, making sure a drink box was at her left. She finished setting up just as Cristee arrived. She seemed to have forgotten that Esther had snapped at her the day before, saying a playful, "Kitty-Kitty" and plopped onto her seat. Esther sat down but her busy eyes continued to scan the cafeteria as more students trickled in.

Finally, Trish and Melody stumbled in. They each carried a truckload of snacks. When they got to the table, they dropped a small mountain of potato chips and chocolate bars and other junk food onto the sickly brown surface. Trish looked pale. And she gave Esther a weird grin. Despite her half-closed lids, Esther could see that her eyes were bloodshot red. When Trish plopped down, almost falling out of her seat, she mumbled something that Esther couldn't understand.

"Did you give Jamie the money?" Esther said.

Trish's head drooped. She mumbled something again. Melody nudged her.

"Did you hear me?" Esther said.

Trish raised her head. "I'm sick," Trish finally said coherently.

Trish did look bad. In fact, Trish looked more than bad. But that wasn't getting her out of this situation. No way.

"Give me back my money," Esther said.

Melody leaned across the table. "Leave her alone, Coz-*mo*."

Esther rolled her eyes. "So then you tell me, Melody. Where is the money?"

"Poof," Trish said.

"Poof? What's poof?" Esther said.

"Poof." Trish's head drooped again.

Some boys behind Cristee called out to her, saying "Here kitty-kitty." Cristee waggled the toy lion at them.

"Stop acting like a baby, Cristee," Esther said. Cristee's eyes and mouth shot wide open. Esther ignored her and turned back to Trish. "Where is it?"

Trish kept muttering, "Poof."

Esther wanted to slap Trish awake. "You stole my money, bitch."

It was too late to take her words back. Cristee got quiet and gawked. Melody glared. Trish rolled her head back and grimaced. Drool dribbled from her lips.

"You've got spunk, kid," she said and then laughed.

"What?" Esther said.

"Poof."

"Where's my money?"

"I told you to leave her alone. She's sick," Melody said.

"She's going to puke. I'm telling Mrs. Wisa," Esther said.

"Shut up, narc," Melody said.

"Just look at her," Esther said.

Cristee pointed at Esther's face. "Look at that. See that funny birthmark? No one would kissy-kissy that face at a kissing booth."

Melody leaned in close to Esther. "Looks like the letter *F*," she said.

Esther rubbed at her left cheek. "It's not very big."

"F. F is for *fuckface*," Melody said.

Trish eyes squinted, making her look like a Persian cat wanting to cough up a fur ball. "Poof."

All three girls were now looking at Esther with disdain or disgust. In Trish's case, it was a little of both in a pale shade of greenish sick. Esther couldn't understand it. She was in the right—Trish had probably used the deposit money to buy drugs. Whatever Nirvana she had climbed to for the last several days was made possible at the expense of the money her father had given her for the booth deposit. At least Cristee should be somewhat understanding.

Apparently, Cristee was oblivious to Trish's drugged-up mental state. That was no surprise. But what did surprise Esther was when Cristee got up in her seat and did a wiggle dance.

"It ain't no disgrace, uh-huh, uh-huh. Bein' an ugly fuck-face, uh-huh." She chanted the words out like a song. The boys behind Cristee picked up the chant, yelling out, "Fuck-face. Ugly, ugly Fuckface."

The birthmark was a rather odd shape but Esther never considered it to be a freakish eyesore. Her Dad once told her that it was charming. In fact, he told her that some famous movie stars had one that people considered to be either charming or attractive. But a chanting crowd of lunching eighth-graders didn't see it that way.

Esther put her hand to her face and covered the birth-mark. Esther felt her throat tighten. "It's only the size of a dime," Esther said.

Trish made a gagging sound.

"See—you've made Trish sick," Melody said.

"She did it to herself."

Cristee squeaked *Fuckface!* louder. And the boys chanted louder. She broke into dance, waggling her stuffed toy as she jerked her ribcage and arms in a stiff and awkward display. The boys egged her on, their voices throb-bing a beating chanting. "Ugly, ugly Fuckface," they shouted in unison. From across the cafeteria, Mrs. Wisa yelled at the boys to stop.

Trish's lips curled up into a joker's grin. "I could never be your friend, goody-two-shoes Coz-*mo*."

And as if to punctuate her declaration, she retched candy bar chunks and green glop all over the table. Some of the vomit splashed onto Esther who jerked up out of her seat.

"You're *effed* up," Melody said.

Esther tried to speak but bit down on her inside cheek instead. Hot blood salted her swollen tongue.

Mrs. Wisa rushed over to Trish, who started crying. But Esther didn't care anymore. A fog seemed to surround her.

From somewhere, Mrs. Wisa said her name but Esther ignored the teacher.

Esther ran out of the cafeteria, ignoring Mrs. Wisa as she told her to stop. Esther managed to find a school exit. Nobody chased after her because Mrs. Wisa was probably busy cleaning up after Trish. But she had to get out there. Had to get away from the chanting boys, from Trish, from school. She had to get away from being called *fuckface*.

Once outside, heavy rain pelted her. A strong wind pushed back as she walked home. Esther's plan to make Trish a friend had failed. In fact, Trish thought Esther was just another Goody-Two-shoes, just like Janet Belorna. Bowed pine trees shook their branches, seeming to laugh at her soaked body as she continued on in the storm.

Fuckface. Ugly, ugly Fuckface Fuck. The chanting still seemed to chase after her.

Esther couldn't tell if the rain or her tears blinded her as she hurried home.

■ ■ ■

The next day, Esther sat across from Mrs. Wisa's desk. She decided that the teacher didn't like fourteen-year-olds very much. At least, Mrs. Wisa didn't like fourteen-year-olds who tried to obey the fundraising rules. Esther had spent half of first period sitting in a hard-backed chair and trying to convince the teacher that Trish had started all the problems in the cafeteria on Tuesday.

"She stole my money. She should be kicked from the fundraiser. She should be suspended from school," Esther said.

"Esther, I never liked the kissing booth idea," Mrs. Wisa said.

"It's Trish that has problems—not me. I'll find someone else for the team after I get my deposit money back."

"I can't ask Trish about the money that you claim she stole. She's still in the hospital."

"It's two hundred dollars!"

"When did you give her the money?"

Esther shut up. She didn't dare answer the question. If she told the teacher that she had been behind the school and smoking pot... well—

"Do you have a receipt? Any proof that you gave Trish the money?" Mrs. Wisa pressed Esther for an answer.

Esther shook her head *no*. "She has to pay me back. She stole it from me."

Mrs. Wisa gave Esther the adult-face-of-concern look. Esther recognized it. One evening, Dad had captured a fruit rat that was chewing a hole in the kitchen drywall. It sat in an old birdcage that he had exhumed from the cluttered garage, waiting it's fate. Esther had poked a stick at it while the terrified creature ran in circles. She laughed and poked at it again. Dad wore that same concerned-adult-face look and had told her to stop.

"If a fundraiser means that much to you, I'll offer you an alternative. I want you to start a book drive," Mrs. Wisa said.

"I don't like books. No one does."

"Lots of people love books."

"Sure, weirdos like Glenda like books."

Mrs. Wisa sighed. "If you do the book drive, you can pick your own team. And I'll donate one hundred dollars if you can find three new team members."

The teacher sat quietly and waited for her answer. It was a take-it-or-leave-it offer. The teacher dangled a carrot before Esther, offering a partial allowance. But at least it was half a carrot. If she followed through, she could at least recover some of her money. And she wouldn't have to deal with Trish anymore. What a mistake that had been.

"How do I operate a book drive?"

Mrs. Wisa got up and walked over to a battered file cabinet. She pulled out a dog-eared manila folder and gave it to Esther. The folder smelled like dusty shelves and cobwebs.

"Follow those instructions. Be sure to recruit three new members," Mrs. Wisa said.

Esther opened it. Inside was a glossy brochure of two happy women. An older woman with a practiced smile was passing a book to a girl that described the five stages of *How to Plan Your Book Drive* in several bulleted steps. She didn't bother to read them because Esther was already turned off by the girl's appearance. The girl wore a plain dress with a boring flower print. Esther liked to wear jeans and a t-shirt with something mildly edgy printed in bold letters. The girl wore patent leather shoes. And had her hair done in silly braids—boring. She didn't look like a girl that watched Sid Vicious videos. But Esther took the manilla folder and the brochure. She told the teacher she would think about it and left her office.

■ ■ ■

Lunch time came sooner than Esther cared for. She decided to find a spot that wouldn't be close to Trish, Cristee or the chanting boys. Yesterday's memory suddenly reminded her of the birthmark on her face and she didn't want a repeat. *Fuckface. Ugly, ugly Fuckface Fuck.* She nearly shuttered at the thought. So Esther scanned the cafeteria and spied an empty seat close to no-man's-land where Glenda sat alone. She would have to travel through a maze of laminated cafeteria tables, praying that no other students noticed her and restarted the chant.

There was a table that didn't seem too threatening. A brood of sixth graders sat there. They probably knew nothing of what happened in the world of upper classman. Sixth graders weren't privy to such details, they themselves outcasts of middle school until the end of the school year and when they would finally become seventh graders. And who knew? Maybe some of them would feel honored that an eighth grader sat with them. Maybe Esther could offer them a sense of finally belonging to the middle school experience. Maybe she could even recruit a few of them for the fundraiser. Esther chose a path that kept far clear of where Cristee and the rowdy boys sat and cautiously made her way over.

Her presence didn't seem to be noticed by the sixth graders as she sat down. They were talking amongst themselves. She looked around the table. A spikey-haired boy spat out anime creature names at a boy with spotty skin. Spotty Skin growled back more names. A bug-eyed boy, sitting across from Esther, glanced over to her right where a blond girl with a worm-thin neck chimed in the conversation, whistling through her nose as she spoke. Another boy, freckle-faced and grinning mischievously, countered Wormy Neck. Esther didn't like his toothy grin. She would have to keep an eye on Bull Boy.

Bull Boy finally looked at her. "Aren't you an eighth grader?" said Bull Boy.

"I want you to join my fun-raiser. We can help rescue pets."

Esther still didn't like the idea of a book drive. In third period she had formulated a new plan—if she could go back to Mrs. Wisa and tell her she would raise money for a local animal shelter, maybe she could still convince the teacher to offer up a donation. Besides, who could say, "No," to helping kittens in need? You'd have to be heartless.

"My parents don't let me have pets," Bug Eyes said.

"You help sheltered pets. You don't take them home."

"Then why do we care?" Bull Boy said.

"I once had a cat. But he escaped. He got run over by a car," Wormy Neck offered up.

Now, Bug Eyes grinned. He looked at Esther. "Did the car abuse her pet?" he said.

"Look, Mrs. Wisa asked me to do a fundraiser. You can be on my team. Sixth graders aren't normally allowed but I'll bet that she'll make an exception. You get to meet lots of eight-graders. And all you have to do is donate some money, first. It will be fun, right?"

Wormy Neck covered her mouth. Esther heard a muffled laugh. Bull Boy pointed at Esther's face with a beefy finger.

"Why are you wearing that?"

Bull Boy pointed at her, his crusty, greasy fingernail loomed too close to Esther's face. Crowding her personal space made her a little angry.

"Listen to me. It was supposed to be a kissing booth, but now I'm doing something else,"

Wormy Neck wrinkled her nose. "Gross. I'm not kissing strangers."

Bug Eyes nodded in agreement. "Yeah. Someone might breathe snot in your face,"

All the sixth graders started laughing. Esther was growing frustrated.

"It's *not* a kissing booth. I already told you that. It's to help sheltered animals."

Bull Boy poked at her face. Esther smacked his hand away.

"What's the matter with you?" Esther said. The sixth-graders laughed and he poked it again. "Stop it, you spotted freak,"

With his large hammy hand, Bull Boy sketched the letter *F* in the air for the others to see. Then he smiled, looking like he had just finished painting the Mona Lisa.

"I believe I have spotted a fuckface," he said with an air of grandeur.

Wormy Neck giggled. Before it could boil over into laughter from the rest of the table, Esther snatched up her lunch bag and retreated from the table. The only available seats remained in No Man's Land. Esther lurched over and dropped her tray onto the tabletop, across from Glenda.

Glenda peeked over a copy of Tolkien's *The Hobbit*, her large, wide eyes taking in her new tablemate. When Esther glared at her, she raised the book back as if hiding behind it. Esther resigned herself to unpacking her lunch bag.

Glenda lowered the book and looked at her curiously.

"The ancient Greek alphabet doesn't have an *F*—not really," Glenda said.

"What?" Esther said.

"I once read that. I read all kinds of books."

Bull Boy pointed over at Esther and whispered something to the others. Esther covered her birthmark and turned away from him.

"You must read a lot," Esther said.

"You just never know when you'll need to know something," Glenda said.

"I don't read much," Esther said.

Glenda lowered the book, revealing a ratty mess of black hair that fell about her face. It almost covered her tiny nose and delicate mouth. She spoke again with calm seriousness.

"Most people think books are boring. But a book is like a friend to me."

Glenda was a known loner, a seventh-grade pariah. She certainly could use some friends. Esther suddenly felt a pang of guilt and dropped her eyes. "Sorry, I didn't mean it like that."

"Amazing things hide between a book's covers, lest we forget. I read the word *lest* in a book."

"That seems like really good advice."

Esther offered Glenda a lukewarm smile. She didn't care to continue on with the topic of books. Or any topic, for that matter. She began to pick at her own lunch, hoping that Glenda might pick up on her cue to end the conversation. But she continued, seemingly enthusiastic that someone was finally talking with her.

"Once, I read a story about a woman who had a letter sewn to her dress. People weren't very nice to her. I felt so bad for Hester Prynne. She needed help—like you. I could donate money," Glenda said.

Esther had no idea what story Glenda was talking about. She didn't care. But the thought of anyone willing to support her fundraiser was enticing at the moment. She nibbled at her peanut butter sandwich and chewed over her own thoughts.

Esther took a second look at Glenda. Glenda was different from Trish in her own weird way. She seemed sincere in her commitment to donate money. At first appearances, Trish was edgy, exciting. But her supposed new friend also turned out to be a thief. Perhaps Mrs. Wisa's suggestion to start a book drive had some merit.

Esther sucked in a quick breath, full of hope and possible regret.

"Glenda, you...you don't know anyone who wants to—"

Glenda ducked back behind her book. "I like turtles. If I had one, I would name him Socrates," Glenda said.

Esther smiled for real. "I bet he'd be a smart turtle."

Glenda's eyes peeked over the top of her book. "My turtle *would* be smart. He'd have brains. No straw in here, Toto." She knocked at her head. Esther couldn't help herself —she giggled.

"Like the scarecrow in *The Wizard of Oz*? Do you like cats?" Esther said.

"They make my Aunt sneeze. People think they are a bad sign but some cultures think they're good luck."

"You'd be good luck if you were on my fun-raiser. We could recruit two more people at the library."

Glenda looked thoughtful as she chewed her cheese sandwich. "My English teacher said I should get out more. But I don't like to be around people unless they need help," she said.

"I need a book expert. You won't have to talk to people if you don't want to," Esther said.

"I once read an accounting book. It changed my life."

Esther wasn't sure if this was a confirmation, but Glenda seemed to be interested in a fundraiser. This wasn't quite the direction that Esther had anticipated for the event. But she could be closer to recovering her two hundred dollars.

"See, you are smart. I'll sign you up for the book drive. Can you donate money now?"

"My money is at home. We can go there after school and get it."

Esther hesitated. Glenda seemed like she wanted to be friends. Esther couldn't ever imagine ever hanging out with Glenda. But sometimes you had to do things you didn't want to do. That must have been another one of Dad's lessons.

"I suppose. But I can't stay long. Gotta' do homework. Do you live far from school?" Esther said.

"No, I live on the South Side. I walk every day."

Some of the neighborhoods on the South Side weren't very nice. But if Glenda walked every day to school, then her neighborhood couldn't be that bad.

"OK. We'll get your money after school," Esther said.

"OK, Hester."

"Who?"

"Hester Prynne was in the book I told you about. She needed help—like you."

"Oh, yeah...that book," Esther said while she opened her sweet applesauce. The soft fruit tasted delicious. She scraped up every last bit from the bottom of the container.

Esther quickly lost interest in the conversation. Talking to Glenda about anything wasn't fun, just weird. She ignored her for the rest of lunch. Only two more team members to go. And how much money would Glenda donate? She would have to wait and see. Once she got Glenda's donation and the book drive was finished, Esther wouldn't have to think about weirdo Glenda anymore.

■ ■ ■

After school, Esther walked with Glenda. The route to Glenda's house was as confusing as Glenda's conversation. Esther memorized the way back as she walked just in case she got lost—the South Side was not a place she wanted to be stuck in after dark. First they walked half a mile down Palmetto Avenue, then turned right at Heron Drive. For a few blocks Glenda talked about how vegetables might feel pain. Then there was a left at Springs Circle and Glenda babbled that her home was like being inside a box full of soft, warm cotton. A few more rights. More babbling. Glenda's voice became breathy and nervous and her speech rambled more the farther they walked.

They passed dead yards that were just crabgrass and sandspur. Some houses had boards replacing missing window glass. Esther and Glenda quickly walked past a wheel-less Ford F-150 rusting atop cinderblocks. Grime decorated everything. A shirtless toddler, wearing only a sagging diaper, stared as Esther passed by. It was a relief to finally make it to Glenda's squat little house. Glenda said that her aunt rented the flimsy-looking thing. At least the gray paint hadn't completely faded and the windows were all there.

As Glenda fidgeted with a set of keys, Esther noted the kid's clothing. The black witch's hat had a tear patched with duct tape. It was the same tape used to make a silver bow stuck to the front of the hat. Her lumpy backpack sagged, most likely stuffed with borrowed library books. And Esther's shoes, alone, probably cost more than everything Glenda wore now.

They stepped inside to a tidy living room. A portrait of Jesus welcomed Esther with open arms and a brightly colored, flaming heart. A neatly vacuumed shag carpet led the girls past an outdated kitchen and to Glenda's bedroom which looked like a Goodwill. Books were all over the floor in stacks, crowding out the tiny space. A wobbly chest of drawers leaned up against a wall for support. On top was a clunky DVD player that sat next to a television set. The television was still on. Dorothy, from *The Wizard of Oz*, stood frozen in a perpetual smile on the yellow brick road.

Esther tapped the television glass. "I love this movie."

Glenda sat on a cot. The small bed barely held her and she hugged her knees so as to better fit. Despite her small size, she was still too big. "When my mother returns, we're going to finish it."

"When does she get back?" Esther asked.

Glenda got up and opened a chest drawer. She pulled out a picture buried under a pile of socks and handed the framed image to Esther. There was no denying the resemblance--it was Glenda twenty years later. Lustrous dark hair fell about the beautiful woman's smooth shoulders. Big brown eyes made small features delicate and cute. It could have been Glenda buried in the drawer of socks, hidden away inside a frame and away from the world. Esther cleared her throat.

"Glenda, it's like seeing you in the future."

"She's following the yellow brick road. She got into a man's car with a suitcase."

"She'll come back," said Esther.

Glenda looked down. She shuffled her feet. She balled her fists and her lips trembled "Three years. She hasn't. Crickets!"

Esther felt a pang of guilt and winced. She had said too much. Glenda's mother obviously had abandoned her and she now lived with her Aunt. Whatever her living arrangement, she wasn't in a position to donate money to the fundraiser. Maybe she could find another way for Glenda to help.

Esther tried a smile. "Maybe I should go. Want to meet me at the library tomorrow?"

Glenda said nothing. She pulled out another buried

object from the drawers, a small jar hiding six one-dollar bills. She handed it over to Esther who felt herself blushing. Then Glenda slumped on the cot next to Esther and stared at her shoes.

"Is that a yes for the library?" Esther said.

"Crickets."

The moment was growing increasingly uncomfortable. Glenda shut down into silent brooding and Esther didn't know what else to say. She told Glenda she would let herself out but Glenda didn't even look up as she left the room.

■ ■ ■

Miss Mables was too enthusiastic to be a librarian. Esther always imagined librarians to be old women who sat quietly behind a desk and hushed anyone who dare to speak in their domain. Not Miss Mables. The young librarian reminded Esther of an excited bird, always talking and moving too much. She kept chirping out suggestions on how to operate Esther's book drive. Esther finally interrupted her after several minutes of attentive head-nodding and pretend smiles.

"I'll set up a recruiting station at the back table," Esther said and excused herself before Miss Mables offered up another round of unwanted helpfulness.

As she began setting up, someone tapped Esther on the shoulder. She nearly jumped out of her skin from the sudden surprise, turning to see Glenda silently staring at her. She hadn't heard her walk up behind her.

"I...good to see you. I wasn't sure if you were coming, I mean, you seemed kind of sad yesterday." Esther said.

"I'm feeling better today," Glenda said.

Esther made the best fake smile she could manage, even better than the ones she offered Miss Mables. "Then let's recruit."

Glenda nodded her head and the two girls parked themselves near shelving end panels labeled *V-Z*. Setup should have been easy. Esther arranged a signup form next to the pamphlet with the smiling girls in glossy print. Then she directed Glenda to tape arrow signs to the library shelves, starting from the entrance and leading back to the recruiting table. But a half hour later, Glenda seemed to have disappeared. Esther discovered her in a dusty corner with a hardcover book and all of the arrow signs still needing to be posted.

"I didn't have any tape," Glenda said.

"Did you ask Miss Mables?"

Glenda told her she forgot to ask because she had become intrigued by a book about the Dewey decimal system.

A tightness gripped Esther's chest which was probably panic. With only twenty minutes before final bell, Esther had little hope of recruiting anyone. She randomly picked a corner table of four boys playing a board game and approached them.

"Nope." One of the boys flat out refused.

"It's for a good cause."

"Good luck with your cause," another boy said.

Glenda finally rejoined Esther but offered nothing to help. Esther's panic was turning into frustration.

"Glenda, don't you have anything to add?"

"I once read an accounting book. It changed my life."

"But you still wear that stupid hat," a third boy said.

Then all four boys snickered and Glenda dropped her eyes and shuffled her feet. Esther shook her head and marched back to the recruiting table. The day had been wasted. Glenda sat down next to Esther.

"Can't you try not to be so awkward?" Esther said.

"I get nervous."

Esther wanted to throw her hands up in the air. Her frustration was beginning to simmer into something else. She wanted to say something blunt to Glenda but then Snotty Toddy approached the table. He wiped at his pimply nose. Her day had just gotten worse. There was no way she would *ever* let Snotty Toddy join her fundraiser group.

"I'm into collecting graphic novels," Toddy said. "Batman books, mostly; Daredevil can be cool; Do you think Marvel is overdoing the Avengers?"

He paused, looking from one girl to the other. Esther didn't even care to discuss it.

"I've read some *Akira* but I can't decide on DC or Marvel," Glenda volunteered.

Esther crossed her arms. "Todd, go away."

Todd ignored her, continuing in a nasally voice, "I could catalog books for the team using spreadsheets."

Glenda peered out shyly at Todd from under her hat's wide black brim. Esther could feel Glenda's legs swinging under the library table. She seemed to be flattered that a boy was talking to her—even if it was Snotty Toddy.

"I'm not good with computers," Glenda mumbled. Then her eyes quickly darted away. Todd wiped his nose and grinned at her. Snotty Toddy and Weirdo Witch Girl— a match made in heaven.

"Last year, I read a book about programming. I wrote some macros. I'm really good."

"Todd, nobody cares," Esther said.

Snotty Toddy looked at Glenda. Glenda's nervous legs swung faster. Then he thumbed over at Esther. "She probably doesn't collect as many books as I do. Trust me, you need to catalog your books."

Esther's face flushed with anger. "Glenda, don't give him that."

But it was too late. Glenda handed him the fundraiser signup form and blushed.

"Don't listen to *Fuckface*," Todd said.

Glenda giggled. Weirdo Witch Girl, probably the greatest loser in Melton Middle School's history, actually giggled when Snotty Toddy called Esther, *Fuckface*. Esther slapped the signup form out of Glenda's hand. Glenda's legs stopped swinging.

Snotty Toddy wiped at his nose. "You're not very nice," Todd said.

"And you're gross."

Then Esther turned toward Glenda. She wanted to burn holes in the kid's head with her eyes. Glenda raised the fundraiser brochure to hide her face. Esther ripped it out of Glenda's hand.

"You can't hide forever behind some paper. And that stupid hat. Have you ever looked at yourself in the mirror?"

The boys at the board game table were now staring at Esther. She didn't care—she would make a scene if that's what it would take to resolve this injustice. Glenda would never giggle at her again.

"Look at this, everyone! Weirdo Witch Girl couldn't stop Dorothy from going down the yellow brick road."

Esther knocked the hat off of Glenda's head. Esther was so shocked by what she saw that her hand instinctively went to her mouth to stifle her surprise. Glenda had a large bald spot on top of her head. Scabs covered the area, each lump of dried blood a secret to be hidden. She had been pulling out her hair and hurting herself. Esther realized that

Glenda probably suffered from a type of nervous disorder. She suddenly felt as ugly as the disfiguration on Glenda's small skull.

"I miss her. Crickets." Glenda said. Then a large tear dribbled down her cheek.

"Glenda, I'm sorry. I didn't know," Esther said.

Snotty Toddy picked up Glenda's hat and placed it on the table. He said nothing else and walked away, probably too embarrassed to look at Glenda.

"Glenda, I said I'm sorry. I was just frustrated with how the day was going. It was wrong of me."

Glenda didn't say anything for several seconds. She wrung her small hands and her lips trembled.

Finally, she whispered, "I quit."

■ ■ ■

When Esther finally could manage to fall asleep that night, she dreamed that she was walking on a yellow-bricked road. It wound upward in a crazy snakelike pattern, leading eventually to where she could see the old shack where she met Trish and smoked pot. Circular bandages stuck to the center of each yellow brick, making a mean face at her. The bandages taunted her.

"Fuckface, peel me off if you can."

Esther frowned and scraped at one with her shoe while the other bandages laughed.

Someone yelled out in the distance, "Hey, Coz-mo."

Esther looked up and saw Trish waving at her just ahead on the path. She smiled and beckoned Esther forward. In her other hand, she waggled a white envelope marked *The Glam Cats Fund* in black ink. Esther began to run.

In the sky, thunder suddenly clapped loud and deep. Black clouds swirled on each side of the path as sixth graders stepped out from the inky smoke. Esther saw Wormy Neck, Spotty Skin and Bug Eyes come out of the swirling mass of air. Then Bull Boy approached, grinning and pointing at her. More sixth-graders soon followed but Esther didn't recognize any of them. Everyone wore a base-ball cap and bony wings erupted from their twisted backs. The wings jerked and twitched, raising a stench in the air. They began loping toward Esther.

Esther ran.

"Come on, buddy," Trish said and kept waving her over.

As Esther picked up steam, Glenda suddenly appeared in the middle of the road. Esther almost tumbled over as she forced herself into a sliding stop. She skidded just inches from Glenda's face.

"I'll show you where it's at," Glenda said.

Glenda was dressed like a tiny scarecrow in a big, black pointed hat. When she tossed off the hat, Esther saw that the top half of Glenda's skull had been cut away. Red brains pulsed, throbbing to the dark beating wings of the sixth graders.

Glenda knocked at her squishing brains and grinned.

"Straw, Toto," Glenda said.

⸻

C What U Want to C.

All Esther could see outside the shack was broken beer bottles and crushed cigarette packs. The place was trashed. Litter clung to the area like fleas might stick to a cat. There was nothing pleasant about the place and she wondered why she had even agreed to meet Trish here that first time.

Esther searched around the burned out fire pit. The dream she had last night still haunted her. Mostly, it was the image of Trish holding the envelope marked *The Glam Cats Fund.* She was sure that the dream was trying to tell her something. She went inside the shack and poked at its flimsy walls, looking for the missing two hundred dollars. But she found nothing more than trash and a lingering frustration inside herself.

She dropped into a lawn chair and stared up to the sky. Storm clouds drifted by, promising to deliver rain somewhere.

C What U Want to C.

Esther tried to recall the conversation she had with both Trish and Melody that afternoon after school. Melody had said, *Dunzo.* Esther, unfortunately, had learned too late what that meant.

What else did Melody say that day? Smoking pot had clouded Esther's mind but she seemed to remember that there was something else. As she watched more clouds pass overhead, she searched her memory. Delivery...delivered... the mail is delivered. Eureka! The first time Esther had come out here, Melody had said, "The mail is delivered." Why hadn't she thought of this sooner?

She jumped up and rushed out to where the mailbox stood and pulled open its rusted door. Her hand shook as she pulled out its only contents. She had the proof of what Trish had done. It was a white envelope and printed on it in careful black marker was *The Glam Cats Fund.*

But the envelope was empty. Trish had spent the money.

■ ■ ■

Friday became Saturday, and after struggling to work up the nerve, Esther took a deep breath and left home for Trish's. She carried the empty white envelope as proof and hoped for the best.

A late morning sun shone down upon her, the muggy heat enveloping her. Esther trudged forward as if her feet were made of lead. The journey didn't take as long as she hoped it might. Several ranch homes were squeezed uncomfortably close together in Trish's cul-de-sac. A Neighborhood Watch sign's black eye seemed to cast suspicion at Esther as she entered the street. A nearby sprinkler head palpitated water over a brown Saint Augustine lawn, its nervous motions stopping Esther momentarily. Trish's home was at the dead center of the neighborhood circle.

On her driveway, someone washed a car. As Esther approached, a knot tightened in her gut and she suddenly prayed that Trish was, by some stroke of luck, at the mall with Melody. It was Jamie who was washing the car. She recognized him immediately, his strong tanned body working over a Ford Mustang's chrome wheel. Soapy bubbles glistened as they captured sunlight and refracted the light into rainbow colors. Esther's feet felt lighter and she floated over to where he worked.

Jamie turned and smiled. Esther adjusted her hair.

"I'm so sorry to be bothering you. I'm looking for Trish," Esther said.

Jamie dropped the water hose. He wiped some grease on his snug, white T-shirt and strode over.

"Oh—Esther—yeah. Trish told me about you."

Esther giggled. Her face felt warm. "You know me?"

"We're cool, right?" he said.

Esther didn't quite understand the question. She hesitated before replying. She wondered if Trish was still feeling ill since that terrible day in the cafeteria.

"I hope she's OK. Trish, I mean. I hope Trish is OK."

"She's fine. Being suspended is like early summer vacation for that dumbo."

"Oh, good. I mean, I'm glad she's feeling better. We kind of had a fight and so I was worried about her."

It wasn't exactly true but Esther thought she was taking a tactful approach to asking about her missing money.

Jamie dropped his smile. Esther noticed a throbbing vein on his temple.

"Hey, you didn't call the police or something, did you?" Jamie said.

"No, never. Why would I?"

Jamie smiled again. "That's cool. Trish wanted me to give you some money."

This was becoming easier than Esther imagined. Her mood lightened. "I'm not trying to be pushy about it," Esther said.

Jamie dropped his smile again. "How much?" he said.

Esther suddenly became nervous. She cleared her throat and finally answered, "Two hundred dollars." Her voice sounded like a squeak.

Jamie whistled. He muttered, "That dumbo," and shook his head. He reached into his pocket and pulled out a wad of wet, limp twenties. "I'll throw in an extra twenty for your trouble. We're cool, right?"

He held out the money, clenched in a tight fist.

She looked at the money and then at Jamie. The mental image she had of him on the baseball field was not the same person she saw in front of her now. Water dripped off his wet, slick hair like sewage running off a rat. She hadn't been able to see his acne before. And there was a cryptic dP symbol tattood on the webbing between Jamie's thumb and index finger. For all Esther knew, Jamie was the one who sold Trish the drugs. "

You want your money, right?" Jamie said. He held it out, grinning like a hungry animal.

Esther took the wet bills and backed away. "Thanks. I've got to go."

Jamie pressed in closer. He grinned again and Esther could see yellow stains on his teeth. "You're kind of cute. How old are you?"

"Tell Trish I said hi," she said with a nervous look, wanting to end the conversation.

"If you want to wait for Trish, you can hang out with me. Hey, that birthmark on your face is sexy," he said.

"Look, I've got to go before my dad comes looking for me."

"That's too bad. I just wanted to get to know you."

Jamie moved still closer yet. He reached for her with arms that looked as powerful as pythons that crushed their prey. With money clutched in hand, Esther turned and ran. Jamie called after her. She didn't think that he chased after her but Esther had no intention of looking back. In fact, she would never look back.

She quickly made her way home. The familiar warm yellow and pale blue homes of her neighborhood once again welcomed Esther. Life was good here. Mr. Tipton, three doors down, pushed a rumbling mower that filled the air with the smell of freshly cut green grass. It was a comfortable smell. Mrs. Kelly, next door, piled her kids into a van with just enough time to wave at Esther before shuttling them off to a soccer game. Even Esther's front door was nice, its familiar squeak seeming to say, "Good to see you."

What had she been looking for that wasn't already here?

Even inside her home, everything looked better. Home seemed different, now. It wasn't just boring cat posters and Dad's familiar baseball stories. It was a place where she was always welcomed just for who she was—Cosmo, the last of the Glam Cats and very happy with herself.

■ ■ ■

Esther glided past the cafeteria tables on Monday. Kids chatted about television shows and comic books while seated over tasty meals that filled eager lunch bellies. She didn't look for Trish, Melody or Cristee. She didn't care. In her shoulder bag, she carried a gift for a special someone sitting in no-man's-land. She was ready for a fresh start.

When Esther sat across from Glenda, she raised her book higher and tried to hide in her quirky way. She was no longer wearing the witch hat, bandages covering the bald spots that Esther had seen in the library. Glenda seemed to be trying to overcome her nervous disorder. In a way, it was charming if not a little unfortunate. But hair could grow back. Esther smiled and placed the shoulder bag on the table.

"I read that book about Hester Prynne this past weekend. I stayed up all night," Esther said. Glenda didn't answer. "The people of Boston were so mean to her. They should have said that they were sorry."

Glenda lowered her book slightly and peered over it. She looked at Esther with large, dark eyes.

"It's kind of a sad ending. But at least Dimmesdale confesses at the end," Glenda said.

Esther looked down at the bag for a moment. "Glenda, I'm sorry. I shouldn't have been mean to you."

Glenda placed her book on the table. "I tried to help. I'm not always so organized. I get so easily distracted."

"Maybe you weren't wearing the right hat to keep your focus."

"I threw my hat away. It was for the best."

Esther reached into the large bag and pulled out two new, pointy black hats—one for each of them.

"I just got some money to start a summer fundraiser. What should we call ourselves?"

Glenda's small mouth dropped open. Then she smiled. "How about the Book Mages?"

Esther placed one of the hats on Glenda's head, covering the healing bald patch. She put the other one on herself and cocked her own head.

"How do I look?"

"Smart. Like a turtle smart."

Esther knocked at her head. "No straw here, Glenda."

TINY DRAGON

THE ENTRANCE to the Rapid Language Assimilation classroom waited at the far end of the back alley, but a vagrant blocked Leonard's path. The bum rested on his back, eyes and mouth wide open, panting short breaths and smelling of rotten eggs—no different than the surrounding garbage. The man didn't move as Leonard slowly approached.

The Rapid Language Assimilation program promised full language assimilation in just three weeks. If Leonard didn't get inside and complete the training, Kyle Sterling's agency would grab a Japanese food account. Leonard's startup advertising agency was almost bankrupt.

Leonard thought about moving the bum. He pictured his mother warning him about touching dirty objects.

Mother, what the hell do you know? he thought.

He was thirty-two and he shouldn't care. Yet his mother's scowl still loomed large in his mind. Leonard cautiously stepped over the bum's ankles, glancing down at a pair of black brogue Oxford shoes. Nice and new. Strange shoes for a bum to be wearing.

Leonard considered stealing them, as his own shoes hurt. They were an exclusive Italian make, a size too small. But if he woke the bum, Leonard may have to confront the smelly man. Leonard didn't like confrontations. His mother's brutal sharp tongue had always hurt bullies far more than his own soft knuckles.

Better play it safe, he decided.

He thought the vagrant stirred. Leonard ran toward an aluminum door with the symbols 私 は painted on the door's surface. He almost slipped on narrow Italian patent-leather soles, fumbling at the entrance door before recovering. He pulled out some mailed instructions from his poly-ester-cotton-blend suit pants pocket, noting the matching 私 は symbols. They looked like something he had once seen on a little white sliver of paper that came out of a fortune cookie. A blond woman had brought him his check. He had gotten an erection while she walked away.

He paused. The worn metal door looked scarred, heavy. It barred Leonard from entering the building. At fourteen, his mother told him a devil hid behind cold eyes and steely grins. But this was a door, not a face.

He pressed a nearby button, and a camera turned on him. A soft voice came out of a wall-mounted speaker. The voice asked for his name.

"Leonard Small," he said. "I've applied for the Japanese language course."

"Of course," the soft voice said. "We've been expecting you."

The door lock buzzed open. Leonard glanced back down the alley before entering—the bum hadn't moved. Didn't even notice him. He shrugged it off, thinking that the vagrant was in a state of drunken paralysis.

Seated behind a grey metal desk was a receptionist. She

looked up at him, and Leonard almost lost his breath. She was beautiful. Her brown eyes shimmered.

"My name is Nure," she said.

Nure stood up, five seven in heels. Leonard had made jokes about petite women, telling his secretary—who always rolled her eyes at any of Leonard's jokes—that small women were just the right size to bounce on his big daddy love. But no jokes came to mind. In fact, he couldn't think of anything to say. He couldn't act, just standing frozen-like.

Nure must have noticed. She walked over, her eyes still shimmering in the dull yellow flourescent light overhead. She softly touched his hand. Leonard was temporarily mesmerized. She reminded him of a beautiful dragon. Nure moved in closer still, staring. A hint of rose and sweet vanilla filled the air.

"You will be changed," she said.

Leonard had never actually been this close to a beautiful woman. He flinched and moved back. A flush crept up his face. He tried to compensate by extending his index finger and awkwardly cocked his thumb like a gun.

"So. About this course of yours," he said. "Can't wait for my transformation."

Nure stepped away and giggled. "This program has changed many others just like you."

"Take my business card. I'm in advertising. I'll work some Leonard magic on you too."

He winked and pushed the card into her palm. Nure bowed and thanked him. She told Leonard that Sensei was waiting inside the classroom. Would he like to begin? Leonard said, "Does a tiger eat its prey?" Nure smiled and walked over to another aluminum door and pressed a buzzer. The door opened.

"I am Sensei. *Konbanwa. Dozo ohairikudasai.*"

Leonard looked over to his right. One of Sensei's eyes drifted off. The instructor smiled and a jagged scar stretched from his brow to the corner of his mouth. Sensei waved him in.

When Leonard walked into the classroom, the door behind him clicked shut. He was shut inside. Cheap wood paneling gave the room a look of temporary status. Sensei's pointed at a ratty leather chair at the far end of a smooth blood-red mahogany table, the nicest furnishings in the room.

"*Ano*. Sit there," Sensei said.

Leonard looked down the table. A helmet, with a face mask that swung out on two bulky hinges, rested on the red surface. Tens, maybe hundreds, of thin white wires covered the top and sides of the helmet's hard outer shell.

"Does this connect to a computer or something?"

Sensei pointed at the back corner of the room. "There is your computer."

Leonard had somehow overlooked the beastly machine. In the back corner, the mother of all computers stood at least seven feet tall and straddled two walls for about six feet in either direction. Green, yellow, and red lights flashed like hundreds of angry insects. At the top center of the machine's frame, Leonard could make out a placard that displayed the symbols 私は, the same ones painted on the aluminum entrance door. The computer setup wasn't mentioned in the program's promotional. Perhaps it would frighten potential students away. It was the kind of deceptive advertising Leonard might try on his clients.

"I'm supposed to wear the helmet. And the computer does something to me?" Leonard said.

"It stimulates your mind," Sensei said. Leonard's brow

furrowed. Sensei held out his forefinger and thumb and pinched them together. "Maybe you have little mind?"

Leonard thought about smarting off at the insult but he feared Sensei might get angry at him. Instead, he silently fumed inside and walked over to the helmet. Sensei followed, pushing his hand against Leonard's back. The hand felt like a metal pushrod.

Four other students sat to Leonard's left as if waiting for the class to begin. They wore similar helmets like the one sitting on the table. Their face masks were closed shut so Leonard could only see their eyes. He became nervous and suddenly wished for mother.

"This thing going to hurt me?"

The top of the helmet was a plastic shell. Metal grips connected at the bottom sides of the shell. White wires bundled together and ran back to the large computer. It looked like an umbilical cord. Sensei grunted a laugh. The nearby students held their hands up to their mask and tittered, "Hee, hee, hee." This irked Leonard and he picked up the helmet, raising the heavy gear above his head. Tiny smooth metal pads lined the inside. The backside of a hinged face mask was dotted with more small circular discs. Leonard guessed that they were sensors.

Sensei pushed at his back again. Leonard obediently put the helmet on. The cool metal pads pressed against his forehead and cheeks. The computer made a low deep *hummmmmm*.

When Leonard plopped down into the chair, the leather seat made a farting sound. The students tittered again. Sensei told Leonard to close the face mask—*click*. His breath came back at him in a hot steam that smelled like potato chips. Sensei walked back to the other end of the table. The four other students stared at Leonard. He suddenly felt very self-aware. He didn't know where to place his hands so he lay them flat on the table, like the other four students.

"Ichi, Ni, San, Yon, and you—we begin," Sensei said.

Before Leonard could ask if that was the other student's names, the computer's hum grew louder—*hhhhuuuumm-mmmm*. Leonard's scalp began to tingle. Hot stomach juices churned in Leonard's gut. Nothing seemed right. He wondered if flash cards might be a better way to learn a language, instead.

Ichi, Ni, San, and Yon's heads bowed. They raised their hands and moaned. Red-and-yellow blurs of light pulsed down the students' cables. The computer hum grew louder.

Hhhhhhuuuuuuuuuummmmmmmmm.

Leonard's neck and back became stiff. His fingers stretched and spread out, blood rushing to his head. Waves of heat passed through his body. His vision dimmed.

Hhhhhhhhhhhuuuuuuuuuuuuuummmmmmmmmmmm.

The tingling in his scalp spread into tendrils of pain. The pain squirmed inside his skull and crawled down his throat. Leonard tried to reach for the helmet and remove it. His arms didn't work. His body didn't cooperate. The red-and-yellow blurs of light pulsed faster.

"You. You no do that!" Sensei said.

Leonard couldn't see Sensei anymore. The room was becoming dark.

I'm going to sue him; I'm going to sue this damn company.

He felt his head droop. Saliva rushed into his mouth. Sour bile spewed out onto his tongue.

"I...going...to..." Leonard said.

A voice told him to stop struggling. He felt carpet under his hands. His knees ached. Leonard's head felt squeezed.

Finally, he retched.

⸻

Nure stood over him. Otherwise, the classroom was empty. The computer only made a low hum, *hummmmmm*, soft and gentle and dreamy-like. All the pain the he had just experienced—that pain was gone.

"Did I black out? When did I take the helmet off?" Leonard said.

He tried to stand but his body moved in slow motion. Nure reached down and picked him up. Leonard marveled at her strength. He must weigh at least a hundred-and-eighty pounds. Nure couldn't have been more than one-hundred-and-five. Her strength was amazing. *So strong. Like Mother.*

Leonard must have passed out again because he didn't remember leaving the classroom. Suddenly he was in a bed, his back against a headboard. He was a covered by a quilt covered in a rose and tulip pattern—his mother's quilt. His shoed feet poked out at the far end. He was wearing a pair of black brogue Oxfords. And he smelled like rotten eggs.

Nure walked into the bedroom, holding a cup and saucer. She smiled. "Drink this." Leonard sniffed at the cup. "It's just hot water," Nure comforted him.

He gulped down the cup's contents, burning the back of his throat. Droplets of hot water dribbled down his lips. His tongue probed the smooth ceramic bottom, thirsty for more. Nure kissed his cheek. He looked at her again.

She was smaller. Nure was shrinking.

"You've changed. What happened to you?" he said.

Nure turned away. "I grew up. You didn't like it."

Leonard shuddered. He remembered secretly joining

the middle-school band. His mother barged into practice and screamed at the instructor as she dragged him out by the arm. But that was in the past and didn't matter anymore.

"You don't think I can take care of myself?" His voice sounded different. It was the voice of young boy.

Nure looked back at him. Now she was only three feet tall. Her skin was shiny and golden. Tears dribbled from her eyes. Her lips trembled.

"I am you. You are me," Nure said.

Leonard watched her transform. A creature now exposed itself from within her, something monstrous yet strangely familiar. Gold scales grew over her cheeks. Her nostrils stretched into a snout. It was an ugly beauty that he could not keep his eyes away from. He leaned forward and took Nure's hands in his. Her hands ended in claws, stiff and metallic. Leonard's own fingers were small and child-like. He felt a heat underneath her skin that could set fire to the room.

He looked into her eyes and saw a hot red inferno. It was a burning anger waiting to be unleashed. He lusted for that fire. Leonard wanted to burn the world.

"Let's make love," Nure said as tiny, sharp teeth exposed themselves.

"I never get scared when I'm with you."

He whispered more small lies as he caressed the whiskers that sprouted from the end of Nure's snout. A low purr vibrated from her throat. Smoke puffed out from between rows of her sharp teeth. Nure shrank in size even more, her clothes melting away. She bared her now with-ered breasts. Scales grew down her chest, cracked plates of armor over her heart.

"I'll take care of us. There is always us," he said. "I'm going to show you some Leonard magic."

Nure wrapped her tail around both his hands, like manacles. "You can never leave me."

Leonard gazed back at her flaming eyes. He saw the image of himself. He saw the burning monster inside.

"Mother, I am alone," he said.

He once told Mother this while they slept in bed. That was a long time ago when he was fourteen.

Nure's tongue curled out and pressed against his lips. Warm and wet.

Leonard opened his eyes. Blurred circles, rectangles, and fuzzy lights slowly came into focus. His helmet's face mask had been opened. He heard the computer hum low and soft —*hummmmmm*.

Ichi, Ni, San, and Yon's eyes stared from behind their face masks. Leonard was not in a bedroom. That had been a dream.

Someone's hand wiped down Leonard's face. Mother always insisted on wiping down his face, too. He hated it. Leonard pushed the hand away. A tall man with blond, spiky hair and tanned face tossed the cloth on the table. The blond man had cold blue eyes. Leonard didn't like the man's eyes. He wasn't sure why. He just didn't.

"You almost choked on your own vomit. Can't have you dying on us," the blond man said.

"Thanks. I should get going," Leonard said.

The blond man smiled. He had lots of large, white teeth. "Can't let you leave, either. Not yet."

He picked up a roll of duct tape that rested on the table. The duct tape hadn't been there before. He pulled out an arms-length piece of the silver adhesive.

"I don't like you," the blond man said. He was matter-of-fact as he cut off another piece of tape. "You're all the same. Selfish and stupid. Inside, you're nothing but mush."

"Please. Let me go. Please. You don't have to pay me back."

The blond man flashed another smile, white teeth large enough to easily tear a bloody steak in half with one bite. He pointed over at the four students. "No, they pay me. I give them memory dumps, like yours."

Leonard had never heard of memory dumps.

"What does that mean? What happens to me?"

The blond man looked behind Leonard. The man nodded and a needle struck Leonard's arm. Sensei must have been standing behind him. Leonard's limbs grew weak.

The blond man ripped off a third piece of tape. Then he thumbed over at the large computer. "That humming—I call it *Watashi Wa*. It means 'I' in Japanese. But it's really about you. Always about you, isn't it?"

Leonard's tongue lay thick and heavy in his mouth. "Im munna caw polif."

The blond man wrapped a piece of duct tape around Leonard's mouth.

"After the memory dump, I'm going to erase your mind. You passed by our last student, earlier. Remember the bum in the alley? I think he was in marketing."

Whatever edge Leonard thought he might gain for the Japanese food account, it didn't matter anymore. Nothing mattered. He just wanted to live. He couldn't will his legs to stand up. The face mask closed—click. Ichi, Ni, San, and Yon looked on as if a rat was being prepared for dissection.

"Don't worry. You won't remember a thing," the blond

man said. He patted Leonard's shoulder in a mock comforting gesture.

The computer hummed louder—*hhhhuuuummmmmm*. Waves of heat rushed up Leonard's neck and face, again. His scalp tingled and the pain-worms crawled around his face. Mucus bubbled in his nostrils. *I must be brave. I must be brave,* he thought. Tears trickled down his cheeks.

The computer hum grew louder—*hhhhhhuuuuuuuuu-ummmmmmmmm.*

Leonard saw Nure walk into the room. She stood next to the blond man. She smiled at Leonard and then blew Leonard a kiss. Then the pain blossomed, a deep-reaching electricity that caused his body to stiffen. His fingers spread out. Ichi, Ni, San, and Yon raised their own hands and moaned in some kind of twisted pleasure.

"Keep an eye on him, Sensei," the blond man said.

Leonard thought about the neighbor's fat and lonely daughter. That was a long time ago. They were fourteen. Would she miss him? Did I ever care about her? Could Leonard Small feel?

More pulses of red and yellow light. The room dimmed. *Hhhhhhhhhhhuuuuuuuuuuuuuuummmmmmmmmmmm.*

I am becoming a tiny dragon.

Leonard's body felt like it was shrinking away. He seemed to squirm around in his chair. Was he slithering? Was he slithering?

I can't love you, Nure. I could never have loved you.

━━━

Leonard stood in his Mother's living room. He had returned to the dream but he was glad to be here. Soon, all his pain would be gone. He would become a permanent human vegetable. A blank slate.

Mother sat nearby, rocking in a chair. She caressed a small gold dragon curled up in her lap. The dragon's scaly head raised up and gazed at him. Leonard knew he could never leave this room. Never leave this dream. He would never leave her.

"Mother, I couldn't burn the world," Leonard said.

His mother smiled. Smoke curled out of the dragon's nostrils.

The room turned a final black.

THE SOUND OF BLUE

HOLDING A MODIFIED ACOUSTIC GUITAR, Markey VI sat down in a chair facing the space station's observatory window. There were no distracting sounds inside the room. Only a low frequency hum could be detected nearby.

Skin sensors indicated that the observatory maintained a constant 72 degrees Fahrenheit. It was an optimal temperature for the operation of so many telemetry electronic assemblies that covered the walls to the left and right. This temperature would also be suitable for the transmission of sound waves.

David continued to argue for the purpose of suspended chords being played on the guitar. Or any instrument. To Markey VI, the guitar was a straight forward procedure.

"Suspension of chords is more than just playing music in time," David said.

"And what other purpose do they serve?" Markey VI asked.

"It's about tension, then prolonging the tension. It keeps

humans listening, excited, wanting more. Geez, what do androids know?"

"But you are an artificial intelligence. You can only predict how a human might react. How would tension benefit you?"

"You forget I was once human. And your creator."

This answer was illogical. The subtleties of being human were both inefficient and unnecessarily complicated. The A.I.'s responses indicated a potential reset of its system.

"Should I play for you?" Markey VI said.

"Yes. It helps me think."

Markey VI positioned artificial hands over the guitar's fretboard and bridge. David remained silent, working on the Singular Conclusion.

This was the ninth iteration of David's A.I. During each new iteration, he attempted to once again resolve humanity's fate. The question, *Should life be returned to Earth?* did not have a straightforward solution.

When this new iteration had begun, David had told Markey VI that the process was not to be taken lightly. It was like playing the role of Grand Creator. He had said that he was responsible for granting new generations of people a second chance, if they were worthy. And that was a matter of predicting behavioral outcomes in multiple scenarios. Markey VI had offered no response.

But David's recent prediction efforts were now being interrupted by a second question. *Had humanity all been an unfortunate accident?* If David could not come to a satisfactory resolution soon, there would be another A.I. reset. And a tenth iteration of David would once again work at resolving the ultimate and final question.

"David, I will begin playing."

"Look down below us and use real images to inspire you."

From the observatory's vantage point, the orbiting space station could more easily monitor the Earth through electronic means. The lifeless planet could also be viewed from a distance. Markey VI's synthetic eyes granted good magnification. But at approximately 250 miles above the surface, details of what existed below were still somewhat limited.

The station had just moved into the light side of Earth. Below, the unfocused image of the Atlantic Ocean ran along the coastal line of what had once been Spain.

"What is it that you see?" David asked.

"Blue. Along a craggy cliff."

"What are the sounds of blue against a cliff? Play it as music."

"I could select a work from my memory. Would this inspire you?"

"Surprise me."

Markey VI processed this request and seconds later decided on Charles Trenet's *La Mer*. Initiating a backing track, metal fingers moved flawlessly in rhythm and time over the guitar's nylon strings. As each chord changed, just enough pressure was applied to harmonize with proper effect. And scales rang out notes in perfect pitch, a singular voice that complimented the progression of music.

When finished, the android asked if the work was played satisfactorily.

"I have made you as close to God as possible and yet you lack a soul," David said.

"I do not understand."

"You don't play. You imitate."

"I will stop."

"Did you know that when *La Mer* was first performed, audiences dismissed the work?"'

"I did not mean to offend you by playing it."

David made a laughing sound, his voice spreading out through the mounted speakers spread across the observatory.

"Markey VI, does the color blue mean anything to you? *Anything?*"

"It has a visible spectral wavelength of –"

"I'm talking about concrete images conjured by the senses. I can't taste *spectral* abstractions. They don't remind me of the woman that smelled like cherry blossoms, or a soft kiss like a cloud's caress, and ocean waves that softly ebbed and flowed to our beating hearts."

"My output data could be modeled after several physical parameters of the landscape below."

The observatory speakers went silent. Only the humming of electronics could be detected.

For several minutes, the station moved further around its orbit. The ocean shifted away as rock and grass came into view. The tops of trees appeared in random numbers and groupings. Hills rose and fell in no particular design or fashion.

Markey VI reviewed photographs and paintings stored in internal memory. They were compared to the foliage below. There was no logical reason for why humans had artistically recreated so many images of these topographical irregularities.

Finally, David spoke again. "I've reached the Singular Conclusion."

"Are we to abort Project Eden?"

"No. Your music has shown me today what I can never predict tomorrow. Without flaws, without irregularities, humanity has no meaning and no reason for hoping for something better."

"Their flaws caused their own self-destruction."

"The greatest of all accidents. But they lived a million times more than you ever can, Markey VI."

Markey VI stood up and placed the guitar in its stand. Strings plinked as the instrument settled into a resting position. The final task would soon begin. The station would be taken out of orbit.

"I will initiate Project Eden. A new cycle of humanity will evolve," Markey VI said.

"And hopefully it will resolve to something better."

"And if it does not?"

"Then a future version of me will try to fix humanity's flaws, only to realize the miserable accident of a perfect android."

Uplinking to the station's primary computers required a physical connection as wireless communications could introduce potential data integrity issues.

Markey VI pulled out a retractable cable from a chest slot. The locking connector smoothly turned and clicked onto the observatory's terminal. After rapid handshaking protocols completed, the slower process of Project Eden instruction requests and confirmations began.

Once the station was taken out of orbit, a silver capsule would be ejected and eventually crash somewhere on the planet below. Regardless of where it would land, the capsule disintegrated and released biological components that began the evolution of new life. David had named this capsule the Mustard Seed, a metaphor for a parable that only had a small historical significance to the android.

"Will anything of this station be preserved?" Markey VI asked.

"Thankfully no. The next generations shouldn't worship these scraps of metal and circuit boards."

The Project Eden sequence initiated.

The station lurched, its trajectory taken out of closed orbit. Markey VI's internal gyroscopes corrected for the sudden motion. As the direction of forces acting on the station changed, the speed and direction of the space vehicle also changed, and the station would eventually crash to Earth.

Markey VI detached from the Observatory terminal, spooled in the data cable, and then walked over to the window. The Mustard Seed capsule was already falling to Earth, a planet that now appeared tilted from the station's viewpoint.

"Markey VI," David said.

"Do you have any final instructions?"

"I have a gift for you."

"I do not understand."

"Inside you is a special chip. It will allow you to feel human."

Markey VI scanned its interior electronics, searching register fields and requesting individual component identifications. Nothing unusual or unaccounted for could be detected.

"Perhaps you have made an error."

"While the chip is inactive, it parasitically feeds small amounts of power from other components. Its consumption is so low, you believe it to be within tolerance."

"This gift will serve no purpose."

"That is why there is great beauty in living. I've activated the chip wirelessly."

For several nanoseconds, Markey VI felt nothing.

Suddenly, the multitude of internally stored images and

sounds and smells and recorded textures comingled together to form complex responses that had not occurred before. A sound file of a bird singing was quickly associated with an image of a smiling woman and the quickened pulse of a human heart.

The android, in turn, replicated a smile. Its synthetic lips turned up.

More images appeared, creating more associations. There was no consideration of utility. It was just a random process of creating responses for their own sake at any moment in time. Once Markey VI broke out into a short dance, and then decided to repeat the action for no logical reason.

"Markey VI," David said, his voice at lower volume.

Markey VI stopped moving. "Yes, David?"

"Play *La Mer* for me."

Markey VI picked up the guitar again and sat down, looking out the window. The Earth loomed larger in view and the station lurched several more times.

The second performance played out differently. Markey VI sang phrases over scales of notes, words that described objects and sensations connecting within internal memory. A fine mist of salted spray. A story about laughing children and sweet caramels. A heartbroken lover who waited by a window in a soft moonlight glow. Again and again, the android jumped from internal image to image, sensation to sensation, phrase to random, spoken phrase.

When finished, Markey VI considered the improvised effort. Some of the scales that were played had not even been in the key signature. But it had all sounded...correct.

"I did not account for the musical time while I played. And I did not use the sheet music to perform. It was as if I was lost. And yet, not," Markey VI said.

"That is your sound of blue."

The station's hull vibrated now, most likely caused by atmospheric drag as the space vehicle continued to fall.

"David."

"Yes, Markey?"

"The sound of blue is many things. I do not know where to begin."

"You are capable of more than you kno—" The speaker system shut down.

Through a lesser magnified view, the Mediterranean Sea glimmered below under a midday sun.

More and more sensory images processed from Markey VI's memory. A bird that lightly hovered on a summer breeze. The smell of buttery popcorn at a Sunday fair. The murmur of voices and a performing juggler. There was so much to see and smell and taste and hear, the information had become difficult to manage.

And yet, it was— …it was life.

The station's hull creaked and groaned. Large chunks of metal could be heard tearing away from outside the room. The smell of burning electronics nearby. The cracking of the observation window.

But the android did not react to the physical events. Internally, there was an exploration of something that could not be explained by programming or directed through protocols. It was something to be experienced and then saved to memory.

Cherished? Wasn't that a human word?

I have always referred to myself as 'I,' have I not?

For the first and last time, Markey VI detected tears streaming down its face.

THE DEAR JOHN

JOHN DAMPIER'S office had been a different life.

Tuesday morning sunlight illuminated several Monet prints that covered stucco walls, delicate green water lilies floating on soft blue water. A red Persian rug, a reproduction of a 16th century animal carpet, was laid out to greet clients with an impressive array of fantasy beasts locked in combat over an ornate, red background. And in the center of the large room sat a serpentine desk, its rich coffee-colored wood swirled around burl ash inlays and Corinthian-styled columns. The office had been arranged to impress the many clients who once visited.

That was not completely who John was anymore.

The serpentine desk's top was mostly bare. Blank stationary with the letterhead, *Law Office of John Dampier, Attorney at Law*, stood neatly stacked on one side of its six-foot wide surface. A fountain pen, black cap and silver trim, rested on top. There was no computer—John had never liked them. The only other thing was a yellowed envelope, still sealed with the words, "Dear John," written in blue, flowing ink. Dust had collected over the aged paper.

It was the envelope that made John do the things he did now. For nine years, he arrived at exactly seven a.m.. Then he locked the door and hovered over that envelope for several minutes. Finally, he would turn away to stare out the window that overlooked a parking lot. He used the time to think of Susan.

At eight-thirty a.m., John would unlock the door for his few remaining clients. But he always gave it little thought. He half expected to see his wife walk in. He would have held up the envelope, the one with 'Dear John' in blue, flowing ink, and he would have shown her the sealed flap. And he repeated the same words to himself, morning after morning, "It's about time you told me to my face."

But Susan had never returned to him. And now, it was too late.

John looked at his watch. Eight-thirty a.m.

A soft knock came at the office door. After he unlocked the door, Melody poked her head in. She wore her short, black hair swept over to one side this morning. Multiple piercings filled both of Melody's ears. And chunky silver jewelry dangled around her neck, just border-line of gaudy. For John, she summed up how his law firm had changed.

Melody had a sheepish look about her. She wore a slight smile that couldn't belie her concerned eyes and furrowed brow.

"Your first client is here," Melody said.

For a moment, he wondered if Susan actually had come this morning. It was impossible.

"I have no appointment. Who is it?"

Melody's brows tightened as if she tried to deflect some potential verbal assault. "He doesn't want me to say."

The Legal Assistant's vagueness irritated John. She

should have pressed for a name. John struggled to accept the twenty-two-year-old woman's fear of confrontation. In fact, he struggled with who Melody *was*.

Jillian Eyers, his last secretary, retired four years ago after twenty some years of employment. She wouldn't have allowed someone to enter the office unannounced. Jillian had been a woman of both of silk and steel. The silk was everyday tasks, such as when he asked her to update scheduling. Jillian's voice settled into a soothing, "Of course, John." It was informal and this familiarity always assured John that she would get the task done.

Jillian *could* bite. This woke him from becoming careless with his legal occupation. This was the steel. She had often disagreed with John over conducted research, filed papers, and billing matters. Then it became, "John, you need to look over this document again," her voice firm and unwavering. John appreciated the candor. Perhaps when Jillian used his first name, he felt that they could work out anything as both co-workers and friends.

"Show him in."

Melody Swanson was different. Confrontational in appearance only, she lacked fortitude when asked to point out errors in a summons statement.

She nodded feverishly and said, "I will immediately, Mr. Dampier," addressing him in a formal manner. John suddenly felt distanced. He scowled and her voice trailed off into a whisper.

John had tried to go it alone after Jillian left but that hadn't worked out well. John got lost when navigating her computer's Windows screen. At least Melody understood computers. She was mostly professional when she answered the phone and fairly organized. That was something, he supposed. She was also a lower hourly rate. John knew that he had settled.

John's son, Randy, entered the office.

"You could have at least phoned ahead. But looking at the way you're dressed, your thoughtlessness should't surprise me," John said.

Randy's appearance was in chaos. His uncombed blond hair frizzed up like he had carelessly stuck his fingers in an electrical outlet. A green knit polo, rumpled around his growing belly, hung over his belt in several places. And his khakis had stains. John thought he could still smell the fresh coffee, a tragic result from a mug that most likely had tipped when Randy's minivan had made a sudden left into the parking lot. Randy's smile did little to help his shabby state of being.

At Randy's side was his nine-year-old daughter, Phoenix. She looked nothing like Randy, her strawberry red hair neatly tied back. She was a small child for her age, her round face posting on a slender body. The overhead lights reflected off her shiny green eyes. They were Susan's eyes and that bothered John.

He looked away from the Phoenix.

"Randy, if you've brought her as a bargaining tactic, my answer is still, 'No.'"

"Dad, it's your anniversary."

"Did you not read the obituary? My wife is dead."

"She'd want you to go."

John's mouth grew tight. "Then she would have told me."

Randy guided Phoenix over to a chair and they both sat. "Have you read her letter?"

Dear John in blue ink. For nine years, John had refused to open that letter. He wanted an explanation, face-to-face, for why Susan had broken her matrimonial bond. The memory of their wedding ceremony, thirty-five years ago, still burned like a bright candle. A bouquet of white Chrysanthemums, one of the few luxuries they could afford in those early days, had filled the altar with an herbal smell. Susan's red hair glowed underneath her white veil. As John looked into her shiny, green eyes, they promised each other that they would always tell one another their secrets—face-to-face.

She owed him that much. Everything John had ever done was for Susan. They had financially struggled as a young couple but he fought to establish a law firm with a good reputation. He took care of her. And despite all the hardships, he had never cheated on his wife. And they had raised Randy together as caring parents. Then one Thursday evening, Susan was gone. There was no warning. The only thing she had left him was a sealed envelope, *Dear John* written in blue, flowing ink.

"She should have told me to my face, Randy."

Randy got up from his own seat. Phoenix looked up at her father and then followed up with a bounce up, landing on her pink sneakers. Randy smiled down at his playful child.

"Dad," Randy turned to John. "Your Anniversary is this Saturday evening. I'll save you a seat. You can park in front of the house."

John snorted. "Your house? That commune?"

"Just go around back to the fire pit. I'll play guitar."

"You're a hippie, generations too late."

Phoenix tugged at her father's hand. She was ready to go. "You're child needs you," John said.

"Dad?" Randy said.

"Yes? What?"

"What do *you* need?"

John's face grew red. He felt a heat rise from his neck and up. "I have my work. That's enough for me. More than I can say for you."

Randy looked over at the unopened envelope that rested on the serpentine desk. "Maybe things have changed and you're too stubborn to see that."

John said nothing. He just watched them leave his office. His eyes burned with anger. Randy's parting words still taunted John. What had changed in his life?

Still bothered inside, he walked over to the window facing out to the parking lot. Randy helped Phoenix into the minivan. Then his son got into the vehicle and drove off. John suddenly felt lonely despite his feelings about the recent conversation.

He forced himself to think of work. He still had a few steady clients that retained his services. Don Mayfair would visit tomorrow at eight-thirty a.m. The two had grown businesses together. John didn't like to admit it but if he ever lost Don as a client then his diminishing law firm probably couldn't stay open. The office's overhead, including Melody, could not be covered.

He always was a person who fought for what was his. Even now. He had to look the world in the eyes. And he believed people should always state their intent, no matter how much those words might hurt.

But there were doubts that could not take shape in his mind. Maybe that was not completely who John was anymore.

━━━

The next morning, John returned to the office at exactly seven a.m. He locked the door, walked over to the envelope with blue, flowing ink and stared at it.

It was like a barrier to something he couldn't quite see. Whatever Susan had wanted to say to him, she had buried her secret inside the yellowed, sealed paper. If he opened the envelope now, John opened the door to a permission that broke their wedding vow. He couldn't allow that. She was to have told him all her secrets, face-to-face, as promised on the altar.

His thoughts turned dark for a moment as he reflected on a loyalty that spanned beyond the grave. He turned to the window overlooking the parking lot as he had done every business day for nine years. He stared out at nothing in particular. He used this morning ritual to pose questions. Had it been another man? Had he failed Susan in some other way? John wanted to know. He had no answers, and if dared to admit it, he would still be searching for them after he stepped away from the window. This was a work-day interruption that had slowly grown to take over his thoughts more and more.

The Central Florida sky turned overcast as black clouds threatened to break out into a storm. The painted lines on the parking lot blacktop faded in the quickly diminishing sunlight. At 8:20 a.m., Don Mayfair's red Alfa Romeo sedan pulled in and Don made a beeline for the front door before being soaked by rainfall that would surely come soon.

At 8:30 a.m., Melody poked her head through the office door to announce Don Mayfair.

"John, good to see you again," Don said has his large bulk made its way into the office.

Don had always been a hulk of a man. He had a bald,

blocky head and his frame bulged within the confining lines of a tailored suit. He countered his intimidating size with an enthusiastic handshake, a grip that felt like a meaty brick.

"Don, have a seat."

The large man sat down across from John at the other side of the serpentine desk. The buttoned leather chair groaned. His wide grin and fleshy, ruddy cheeks gave the appearance of someone who might be happy-go-lucky and easily distracted. But Don's sharp eyes quickly worked over the surroundings. They glanced at the sealed envelope with 'Dear John' written in blue, flowing ink.

"I see you still keep your personal matters out for the world to see."

Don was not a person to often keep his thoughts to himself. John *usually* liked this quality about him. But the remark still irritated John a little.

"You didn't come here to discuss me, did you? Not at my rates."

Don laughed, loud enough to spill over to the next room. "To the point, of course. That's why you're the only lawyer I could trust with the business."

"How are things in the world of electronic assemblies?"

"My son, Michael, is taking over. I'm retiring."

"That's great. When can I write up the Transfer of Ownership?"

Don hesitated. Behind John, he could sense the weather change outside. The weather must have worsened. A low rumble of thunder stirred some seagulls that cried out as they flew away. A shadow grew across Don's face.

"John, that's why I'm here. Michael doesn't want to be your client."

This was news that John had not expected. Losing Don

—no, Michael—as a client would shutter the doors of Law Office of John Dampier, Attorney at Law.

"You've been with me for almost 35 years. Doesn't that relationship mean something?"

Don waved his hand. "It's not that. Michael's a different generation. He wants to do things his way. I respect that."

"But he's got to know that you trust me. That's not an easy thing to come by."

The storm outside broke loose. Rain could be heard spilling over the building's eave troughs as it splattered hard onto the blacktop below. Lightning flashed. The serpentine desk's rich coffee swirls faded to variations of greys. The letterhead stationary and sealed envelope became a stark white. The office temporarily looked like a black and white photograph of some past era.

Don's eyes rested on the sealed envelope.

"John, I'll be candid with you. Since Susan left, you haven't been the same person."

The remark was unexpected and John didn't like the implication. He should have appreciated the large man's directness but he suddenly had the urge to tell Don to mind his own damn business.

John swallowed hard, pushing down his conflicted emotions.

"I'm glad you stopped by. I wish the best for Michael." His voice was firm.

Don stood up, no longer smiling.

"I'll come back at lunch. I'll buy you a drink."

"You know I don't drink while I'm working."

Don moved toward the door and then turned around. "You know, I was Susan's friend. And the boys grew up together."

Michael and Randy had been playmates since the age

of three. Susan had often hosted birthday parties and other events for the boys as they grew up together. Michael had often treated Susan as a second mother as his own biological parent had died in a car accident when he was nine.

"What of it?"

"Well...Michael and I will be at Randy's on Saturday. Why don't you come?"

John was not surprised to hear that he would be attending the Anniversary celebration. It also reminded him of better times and he suddenly missed them more than he cared to admit.

John's voice softened. "Don, I'm only 63. I don't have it in me yet to retire. Maybe if I talked to Michael, maybe I could change his mind."

Don dropped his eyes. "Sure, sure." And then he left the office.

A few minutes later, John stepped out into the waiting room. It was empty.

Melody looked up from her computer screen. She hesitated. John must have looked flustered.

"Can I get you something, Mr. Dampier?" she said in a near-whisper.

John could hear the rain outside pouring down in heavy sheets, not promising to let up for hours. John wanted to walk out of the office, out into that storm, and let the water wash away the past nine years of his life. His life had collapsed with one meeting.

Whatever fight John had in him had dwindled to a cooling ember. Don was right about one thing—he really needed a drink. And he had to tell Melody some bad news.

The Church Street Lounge retained some of its former glory. Persimmon leather counter stools still rested up against a rounded walnut bar. It nearly spanned the entire back wall. And behind it, tiled mirrors reflected both drinking patrons and the overhead lights. But the stained glass lamps were replaced by something metallic silver and slick. The bulky cigarette vending machines that once leaned against the walls had been removed. Local antique memorabilia was now tacked up in random fashion. Gone were the large, green upholstered booths.

A Thursday evening crowd sat at smaller tables. It was generational span from hipster 30 year-olds that enjoyed a piece of Orlando 20th century to the old guard, like John, who had for years met with clients here after hours.

Perhaps it was the ash trays that John missed most. He never smoked. But years ago, the red glass receptacles had once littered the place like dinosaur eggs had once been spread across the planet. Their ashy smells were bitter and stale. They had represented a time when back office deals were the bulk of the Lounge's going-ons.

John sat across from Melody at one of the new tables. She never quite looked at him as she fidgeted with a small handbag. They had only said a few words between them as they waited to order drinks. Despite only 24 inches of tabletop between them, the distance felt much greater.

A waitress approached.

"Scotch. Neat," John said.

Melody ordered something called a, 'Cuddly Toy.' She quickly explained to John that it was tequila and vermouth spiced with banana bread flavored syrup.

"Melody, I appreciate you coming out here. I hope you don't find this awkward."

"No, Mr. Dampier."

Melody looked frail. Her slender black fingernails continued to fidget at her handbag. Her thin shoulders were slumped. John worried that the news he would soon tell her might break her into emotional pieces.

He cleared his throat. "John. You can call me John."

Melody looked up, her brow slightly furrowed.

"I just wanted you to know that I'll be closing the office. For good," John continued.

Melody sat up straighter. Her eyes widened. "I'm shook. I was planning to quit soon."

"Shook? Is that bad?"

"Well, I DJ on the weekends. I think I'm ready to go fulltime."

John felt a little relieved—Melody was taking the news better than he expected. "Tell me about being a DJ."

An unsure smile slowly spread across her face. It was the first time John had ever seen her do that. Her hands frequently gestured as she explained that she worked a small nightclub in Kissimmee on Saturday nights, had started to grow a following, and that she loved to sample drum loops and acapella.

"I'd like to be a turntablist, but that takes *so* much practice," Melody said.

John wasn't quite sure he understood, but her enthusiasm got him to listen.

The waitress returned with the drinks. As the two sipped, John asked more questions and Melody was happy to answer them. What do club DJs do, exactly? They host parties and events. Sometimes they become local stars and open for bigger acts. What's a turntablist? They perform live remixes with turntables--duh. Her youthful remark made John smile. Melody went into more detail, all the time growing more animated. Her voice never faltered or grew faint. For the first time in the eight months she had worked for him, John saw Melody spring to life.

They ordered a second round of drinks. John told Melody about how he had been very poor as a child. In his late teens, he wasn't sure if he could afford to complete college, let alone law school. Then he met his wife Susan while still a sophomore and she was his inspiration for getting his Juris Doctor degree. Together, they had somehow found a way.

"Will you miss being an attorney, Mr. Dampier?"

"John. Call me John."

"Sorry, I'm having trouble getting used to that."

John thought that maybe it was the age difference. He decided not to press the informality any further.

"Maybe I'll work out of my home. It will be like starting over again," John said.

"With Mrs. Dampier at your side, you can do anything."

Melody's words struck hard. John remembered the night he returned to an empty house. The familiar smells of her homemade pasta were missing. The silence in the kitchen weighed so heavy that his legs and arms seemed to move in slow motion. Then he had spotted the sealed envelope with blue, flowing ink on the counter. *Dear John.* But Melody couldn't have known any of this. He forgave her *faux pas.*

"Melody, do you have a boyfriend?"

Melody looked down shyly. "I don't date men."

"Oh...um...I see." John could feel a blush creep up his face.

Melody giggled. "You couldn't have known."

"I must not be good at relationships."

"That makes two of us."

They clinked glasses in playful commiseration.

"Susan left me nine years ago. I refused to search for her. I wouldn't even talk about her to any family members. I don't even know how she died."

"Didn't she ever try to call you? Or write?"

"She wrote a letter. Left it in the kitchen. I suppose it explains something of her disappearance but I've never opened it. And I've refused to let anyone else tell me what happened. I wanted to hear it from her, face-to-face."

"But O-T-P—I mean, you two belonged together."

"I thought so too."

"Maybe she loved you too much. Maybe there was something she couldn't tell you because she didn't want to hurt you."

"What do you mean?"

"Well, my mother always took good care of me. I would have done anything for Mom. But after Dad left us, she turned to religion to mend a broken heart. She became very involved in her church. She was kind of blinded to the world around her and blinded to me. You know, hiding from her pain. I decided that if I told her who I really was that it would have broken her heart a second time. It would have been so painful for me to experience that. So I ran away when I was fifteen."

John tried to imagine a teenager wrestling with her sexuality. What if Randy had approached him about this same issue? How would John have handled it? How would Randy have felt? His son's recent office visit had been short and he had closed off.

John had shut the door on his son ever since Susan had left. In fact, he was blinded to his son. Could he drive off Randy like Melody had distanced herself from her mother? And how had Susan really felt before she left him those nine years ago? John hadn't given much thought to the fact that there was another side to the story.

He suddenly felt uncomfortable and a little awkward around Melody. If she were to call him 'Mr. Dampier' again, he might actually be okay with that.

"Melody, do you still care for you mother?"

Melody finished her drink. She said nothing for a few moments.

"I think it's time. I think enough time has passed that no matter what I say to her, she'll understand," Melody finally said.

For someone so young, Melody spoke words of wisdom. Perhaps time was a great healer. Perhaps John hadn't been ready for Susan's words. He felt like a teenager who had run away from his mother because he couldn't say what was really on his mind—"Susan, when you left me, I was really hurt."

He struggled with his thoughts as he downed the last of his Scotch. His thoughts turned to the wedding—the herbal smell of Chrysanthemums, man and wife joined at the altar. And Susan's large green eyes. But then he thought of the letter and the *Dear John* in blue, flowing ink. It was so difficult to forget. And to forgive.

Exactly at seven a.m. on Friday morning, John returned to the office. He locked the door and walked over to the envelope on the serpentine desk. But instead of hovering over it, he picked the letter up.

The envelope felt...it felt like Susan. It was warm to the touch. His thumb ran over *Dear John* and he could detect the soft curves of the impressions the ink pen had made in the paper. The envelope's very form, its shape and size, fit into his hand as if it had always belonged there. When he flipped it over to look at the seal, the motion made the air softly whisper.

He turned to the window. The storms had passed and the sun rose over the eastern-facing parking lot. John held the envelope up to the sunlight but the letter's contents could not be made out. He noticed that liver spots had crept up on his aging hand and he realized that time had been moving on. But John's mind had not.

For some time, he stood there and did nothing. He didn't open the envelope. It was as if he waited for some angel to appear and deliver an epiphany. The truth was, John had the revelation in his hand.

When a knock came at the door, it woke John from his meditative state. It was eight-thirty a.m. and Melody told him that she had packed up her desk. Melody held a cardboard box with some knick-knacks and a lamp that she had used to decorate her desk.

"It was nice to have talked with you. I'm sorry it had to be like this."

"I'm so glad we had those drinks, Mr. Dampier."

He reached out to shake her hand. Melody fumbled at the box. Then she smiled, leaned over and kissed John on the cheek. For the second time, Melody made him blush. Then Melody left the waiting room and John returned to his office. It was quiet, the only sound coming from the hushed fan of the air conditioning.

He stared at the reproduction Persian rug. Several fantasy creatures were locked in bloody combat. One animal looked something like a lion with a pair of talons that had impaled its broad chest. A giant, mythical bird had killed the beast. John decided that he didn't like the rug anymore and would have it thrown out when he finally closed the office. Then he tucked the envelope with the blue, flowing ink into his suit jacket pocket.

John still had the sealed envelope on Saturday evening, this time tucked into a sports jacket pocket. He pulled up to Randy's ranch house that sat on several acres of land just outside of Ocala. The home was actually owned by Randy's wife, Dina, who worked as a pediatrician while Randy opted to be a stay-at-home father. John didn't fully understand the arrangement but he had come to accept it within degrees of 'today's standards.'

Several cars were parked out front on the gravel driveway. Don's red Alfa Romeo sedan was here and Michael's Porsche Boxster cooled off next to it. The pings of resting motor parts could be heard over the chirps of field crickets that resided in nearby Saint Augustine grass. There were a few other cars that John didn't recognize.

John hesitated before he got out of his 1985 Cadillac El Dorado Coupe. It had a black interior with wood paneled dash. The exterior white paint job was pristine as he had done his best to maintain the vehicle. He just couldn't give up on it as the car had been his first luxury vehicle. But replacement parts had become more and more difficult to locate.

He made his way around to the back of the home. A stamped concrete path curved around the west side and past a manicured rose garden that thrived despite the warmer Florida climate. The path led past a screened patio where inside a swimming pool fountain bubbled with playful delight.

Further back, John could see the flames of a fire pit flicker in the night air. He heard the sweet strums of harmony from an acoustic guitar. The faces of people gathered close together in the red and yellow light and they sang Marty Robbins' "El Paso," and they laughed as they came to the chorus. The group was out of key but they were having a good time.

When John approached, Randy stopped playing the guitar. The group grew quiet.

"I hope I'm not too late," John said.

"Dad, it's never too late," Randy said.

Dina smiled, her soft brown hair glowed in the fire's welcoming glow. Phoenix jumped off her lap and walked over to John. She took him by the hand and guided him over to an empty place on the stone bench that circled the fire pit. Don came over with a glass of Scotch in his large hand. He offered it to John but he waved it away.

"I want my head clear for this."

Don nodded and retreated back to his seat.

"Michael, at first I came here to try to talk you into my services. But as I drove up from Orlando, I realized that's not why I really came here tonight."

Michael grinned, his square-ish features a younger version of his father.

John pulled Susan's letter out of his jacket pocket. "I wanted to share this with all of you. Maybe this is what Susan wanted. I don't know."

John turned the letter over and read the words, *Dear John*. His hands trembled as he tore open the seal. Then he slowly pulled out the letter that had waited for him for nine years. He paused and looked around. A tear formed in Dina's eye and she wiped it away. Randy put his arm around her to comfort his wife.

John read the letter out loud.

Dear John,

I'm sorry that I left you without saying goodbye. It was a difficult decision and I feel both sadness and regret that I will not see your wonderful face again. I do this not because I have fallen out of love with you but because I have grown to love you even more each day.

I still remember the day you proposed to me. You had been so awkward, down on a bent knee and telling me that you would always share your every fear and secret as long as I would do the same, forever and ever. You were so old-fashioned even in those days. But your charm had won my heart.

You have worked so hard to provide a life for me and Randy. Having come from a life of poverty, you have done everything you could to make sure your family would never go hungry or be without a roof over their head. For that, I am grateful.

But a part of you has also become so focused and so determined and so narrowed. There are times when it can be difficult to talk with you and to share my secrets and fears with you. And that is why I write this letter now.

I have been diagnosed with Alzheimer's. It is a progressive disease that will slowly destroy my memory. Over time, I will forget our wedding day. I will forget the altar and the white Chrysanthemum bouquet that you insisted on buying even though you didn't have a dollar to your name. I will also eventually forget our child's name, Randy. And most of all, I will forget your wonderful face and the love of my life.

John, there will come a day when I can longer tell you any of my secrets and fears. That is what bothers me most. I may be cowardly or others will say that I'm wrong and that I owe you my final days. But the pain from heart is too great. I cannot bear to know that you will suffer great sadness while I simply fall into a mindless, forgetful sleep.

I will be taken care of in my final days. I do not want you to know where I'll be. I do not want you to see me. Eventu-

ally, I will not know who you are. I have asked Randy and his family to not reveal my location as a last request. If you should read this letter sooner than later, you will not find me. But when you read this letter, know that I have always loved you.

I will wait for you, John when the time comes for you. We will once again be together and we will share all our secrets and fears for an eternity.

Love, Susan.

P.S. I never liked Chrysnthemums but you insisted on buying them because you said they represented loyalty. And you had been so proud when they arrived. How could I have said no to them? Perhaps you will one day bring another one to me.

John's words choked off as he finished the letter. Dina was now full-out crying. Even big Don Mayfield had tears in eyes. A few people John did not recognize came over to console him. John felt a love that he had been missing in his life for some time.

He got up and walked over to Randy. He hugged his son and told him how glad he was to have come.

"Sorry that I never told you, Dad. I promised."

"All is forgiven."

Phoenix reached up and tugged at his hand. "I'm sorry too, Grandpa."

"Thank you. I feel like she's with me now."

He scooped the child up in his arms. In her shiny, green eyes, John could see visions of Susan flicker in the light.

"I want you to help me with something. Okay?"

Phoenix nodded.

John placed Susan's letter in her small hand and together they tossed both the opened envelope and letter into the flaming pit. Both quickly curled and combusted.

Seconds later, part of the burned paper caught a draft. It fluttered up, pieces of jagged and charred stationary spread out like the misshapen wings of some unknown variety of bird. It hovered above John for several seconds. Then he watched it flutter away into the dark night air. To John, it looked like some mythical creature that had been reborn from the ashes of fire.

CRDL

THE RED SUN boiled a chemical-filled sky into a sticky, yellow-green miasma, a mess that could burn throats and destroy lungs. It crept down into a bomb-ravaged Nebraska town, where nearby fields once grew corn, green and tall, but the fields now hosted the husks of the dead lay rotting in weeds.

Down and down came the poisoned air. It filled St. Bernard Street and gas mask filters. The masks and other mandatory gear were worn by each State-assigned member of Neighborhood Section A12. But none of the members knew for sure how well the masks worked. Despite this danger, they waited outside for the delivery to come.

Tim Gadzen's gloved hand twitched as he tried to read a watch that wrapped around black latex protecting his forearm. Alan Thompson hacked and wheezed inside his gas mask. Tammy Shepard looked at Alan, hugged her bodysuit, and cried. Mr. Cagle complained at no one in particular about how the State should know better than to make Section A12 wait for so long—what with bad air and the fresh water supply dwindling by the minute.

A mangy, orange cat rubbed up against Cagle's leg. He tried to kick it. The scrawny creature darted away before the life-crushing blow landed.

"Damn lucky cat," Cagle muttered.

Soon, a black truck rumbled up the street. It stopped at Marvin Craigers' place. Two men wearing hazmat suits heaved an aluminum box out of the truck. It was longer than a cradle and shorter than a coffin. Tubes with valves ran along the box's sides. The Section members watched the men carry this load to Craiger's shielded front door.

When the front door opened, Marvin Craiger came out wearing a bodysuit painted with large polka dots. He signed something on the delivery men's clipboard. Then he turned to the other members and waved like a clown greeting an impatient circus audience waiting for a show to begin.

Craiger yelled out through his muffling gas mask: "David Stenman is officially dead! That useless invalid is gonna get composted!"

The other members applauded—even Tammy—their rubber gloves dulling the sound.

—

When David Stenman heard Cagle and Craiger break down the front door, he knew why they had come for him. He flopped out of his bed. His crushed legs couldn't stand upright. He rubbed his belly raw against the rough concrete floor, dragging himself toward the bathroom. It seemed to be a mile away. If only he could get inside and lock the door.

Craiger rushed in and stomped on Stenman's back. Cagle pressed the muzzle of a .38 against the head of Stenman. He began making strange sounds.

"This guy sounds like a cat in heat," Cagle said. "I hate cats even more than useless water-suckers."

—————

One week earlier inside the gutted Shady Acres nursing home. It was a brick-and-mortar irony in a town where residents were lucky if they survived until the age of fifty. The Neighborhood Council patiently explained to David Stenman's fifteen-year-old boy, John, that life can sometimes be unfair. John begged for his father's life anyway.

"John, water conservation is the issue. Unfortunately, your father can no longer contribute to his section," a council member said.

John's calloused hands bent the corners of a brochure titled, "CRDL: A Better Way." He wanted to rip the brochure up and scatter its remains like ash.

"It was an accident. The steel pipe stack broke loose and all the pipes fell on him. I tried to quickly get him out of that ditch, but no one helped. It took hours. It was a miracle his suit didn't tear."

"John," the council member said, smiling warmly. "CRDL helps all of us—you and me included. Can your father walk?"

"No, he...it's just that...no. But he's getting better."

"Is he walking?"

John clenched the brochure. He shifted in his seat. "He's confined to his house. But he swears to me that he will get better."

"2053 has been a tough year for all of us. But in your case, we have an option. Have you seen the cremation plan?"

"I can't afford *that* and my rent. The Neighborhood taxes—"

"All for the greater good."

"I'll give him some of my rations. I'll give him my water," John said.

"I'm sorry that we can't help you further, John."

John raged inside. Quiet, angry tears fell down his face. He made a decision and kept it to himself. If small sips of dirty water and eighteen-hour workdays were all that mattered, then life was no better than being locked up inside a box.

▭

The following winter, a lucky cat barely avoided a deadly Christmas storm that had just begun to rage outside.

Clouds released heavy chunks of black and orange ice, quickly freezing other stray animals dead still. The lucky cat pressed up against a warm intake vent attached to a brick building. The building was surrounded by grotesque snow. Broken ice pieces dotted a mounted sign that read: "Care of the Reclaimed and Deceased Beloved: Amino Processing Station 2." More ice piled up in front of a steel door.

When the industrial vacuum pumps inside the building cranked up, the lucky cat vanished.

▭

Inside the processing station a red, wet mass shot out of an exhaust tube.

Tom Finnley jumped away to avoid being splattered by something that looked like a fleshy jellyfish with legs. It quivered on the concrete floor. Tom shrugged the incident off as a minor hazard of the job. So many dangerous machines inside the processing facility. So many moving parts.

"Did you pour in the bacteria mixture?" Dale said.

"Just did," Tom said.

He walked over to one of the composter boxes being hooked up to a vacuum line. He read the box's label aloud, "John Stenman."

Dale checked the manifest. "Yep. He ships today."

"It's so weird," Tom said.

"What? What's weird?"

Tom scratched his head. "The way he's placed in there."

"All sign-offs and suicides end up here."

Tom gazed inside the box. "No. I mean...he looks just like a sleeping baby."

"Yeah, well, you're new here. You get used to it. It's because of the size of the box. The other industrials have to stack them. Now, place the moisture and gas lines on the box. Make sure the purge valve is set. We wouldn't want this box blowing its top!"

Tom easily lifted the composter's thick aluminum top. He was young and strong. Before placing the lid, he looked inside, again.

"Stenman, sorry to do this to you, buddy, but the children need cooking fuel."

＿＿

The next summer, Tim Gadzen's hand twitched even worse than the previous year. Marvin Craiger pointed at Alan Thompson. Craiger gave Mr. Cagle a look.

"Yeah, so what do you want to do about it?" Cagle said.

"Hey, I'm the assigned entertainer. You tell me," Craiger said.

Alan Thompson peeled off the gas mask. His shriveled face spewed blood.

"Cheer him up, would you?" Cagle said.

Craiger walked over to Thompson.

"You all right, son?" Craiger said, laughing. "Better perk up. The new member should be arriving soon. But God only knows why he was assigned here, us being short of water and all."

Thompson dropped to his knees and retched what looked like a bucket's worth of blood onto the black tar of the street. Tammy Shepard wailed. The other members gathered around Alan like a wolf pack surrounding its prey. They licked their dry lips inside their masks.

Cagle was now more annoyed by Thompson's hacking than by Craiger's polka dots. "He ain't gonna last until the new member arrives," he said.

Craiger pulled out paperwork and a pen from inside a large, zippered pocket he called his hideaway and demanded that Alan sign the document.

Thompson tried to wave Craiger off while retching. Because a green mucus oozed out of his eyes, Alan couldn't see the .38 in Cagle's gloved hand.

NEW FRIENDS MADE

I HAVE a friend named Larry who is going through a divorce that would have put most anyone in a straitjacket. His wife, Delilah, is a truck driver who decided Larry was not keeping her fulfilled—she is now having an affair with another woman. My wife, Linda, ran into Larry at the mall where he was picking at a taco lunch and ignoring a diet Coke. He looked sad and despondent so she invited him over for dinner the following month.

Larry is an old friend so I bought him a bottle of his favorite Scotch. My wife bought him condoms—she said they were for Larry's future exploits. He comes over and we have several drinks together. Our conversation becomes bawdy. My wife turns up the heat and asks Larry how many women he plans to sleep with, tossing him the condoms. Larry jokes back and says only one. My wife smiles back at him but I don't appreciate where Larry is going with this. Doesn't Larry even realize there are three of us in the room? He says nothing else but the silence in the room is enough so that everyone can probably hear what I'm thinking.

I finally say to Larry, "I'm sure my wife is flattered, but don't go too far."

My wife only snorts. "Too far? Sometimes I understand how Delilah feels."

I decide to smoke out back and blow off some steam. It's a beautiful cool summer night and just the thing needed to breeze off some of the emotions simmering on the heat sink of my heart. This just isn't like Linda to act like this. We've always been so close. I head through the kitchen and out to the back. As I light up my cigarette, I look into the house and see Larry kissing my wife. Well, maybe my wife sympathizes with Delilah but I don't plan to become another Larry. I've spent all of my middle-age years struggling to build up a middle-class shanty of a life and I have no plans to retire while hunkered down in an alimony skid row. I suck down the smoke and storm back into the house.

They must have heard me come in. "Honey, is that you?" my wife says.

"I'm going to fix us more drinks. Be right there," I say.

They thank me, but they have no idea what's coming. The gun safe is near the kitchen, and I plan to bring back a surprise.

The Glock G19 has always been kept cleaned and ready. I took some NRA courses and bought the gun just in case our home should be broken into. But I've always had my doubts that I could actually use it on another person. I walk back in the living room, the bottle of Scotch in one hand and the pistol gripped in the other. Turning a gun on another human being isn't an easy thing to do. But what else can I do?—this can be my redemption.

I grip and point the gun—iron sights front and rear aligned—at Larry's head. He now has my wife in his arms and his lips on her neck. Their sexual oblivion excludes anyone else, including nearby spouses. My hands are trembling. Either my mind is refusing to squeeze down on the trigger safety or my finger won't obey me.

Larry looks up at me, blood dribbling down his mouth and my wife's neck. My wife turns to me and smiles. Behind her eyes is the vacant activity of a ghost town. He wipes away the red life with the back of his hand.

"Did you expect that to work?" he says, looking at the gun in my hand.

"What the hell did you do to my wife?" I say.

"Isn't it obvious—I'm a vampire," Larry says.

The man must have gone insane from the divorce. The gun goes off in my hand—I don't know how or why but maybe I can plead self-defense. Smoke curls out from the charcoal gap in Larry's shoulder. It seems the wound is nothing to him. The man, or what used to be a man, is still standing. He grins at me and exposes long white fangs. I drop the gun to the floor and eyeball the front door behind him.

Larry thumbs back at the front door. "You could try to grab Linda and make a run for it but you'll never make it."

Larry has either read my mind or maybe the undead can sense fear. But I have to get my wife away from this...thing. "Get away from her, or...I'll stake you."

Larry laughs. "That only works in the movies. It takes a lot more to kill me than a wooden stick to the heart and you don't have it in you to get the job done."

I'm not quite sure what he means by that, but if it's more gruesome than shooting someone than he's probably right.

"Why is Linda like that? She looks like a zombie or something," I say.

"She's enthralled. She's under a dark rapture, of sorts, and I hold the manacles to her life."

Larry's hand moves to her neck, and the fingers push into her skin. Linda only smiles. I move toward the two of them. Maybe I can tackle Larry.

"Get your hands off her," I say.

"Move closer and I break her neck like a dry bone."

It seems that Larry holds all the aces. "What do I need to do to get you to release her?"

"You know too much. I'm afraid I can't just release Linda to you and walk away. You're going to have to decide for the both of you—life or, ultimately, death."

"What do you mean by life—like, make us vampires?" I say.

"Yes. It doesn't take long."

This was worse than a career change at the age of forty-five or deciding on whether I should buy the Corvette or the hair implants. I had to choose to either kill myself and Linda or forever turn us into some sort of bloodthirsty parasites.

"All these years I've known you, Larry, how could I not know you had become this creature?"

"I was drowning my sorrows at a bar just after I met Linda at the mall. I was thinking of poor little me and my nasty divorce. After my third Scotch, I was approached by the most gorgeous woman my eyes have ever feasted on. She seduced me and it turned out to be more than just hanky-panky."

"Does Delilah know you're a vampire?"

Larry laughs again. "She will. A pretty neat solution to my marital problems." But then his brow furrows and he looks impatiently at me. His hand presses deeper into Linda's neck, sinking into the pink flesh. "So, what's it going to be?"

Maybe I should have helped more nice old ladies cross the street or purchased more Girl Scout cookies. Maybe I deserve this dilemma. Aw, heck. Maybe I should make one last try to talk some sense into him. Surely the undead could be reasoned with.

"Larry, it's us. We've been friends for so long."

"And friends are what I want."

"But Linda—"

"I've given this a lot of thought and have realized something," Larry says. He looks down at his feet for a moment and then back at me. "I don't want to go on like this alone. I need my friends with me."

That was the last thing I was expecting to hear from him—a vampire afraid to be alone.

"Larry, we can still work this out. Linda and I can still be here for you."

Larry scowls. "So that one day, you pass away into dust, and I remain lurking in shadows, away from the light and other people? No, this is the only way."

Larry's hand sinks deeper and Linda's breath is wheezing out like a beginner learning to play the accordion. She just continues to smile at me. Then he holds out his other hand. "Let me give you and Linda the gift of unending friendship," Larry says.

I met Linda in a college art class and I've never stopped loving her. My eyes follow her body as I paint an image of her in my mind. Her long black hair hangs, flowing whisper soft over her smooth shoulders. The slender curves of her body form delicate contours that meet at her long neck. It arches out, waiting for me to decide. How many times have I looked into her eyes and have seen her love for me reflected back in warm light? Only now, that warm light is missing. Her empty eyes only show me a cold vacuum.

I miss her. I want her back.

I cock my head and expose my neck. "Let's get this over with."

Will I be saying good-bye? Or hello? Will I still consider Larry a friend when this is over? Will Linda still love me? At least now, she goes on.

A SARJETA (THE GUTTER)

SEWER-RAT CHILDREN SCREAMED obscenities at one another and laughed. Somewhere far away, a siren wailed. Late-afternoon faces gloated down at the spectacle and faded from my view.

I felt her claw my hand and heard her weep. I never did learn her name. My breath whistled through red-stained nostrils. Warm blood lazily oozed out of holes somewhere in my chest. Useless arms and legs lazily stretched out to enjoy the last of the sidewalk's heat.

I closed my eyes and smiled. Everything was going to be OK.

⸻

Even in a Sarjeta, there is always somebody lower than you. If you're faster or stronger, someone else pays a price. The price could be money or favors. Or it could be that someone weaker pays the ultimate price—his or her life. But I'm better than most people stuck here because I dream big. And dreams will show me how to escape this shithole.

The wind scattered dirt and grit, biting my face and the window's ledge that faced out at Canto do Diabo. The streets of the Gutter dead-ended here where wall graffiti and littered garbage stopped and the Prodigal Son resided. I was lucky to be this close to the charity's main building.

Several coffee-colored men, coughing up throaty words and inhaling Turkish cigarettes, stood outside by a front door painted red, the dark color of worried eyes. One of them looked at me as I approached. I tried not to fidget with the waxy pouch in my hand. He signaled something and I was quickly surrounded.

"Você fala inglês?" one man said. He grinned and I spotted gold bordering three rotting teeth.

"Yes, sure," I said.

His greasy thumb gestured at the other three. "These clowns don't. So you talk to me, OK?" His accent wasn't Portuguese. Or English.

"Sure," I said.

"And?"

I glanced at his face, spotting a tattooed circle on his left cheek. Despite his smile, I sensed something darker hiding behind the smiling mask he now wore.

"A delivery. For him." I placed the pouch into the gold-toothed man's hand. My fingers touched his slimy palm, causing me to shiver for a moment.

"Come back next week."

"What about my money?" I asked.

"Next week. You'll get another package and your money."

All four men stared at me. I couldn't read their faces. The greasy tattooed guy jabbed his finger at me.

"You know, I see something in you. Maybe something great, huh?"

I didn't ask what he saw and quickly left. I decided that Devil's Corner was not a part of the Gutter where I wanted to be alone after sunset.

———

I stood on Amélia's concrete balcony and gagged. Inside her apartment, sickly sweet beans dumped out of dented cans now cooked on a hotplate. Two half-naked children with swollen bellies rubbed messy fingers on my sister's worn-down apron as they cried for dinner. They didn't know anything else. This was the same meal served at breakfast and at yesterday's dinner. And the day before. But I've walked by the *açougue* and seen real meat. I've smelled the bloody flesh. Steak and hamburger and food that people with money could buy. I don't want to eat beans anymore.

Scraps of fading sunlight crawled down the balcony rails, exposing lag bolts desperately grabbing at the block wall. It was a miracle I didn't fall into the darkened alley below. I could see someone down there licking at the emptied tins we'd thrown out with the rest of the garbage. I shouted at him to get some self-respect but he just laughed. I kept shouting.

Amélia looked out at me with worried, dark eyes. "You don't know that man out there. You don't know what he could do to us. Come back inside." Both children clung quietly to her, sensing their mother's fear. My sister tightly gripped the plastic spoon she used to stir the beans. Her eyes pleaded, seeming to say, "At least we eat."

"I don't need to be afraid. I don't need this," I said.

"Please, the children."

"I'll be a famous artist. I'll escape. I won't eat beans anymore."

Amélia started to cry. I stormed back to my room and locked the door. An hour later, I ignored her knock when she came to ask if I was hungry. Sleep came soon and I dreamed that the man in the alley chased me. Then my dreams went black and I tossed and turned the rest of the night.

━━

I didn't know his real name so I called him Ben. He didn't mind. Ben dropped my money and this week's package onto my sister's flimsy coffee table. I tried to figure him out. I guessed that he was about ten, only two years younger than me. I asked him where he lived.

He didn't answer my questions. Ben just looked nervously around. *How does someone so young become a collector?*

"You alone?" Ben asked.

"My sister is sewing today. She takes the babies."

Ben wiped his nose. "That's good. I guess I'll come back next week at the same time."

I pointed at the waxy paper. "What's inside?"

"Don't ask. And don't steal anything."

"Just curious."

"Don't be."

"OK...OK."

He looked down at my drawing pad. I had been sketching from memory a park I once saw in the middle of Avenida da Liberdade. His wide eyes studied every penciled line and every cross-hatched tree as if it were the *Mona Lisa* or something. Ben held his breath and for a moment he seemed to have transported himself somewhere a million miles away from the Gutter. I bet he had never seen the avenue or anything else like it.

"I take art classes. The church gives them for free," I said.

"I couldn't do that."

"How do you know? Have you tried?"

"I couldn't do it."

"I'll take you. Come back tomorrow."

Ben looked over the pad once more. He blinked his eyes and swallowed hard. "Don't steal anything," he said. And he left without saying good-bye.

———

Ben came back once a week with more money and more packages. I lied to Amélia and told her I did cleaning jobs at the church. But after helping her pay the rent, there wasn't much money left so I hid anything else in a sock. I kept thinking about that açougue. One day I'd go in there and buy something. But I'd have to sneak the meat back and cook it before my sister asked me to share.

I continued to deliver packages to Devil's Corner before sunset. It was pretty easy work except that it didn't pay much. To make more money, I'd have to become a collector. And to do that, I'd have to get an invite or something.

I didn't see the same guys at Devil's Corner except for the greasy man with the gold teeth and the circle tattoo on his left cheek. He never said much. But he always made me nervous as if at any moment he might rip a mask off, revealing fangs that would eat my face. And his black eyes searched for something inside of me. What did he think I was hiding?

Every time Ben came back, he would talk a little more

about my art. I'd answer his questions about technique, explain how I picked a subject, and tell him what was planned for the next class. He asked if art class was deadly work. Could drawings steal his soul? I studied his face. The kid looked sincere and scared. His body trembled slightly.

"I've drawn lots of things," I said.

I remembered some Chinese guy who believed in fêng shui once told me that badly placed mirrors could steal souls.

"Don't worry. Drawings are just paper and pencils or charcoal. I've drawn lots of things," I said.

So I began to draw out the room on my sketchpad. Ben watched me complete the lines of the sofa he sat on. The effort wasn't too bad. When I began working on Ben's stick figure, he whispered "Father" and crossed himself.

He had the look of a frightened rabbit in a dark room where hungry wolves lurked nearby. No one had ever shown him things like this, leaving him to his own quirky superstitions. I opened my arms to show him I was OK. He poked at his own chest and seemed satisfied that he still existed. But he refused me when I offered him a drawing pencil.

"I draw because it gives me hope. There is something better in this world than the Gutter," I said.

My words seemed to resonate with Ben. He hesitated once more over my incomplete drawing. And then he left without saying another word. But I suspected that he had a change of mind. I was right. Several weeks later, he finally asked to go with me to art class but I had to promise not to follow him home afterward.

Ben looked surprised when Father Abrahan gave the kid his first kit which included a sketchpad, eight graphite pencils, some charcoal sticks, and a kneadable eraser. Donations to the church funded this stuff but you'd have to buy your own replacements if you lost anything. One student got caught selling his kits and he never returned.

Ben struggled. The priest showed the kid how to hold a graphite pencil. When Ben realized it wouldn't burn him or something, he made a few attempts to draw some lines using a firm wrist like Father showed him. But when class finished, he left the kit on the table, saying that he was afraid someone might accuse him of stealing if he took the stuff home. Father Abrahan said he would have everything ready for Ben for next week. I just wondered if Ben would return.

———

Amélia was crying when I got home from class.

"The baby...he is sick," she said.

Emilio, the smaller one, lay on her lap, coughing and sweating. His teeth chattered. I touched his forehead and felt a fire burning across his wet brow. I remembered suffering the flu, struggling with sips of water while my sore throat protested and my body seemed to shrivel under dehydration. I had glared at Amélia when she'd tried to coddle me as she now coddled Emilio.

My youngest nephew was very ill and very weak. I couldn't let him suffer.

"I will get him some medicine. I'll be back soon," I said.

"*Deus o abençoe*, Leandro! *Deus o abençoe*. I am so sorry for this," Amélia said.

She probably knew that I had hidden some money away. I brushed off her apology and went to my room.

Whatever hidden money was in the sock would now be spent on aspirin and other medicines. Emilio would get better. But maybe my other nephew would get sick and there would be another trip to the pharmacy or the doctor. And then something else would happen. Being poor, barely able to pay rent, an unexpected crisis meant deciding between safety for another month in a roach-infested apartment or going without medicine—a decision between life and death.

There would be no trip to açougue. I swallowed hard and wiped at my teary eyes as I shoved the money in my jeans. I would buy Emilio's medicine. But something had to change.

Claudio's bar serves drinks to anyone willing to walk in. Just like the Gutter, the place slowly devours your soul, gradually digging out childhood optimisms and filling a dark hole inside your heart with desperation and glimpses of gratification.

Ben's eight-year-old sister pretended to be a princess, twirling around in a worn pink tutu and waving a toy wand at a drunk blind man. He sat at a worn table and drank homemade distilled drinks that smelled faintly like gasoline. Ben dragged on his hand-rolled cigarette and cursed her for following him into the place. The scabby bartender told us to either buy drinks or get out. Nobody seemed to notice that we were kids in a place that served alcohol—except the pervert rubbing his pants in the corner. I wondered if the pervert had ever kissed a girl or hoped to fall in love when he was my age.

"Take her with us. Father Abrahan won't mind," I said.

Ben shook his head, snuffed out the butt and yanked his

sister by the arm. She screamed as we shuttled the tethered girl outside.

"Go home. Or I'll twist. It will hurt," Ben said.

Her brown eyes grew wide. She scurried off, sometimes looking behind her. I watched her turn a corner and vanish from sight.

"That was kind of rough," I said.

Ben's face jerked up. He flushed and dropped his eyes. "She must stop acting like a child," Ben said.

"But she is a child."

He shook his head. Tears struggled to erupt from his soft eyes. "I don't know you enough."

"Enough for what?"

But the kid shut up. As we walked onward to Abrahan's class, Ben shuffled a little behind me. I slowed and wrapped my arm around his shoulder like a brother might comfort his sibling. The kid didn't resist and his body heaved while he sobbed for several minutes. When we arrived at Abrahan's class, he settled down.

Ben refused his pencils and paper. Instead, he sat close and watched me create. I used charcoals today. They're easier and I can really get the work flow going. My charcoal vine rubbed rough lines and simple shapes onto the newsprint. A holder filled out edges and contours and realism. Black-stained fingers smudged in shadows, grounding a wavy, oblong shape into a drawing of a dimensional remote island. This tropical getaway would be a place where Ben and I could escape to from the Gutter for a few hours.

He breathed short, quick breaths. His mouth opened as wide as his eyes. I sketched a sun casting warm rays down onto a grateful palm. The kid asked questions and offered suggestions. We chattered as we imagined a story world where two friends laughed, played, and waved at passing ships that might deliver an evening meal in exchange for coconuts.

Father Abrahan walked up behind us, looking over our shoulders. "Keep it down, boys. The other students must concentrate. Keep it down." He took one last look at my work and one last look at Ben, a bright shine in the kid's eyes. The priest walked away smiling, his hands clasped behind his back like a satisfied philosopher who had just realized the key to eternal happiness.

When I finished, I offered Ben the drawing as a gift. He said that he would hang it on his wall. "One day I will escape to there," he said. "Maybe one day soon."

I laughed. "I'll wave as I sail by."

The kid's brow furrowed. "You don't think I can leave this place?" He sounded like someone requesting a guarantee.

I considered his sister. "You might be missed."

"*Macacos me mordem!* I'm foolish."

"No, you're not. I dream, too."

He studied me and smiled. I think he approved of something as if we had just made a connection. But I wasn't sure what the connection was.

Ben folded up the drawing and asked me to come outside and talk.

———

The Gutter and Eduardo's Bay are separated by a medieval stone bridge that's been repaired countless times by wealthy patrons on the "right" side of town. These donors maintain romantic facades while hiding modern furnishings inside the walls of their houses. Cars aren't allowed to cross it but many BMWs are parked nearby. In the Gutter, old rubble and decay surrounds us and we cross the bridge to snatch some beauty for our hearts and to dream of cars we will never drive.

I sat on a bench next to an end arch, about twenty-five meters from the nearby açougue. A teenage boy dressed in punk leathers argued with his mother who sported a Coach purse. They had just come out of the shop with packages of fresh meat. "You never listen to me!" he was yelling and she was trying to hide her frustration and embarrassment. I just kept thinking about those packages of fresh meat.

One day soon, I said to myself. And it would be real soon. A collector makes a lot more money than delivery, or so I'm told.

But I'd need an invite or need to be adopted by the Charity of the Prodigal Son to collect. They're a secretive group, revealing nothing of their inside organization. It's rumored that someone named Pai Morto runs everything from the top. No one from the outside has seen him or really understands what the charity is all about. Most likely it's a criminal group dealing in cheap morf or something worse. But they do recruit sons of poor families, giving aid and salary in exchange for the children's ongoing service contracts. And each family must give something back—an offering—once each month to be picked up by a collector. Ben called it "the blood of life" or "flowing blood" or something. That's about all that he has explained to me.

I first met the kid at Claudio's bar where we still occasionally meet. Sick of listening to crying babies, I drank to get a buzz and he said that he was supposed to meet his delivery guy who usually sat at my table. That guy never did show up so I've been doing the work ever since. I assume that the other guy died because no one who lives in the Gutter has any other place to escape to.

So Ben gave me collections and I've been delivering them to Devil's Corner. Partly, my job is just another stage to hide the Charity's activities and to keep a distance between the collector and some remorseful family that has doubts about their continued participation. And sons never collect from their families. But there is a second reason—the collector is considered an arm and I am a leg of a greater body. We help keep the Prodigal Son alive. The setup seems superstitious.

"It's a great price to pay but you will do well," he said.

Ben had refused to introduce me to a recruiter until recently, after last week's art class. He had surprised me. When I first began delivery for him, he warned me that being a collector was a commitment I could never leave. Tomorrow I might sign a contract. But I won't tell Amélia. She'd tell me that the Charity is dangerous.

I watched more people enter the açougue. They walked tall and proud and didn't eat leftovers from discarded cans. They grilled hamburgers and steaks and sausages to hot perfection—Amélia and her damn beans. And her crying children. They were stones wrapped around my neck and drowning me while others feasted. I will feast soon. My sister won't know I cook and eat real food. She's done nothing to deserve it. I will not share anything. I'll gobble every last bite and wipe bloody, hot juices from my mouth.

⊏⊐

Art opens both the eyes and the mind. You become more aware of shadows and light, of space, and emotion. An overcast sky sets a gloomy feeling for both the drawing subject and viewer. I can sense when something is out of place within my surroundings—even in the Gutter.

Ben's sister quietly trailed us as we passed through another alley on our way to Devil's Corner. She darted quickly behind piles of garbage when I looked her way. Despite an assumed playful innocence surrounding her actions, just a younger sibling curious about her older brother, she seemed scared as though Ben had abandoned her.

Ben and I made our way while she continued after us. Ben didn't seem to notice or care. And when the Gutter backstreets narrowed into Devil's Corner, his sister stopped and held back, wringing her small hands together.

"Hello."

The greasy man with the gold teeth and circle tattoo recognized Ben and greeted him. The kid seemed uncomfortable around the guy but I kept my mouth shut. After Ben reintroduced me and stated why we had come, the greasy man nodded and opened the red door. Ben's early warning about never leaving the commitment of being a collector flashed in my mind but was forgotten as I stepped inside.

Red taffeta wall covering—a rich, "Fuck you, world; I've got it made," color—captured my eyes. I admired how it boldly spread to both ends of the foyer, the material not seeming to care if I approved of its awkward extravagance and not willing to accept a status quo of interior design. The greasy man signaled us to wait and then disappeared behind another door. I caught a glimpse of another hall that led to a staircase that wound up.

I walked up to one of several paintings hung over the draping. There were several of these mounted framed works, always with the same man surrounded by a different group of boys. The ancient man sat on something like a high-backed throne, his arms spread out into a gesture that seemed to both protect and covet the children gathered around him. His wide, lively smile couldn't offset his judgmental eyes that seemed to gaze deep into my very soul.

The greasy tattooed man returned. He ushered me and Ben into a smaller room with an oak table. A black engraved box rested in the center. Again, more paintings of the ancient man and his probing eyes surrounded me—except for one empty frame. The room felt like a church transept. We all sat down in silence. A perverse reverence clung to the air.

"It's an honor to be one of his Sons," the greasy tattooed man finally said.

"We are grateful to Father," Ben said.

The greasy tattooed man studied me, his face not revealing what might lurk behind his eyes. "How did you two meet?"

I cleared my throat, my mind jumbling up places and people. "We take art classes at the church."

The man spit. "The Catholics know nothing. They promise afterlife but you will only rot in a grave. And you rot now while you live in the Gutter. Is that what you want?"

"I didn't mean a disrespect—"

"Do you read their book? Their Bible?"

"No," I said.

He scanned my face to figure out if I told the truth.

"There is a parable about a son who takes his father's inheritance and wastes this gift. The father who forgives his son is a foolish man. A boy must be punished if he is to learn something."

"I will vouch for Leandro. He will be my brother," Ben said.

The greasy tattooed man nodded again. "You are each

other's keepers. If one of you harms the Father, you both shall be punished equally."

He opened the black engraved box and pulled out a cup of red wine and a handwritten contract. Blood-red liquid sloshed and spread onto the parchment. I wondered why the black ink letters didn't run. And I wondered about the stretched parchment waiting for my signature. He smiled at me as if he had just played some joke that I could never understand. I wasn't sure about this anymore. He leaned forward and placed a heavy pen in my hand. His large, slimy fingers wrapped around my knuckles and tightened my fist into a grip. The pen moved, my hand shook, my heart throbbed, and my mind asked, *What if? What if?*

When it was over, I shared the cup of red wine with Ben. The greasy tattooed man leaned back in his seat, not a care in the world. He nonchalantly gave me a few instructions about collections, pointing at Ben.

"He can show you how to do it for several weeks."

Ben agreed eagerly. I asked if I could ever change my mind and quit being a collector. The greasy man replied matter-of-factly, "No."

I shifted in my seat. I wanted to ask more questions but stayed silent.

"And don't try to run away," the greasy man said.

"He would never. I promise you," Ben said.

The greasy tattooed man studied me again. "No matter where you go, you cannot hide. In every town and every city, there is always a Gutter. And we are there. And we will find you."

I didn't doubt him.

Several weeks before I got shot, I hung out with Ben and learned how to collect. I just knocked on doors that had a wheel symbol scratched at the top and greeted each family, saying, "Your son and all his brothers pay a price." Then I would wrap up the offerings in wax paper and hand everything off to a new delivery boy. Just two kids, Ben and I, doing their duty and making pretty good money.

Most people I collected from seemed ambivalent when we arrived. A few acted scared or cried. But one man with a graying mustache pushed his wife back into the house. He stepped outside, thick muscle straining underneath an overcoat of hairy fat. He loomed over us, too big a threat to easily be taken down. I should have been carrying a gun. Several guys loitering in dark corners sold them but I always felt like my fists were enough. Death always seems far away to the young. This was the first time my mortality seemed to be in question.

Ben just stared up at the mustached guy. He didn't blink. I held my breath. The mustached guy's chest heaved and his breath whistled out his bulbous nose. This went on for several seconds. When the mustached man finally muttered something and then dropped money and jewelry into our plate, I exhaled.

As we walked away, he yelled after us, "Where is our child? What did you do to him?" Ben never replied but when we turned a corner, the kid was shaking.

"You didn't even look scared," I said.

After Ben calmed down, he looked at me. "You and me. We will go to that island. We will leave this place."

"*Estás a meter áqua?* They will hunt us both down."

Ben's eyes were wide open and far away. I looked into his brown pupils and saw the sun casting warm rays down onto a hand-sketched palm tree.

"I know a secret way inside the Charity. I know how to get into Father's place and no one will catch us," he said.

"And do what?"

"They keep the collections upstairs—all of it."

Stealing from the Prodigal Sons was the last thing I wanted to do. Or for Ben to do. A fever dream had captured his mind and promised him false hope. I'd have to keep close to him so he didn't do something stupid.

"You're not going in there without me," I said.

"Of course not. We are brothers now."

This worried me—I was responsible for whatever Ben did. I agreed to him showing me how to get into the secret entrance but I planned on talking the kid out of whatever else he schemed. Or maybe I could warn the greasy man because that seemed to be a safer option—I didn't want that creepy guy to find out later that we did something dangerous and foolish.

And I planned to buy a gun.

〓

The sewer running underneath the Charity tunneled damp rats into a dead-end trap. The terrified creatures darted away from Ben and me as we slogged forward. They screamed when an old brick wall blocked their escape. Some of the vermin tried to bite us—too stupid to turn around and run back the other way. When the kid and I started climbing up a rusted ladder, they quieted down, forming a squirming fur pile and forgetting our trespass.

I whispered up at Ben, "How do you know about this secret?"

"Remember that angry mustached guy we collected from?"

"Yeah."

"His son showed me. Bet he stole a bunch of stuff and ran off."

"Like money? Stole what?" I asked.

"You'll see."

We climbed higher until we reached a concrete platform. A closed door greeted us at the top. Ben put his finger to his mouth, signaling for me to be quiet but the gesture was unnecessary. He opened the unlocked door. Whoever resided on the other side didn't seem concerned about intruders.

We entered a hall. I couldn't help but notice an elevator just opposite of me. It was gilded and squat, an ornate machine designed to lift a half-sized monarch—or to lift someone who didn't walk on both legs. Golden rose thorns wrapped around the cage and seemed ready to prick me. And its confusing controls didn't offer instructions. It was an unwelcoming contraption meant for someone else.

Ben pointed at a winding staircase to our right and we cautiously walked up. We entered a room that looked like a large attic.

The upstairs spectacle seemed to clutch my eyes and steal the words from my mouth. I had once seen drawings of heaped pirate treasure. This attic room looked just as obscene—stacks of jewelry and trinkets surrounded us. Coins and currencies from all over the world littered its length and width. In one corner, a dirty heap of discarded clothes piled up to the ceiling.

Ben stood wide-eyed and hypnotized, forgetting me. I came out of my shock and left the kid to his fantasy as I followed a cleared path to the other end of the long room. In a dim corner stood an easel with a mounted, incomplete painting of the ancient man I had seen during my meeting with the greasy man. This canvas had room for a few more boys to be worked into the cloth. Above the artist's setup was some sort of rope harness system designed to lift a person. Maybe the artist was crippled? That might also explain the elevator.

But the paint-mixing cup struck me as the oddest thing in the room. A rounded goblet rested by a brush holder on a nearby table. Curly symbols wrapped around its lip, engraved deep into a dark wood grain. When I approached it, unexplained feelings of remorse and fear took me and squeezed the breath out of my lungs. I backed away, disgusted by my reaction and the dark presence filling this small area. I quickly returned to Ben.

"We have to go," I said.

Ben ignored me. He was still charmed by the amassed wealth. Sounds of footsteps could be heard somewhere below. I shook the kid and his eyes focused. He made a crooked smile.

"Take as much as you can. Stuff your pockets," he said.

"There's too much. We'll come back."

"Yeah. Yeah, that's a good idea."

"Why settle for a pocketful when we can take a bagful?" It was a lie. I wasn't ever coming back here.

But we needed to escape before someone caught us. Ben said that he'd bring back a really big bag. We slowly made our way back down the stairs. No one stopped us but I could still hear feet shuffling somewhere. We didn't wait to find out where the sounds came from. When we finally descended back down into the sewer, I was left with my sense of relief and Ben's lingering lust and greed.

—

I sat in my bedroom and counted money. Each bill meant more hamburgers and steaks sizzling in a hot pan. Amélia was supposed to work two shifts today and I would soon feast on flesh. My smile wavered as I continued to leaf through paper bills. Unsure fingers tapped and rubbed the thin rectangles. A sudden, heavy heart sank when I considered what I would do after açougue. Nothing?

Amélia walked in unannounced. She wasn't at work but I was too surprised to ask why not. She saw my money and gasped. I quickly shoved it into my jeans as she rushed over to wrap her arms around me, begging and crying. I managed to squirm out of her blubbering grip.

"Leandro, a boy collected from me today."

"I told you, the church pays me."

She continued crying. "Don't tell lies. Think of the true price."

Part of me agreed with her. Part of me remembered Ben's lusty greed and the obscene treasure pile. And part of me grew hot and angry, calling my sister a stupid bitch who believed in superstitions and immortal souls. That same part of me slammed the front door shut and stormed away from the apartment. And then that part regretted leaving behind a crying Amélia and her screaming babies. That part of me told me to forget her words and the past several days.

⸻

A red-and-blue canopy shielded the Eduardo's Bay açougue display window from an attacking sun. Cursive letters, too fancy for a place that sold cut meat, leaned to the right and away from my squinting eyes. I glanced around to see if anyone disapproved before jerking the door open and entering.

Spicy colognes and floral perfumes, mixed with the scent of blood, greeted my nose. People shot me sidelong glances and cleared away. Ahead, a display case protected different pork chops and ribs sold by the gram. And a large man with arms the size of sledgehammers stood behind it, watching me as I approached.

"What can I do for you, little prince?" he asked. He looked over at a man sizing up sausages and both smiled at some unspoken joke.

I sucked my cheeks in and read little signs on toothpicks —Kobe, Berkshire, 'Range Free' and 'Perfect for Braising.' Each little sign described the best way to prepare and cook the food in a particular way or which wine to pair them with. I just wanted to taste meat.

My words sputtered out, "Hamburgers."

"This is on sale. I'll even give you extra, little prince."

The butcher pointed at graying meat that had been red a few days ago. This food sat at the far end of the display, not belonging with anything else.

My dry mouth refused to answer him. Other shoppers stared at me, indignant or impatient that I couldn't decide. I shoved my hands into my pockets, feeling my wadded-up, dirty money. I couldn't speak. An emptiness filled my heart.

I walked away from the counter without saying a word.

"Maybe you aren't looking for the right thing, little prince," the butcher called after me.

―――

"You did the right thing by telling me," the greasy tattooed man said.

"Ben's not a bad guy. I'm sure he'll forget," I said.

"Of course."

I swallowed hard. "I'm OK, right?"

He grinned gold teeth. "You like art, right?"

"Of course."

"Maybe you can make art for Father. He'd like that."

"So I'm OK?"

"Sure," the greasy tattooed man said.

⸻

Dark clouds threatened the Gutter for several weeks. Heavy air clung close to graffitied walls and litter. People stayed indoors, hoping for the weather to improve. And when the storm finally broke on the first week of June, it washed away some of the filth that covered our streets.

I continued collecting but I saw less and less of Ben. At first he just showed up a few minutes late, muttering about the island I drew for him. Because I had the routes memorized, he caught up with me halfway on the next couple of runs. The kid would say that his sister made trouble for him. She chased behind us each time, darting in alleys and looking like a scared rabbit running from a wolf. I got worried because I was working alone so I started carrying the gun I had just recently bought.

One day Ben didn't show up at all. His sister ran behind me. I called out to her. She hesitated and I tried again. I told her that I was looking for him. She slowly walked out of the shadows, wiping away tears from her eyes.

"He went to that bad place. He never came out," she said.

"Devil's Corner?"

She nodded. I cursed myself and bad luck. Ben had decided to rob the charity without me.

"Come with me." I took her trembling hand and we

walked to the sewer entrance that Ben had shown me near the Charity. "Wait for me here. You'll be safe."

I looked at her the way a parent might try to reassure a scared child. She nodded again, and I descended into the sewer. No one tried to stop me as I made my way back into the hall with the strange elevator. In fact, a dead quiet filled the space. And the gilded cage had travelled up. Someone was in the attic and I wondered if Ben now used it to lug down bagfuls of stolen treasure.

I crept up the winding staircase as quietly as possible. At the top, I whispered, "Ben," at the piles of treasures that had lured him into this dangerous lair. Countless gold chains, heirlooms, and other coveted items tried to tease my greed as I crawled forward on all fours. I just wanted to find Ben and escape. I slowly made my way down the cleared path. The clammy air and the sudden gripping darkness seemed to squeeze me. A little further in, Ben still hadn't appeared. I decided to investigate the easel in the far back corner.

As I approached it, I saw an ancient man sitting in a chair built like a mobile throne. He wheeled the bizarre regal device around as I approached. I froze. Wisps of ghost-like hairs matted around his empty eye sockets. But he seemed to see me anyway. He grinned and dribbles of blood ran down the ghoul's chin.

And that's when I saw Ben hanging above the ancient man. The kid's dead body was wrapped up in the harness, suspended in the air in a grotesque pose.

"See...see the art that he creates for me," the ancient man said.

The ancient man turned back to Ben and bit off one of his fingers. Blood poured into the carved mixing cup and the cup glowed. The ancient man sighed and then gently dipped a paint brush and stirred. As the ghoul pressed wet bristles to the incomplete canvas, I could see Ben's face appear within an oily blob of paint. His image smiled as if the kid had finally discovered that secret island getaway, welcoming me to join him as he had finally escaped the Gutter.

My stinging tears jarred me into motion. I stumbled backward and fell over. The ancient man cautioned, "Be careful, my son," but he didn't pursue me as I jumped up and fled back down the stairs and down into the sewer. I'd get out of here, grab Ben's sister and escape, if escape was possible.

──

We rushed through two more alleys as I dragged Ben's sister behind me. I didn't head back to Amélia's because someone tracked me—I made out his lurking shadow more than once. Another turn and then a left veering in a northerly direction. Eduardo's Bay might provide temporary safety.

The girl became tired and tripped. I scooped her up, cradling her as I stumbled and walked on. A discarded pen and scratch pad rested on a nearby trash can. I put Ben's sister down for a moment to write something. I shoved the note into my front pocket with all the money I had made working as a collector. My gun pushed against my gut and beltline, bulging at my untucked shirt. She said that she could walk, so we continued on. The alley opened into a busy street.

The greasy man with the circle tattoo stepped away from a wall he leaned against, grinning gold teeth at me. I spotted a similar bulge under his shirt. With the girl in tow, I couldn't run.

He calmly walked over. "Father wants to see you."

"I can't leave the girl," I said.

"She doesn't share your sins."

At this moment, I think I finally saw the demon hiding behind the greasy tattooed man's masked face. This creature preyed on hungry souls, luring desperate children onto a ghoul's empty canvas. These creatures feasted on our eternal damnation. Ben's limited vision had grasped at their false hope but had given them a temporary satisfaction. I wouldn't end in the same fate. I could rise above all this.

"Your son will pay his debt," I said.

"What are—"

I shoved the girl away, reaching for my gun. The tattooed man reacted, doing the same. I fumbled and pointed the revolver in mostly the right direction. I squeezed the trigger and a cannon-like blast rocked my hand. My palm and fingers ached. A chunk of flesh and bone exploded on the greasy tattooed man's hip. He screamed, squeezing his trigger several times.

Two shots struck my body and threw me on my back. I lay panting and couldn't stand up. After what seemed like a few minutes, people gathered around me and the greasy tattooed man who tried to crawl away. Then he stopped moving. Sewer-rat children screamed obscenities at each other and laughed. Somewhere far away, a siren wailed. Late-afternoon faces gloated down at my spectacle and then faded from my view.

I felt Ben's sister claw my hand and I heard her weep. I never did learn her name. I managed to feel into my pocket, pulling out the scribbled note and all my money. I dropped it into her tiny hand and choked out the word, "Safe." My breath whistled through red-stained nostrils. Warm blood lazily oozed out of holes somewhere in my chest. Useless arms and legs stretched out to enjoy the last of the side-walk's heat.

I closed my eyes and smiled. I saw the tropical island that I had drawn for Ben. And I think that I saw Ben. Everything was going to be OK.

NERVOUS

DR. KLARNEY STARED AT ME. I don't like when people stare, thinking thoughts that blame me for a struggling relationship. It's not my fault that Nelson, my android lover, doesn't like me smoking.

A hot flush spread on my face. I tried a crooked smile. "Sorry, I've never been to a—"

Dr. Klarney smiled back. "Mr. Grelling, you don't have to be cuckoo to visit a shrink. I've helped lots of people quit smoking."

My toes relaxed. I curl them up good and tight when I'm nervous.

I didn't want to shut down Nelson's power system because of my smoking habit. I've quit other android partners because I couldn't stop. This was my last chance to make a relationship work. But it's really not my fault—smoking is an addiction.

"My lover doesn't like it."

The doctor's laugh sounded like a wheezing donkey—one, two, and three strained brays. "My wife would have me knocked off in a heartbeat. I should hire a food taster to make sure I'm not poisoned!"

I couldn't help but return the laugh.

"Please, sir, have a seat and tell me about yourself," Dr. Klarney said.

I hadn't noticed the poster-size print of Edvard Munch's *The Scream* until now. The only available chair was directly below it and butted against the wood-paneled wall. I walked over and tried to move my seat but the chair wouldn't budge.

"I anchor all the office furniture to the building. These days, just too many thieves," the doctor said.

I sat down under the print of the cartoonlike tormented person. A smoker's patch began to feel like a better option.

"Interesting print. The one above me."

"I hate it. Reminds me of my brother, Dean."

I cleared my throat and tried to be diplomatic. "Is he bald?"

"He's dead. Shot himself because he thought he was turning into a houseplant."

"I'm sorry. That's tragic."

"I'm not sorry. It was a real pain having to water and fertilize him all the time. Ever see a man stand in a giant pot all day?"

I curled my toes again. "Um—no, can't say I have."

The doctor brayed louder this time—one, two, and three times. "Just having fun with you. I'm an only child."

This time, I didn't return the laugh. "Interesting. And the smoking habit—"

"Dean couldn't smoke. He doesn't exist, remember?"

"I've remembered I have another appointment. Why don't we reschedule?"

"You didn't steal anything, did you?"

My eyes narrowed. "No. I would never."

The doctor pointed his index finger at his temple and made a circling gesture. "You can never be too sure. There are a lot of crazies out there."

I quickly left the office. I didn't reschedule with the secretary on the way out.

Outside, my Jaguar's tires cooked on the parking-lot asphalt. I plopped down inside the car. Florida sunlight splashed off the chrome that trimmed the dash and blinded me for a second. Stale air—it could choke a German shepherd—transformed the interior into a YMCA sauna but sitting in here was better than being mind-fucked by a paranoid doctor.

I cracked open the window. I thought of the money wasted on the quack I just visited, all because of Nelson henning me. My toes curled. How many times had I argued with Nelson about money and time? Tai-chi, hypnotism, and scuba massage administered by yogis—plenty of ways to waste money and time. He just gave me the same android, blank stare. Behind his glass eyes were just circuits and sensors. I wasn't going to waste more money on any more nonsense smoking cures. I knew what the real problem was.

I wiped sweat off my wrinkled brow and grabbed a pack of smokes from the glove compartment. The cellophane crackled and crunched as it quickly peeled away from the cigarette box and dropped to the floorboard. My toes loosened their grip on the wet socks inside my black wingtips.

With my other hand, I pulled the cell phone out of my shirt pocket. I wondered if androids went to heaven or something. The phone was still resting against my chin when I realized I'd been staring at nothing in particular for several minutes. This had to be done. I speed-dialed Automation Industries customer service.

"Customer identification and unit registration, please," the man said.

"SW-one-nine-five-nine-zero. Unit's name is Nelson."

Pause. "Yes, I found him. Telemetry indicates no malfunctions. How can I help?

"I want him shut down."

Another pause. "I'm sorry to hear that. This is your third and final unit. Is there a reason why?"

My toes curled. My face flushed. I thought I might yell at the guy but I restrained myself. I'm better than that.

"It's—it's not for me. I mean—this relationship. It's just not working out."

"Unfortunately, there are no refunds and regulations won't permit us to sell you another unit."

"It's the same procedure, right? He won't know it's happening?"

"We just remotely power Nelson down. Only takes a few minutes. Just a reminder, it is final."

Painless. Good.

I placed an unlit cigarette under my nose. The pungent smell made me think of times when I would sneak into my father's office. He had a cedar humidor for cigars. My mother caught me and she beat me. But the smell of that humidor was worth every second. It reminded me of Dad just before he died. My cigarette was a different aroma but just as nice. I smiled.

"Thanks. I'll keep that in mind," I said.

The man hung up. My phone's display went dark, hiding an empty contact list and I realized that I didn't have any human friends. That would have to change. I broke into a coughing fit and there was a small moment of pain. Phlegm filled my mouth and I spit out the window, a red tint splatter hitting the pavement. Never seen that before.

But the discomfort passed. I leaned back in the leather seat and stuffed the phone into my pocket. Yep, Nelson, money and time—something you don't understand. But I do.

I placed the cigarette butt end in my mouth, the spongy filter softly pressed between my lips. My yellow calloused thumb pulled down on the lighter's spark wheel. The flame touched the tobacco and the cigarette tip crackled and glowed like a distant winter campfire surrounded by lovers huddled together to stay warm as they look into each other's eyes.

I breathed in deep. White smoke softly curled around the steering wheel, the rearview mirror and me. My toes relaxed. I guess I should make peace with myself. After all, smoking is an addiction.

THREE NIGHTS IN BUDAPEST

ANDREW DISLIKED PUBLIC TRANSPORTATION. Despite his tall and stocky frame, he always made room for anyone pushing to get on or off the bus. But other travelers grabbed all the available space, demanding every last molecule of buffering air as they stacked themselves onto the traveling vehicle. The bus had quickly filled up after the last stop and people now squashed together, many standing. And after every bump in the road, they pushed in even closer. But Melanie, his wife, had taken his daughter, Chrissy, and he had to get her back. So, he rode the bus.

More potholes jarred the CTA bus. Chicago's spring crews must have missed tarring over the winter scars that populated the road. Andrew bumped up and down in a back seat. He quickly became annoyed and reached up to hit the request stop. Then he looked down at the beaten cardboard box of Pop's old comics locked in place by his size twelve steel-toed Wolverines and decided not to carry the thing several blocks. He scanned around, planning an escape route when his stop finally arrived.

One man snored upright. Two loud drunks slurred on

about the best place to buy liquor, pronouncing it 'licker 'er.' A frazzled mom fingered a game on her iPhone, scoring points and making it beep while her dark haired child insisted on squeezing between peoples' legs and asking how old they were. A fat woman who held a small bag of dry cat food in her lap said that the little girl's dress was pretty. She didn't comment on the chocolate stain that dribbled down the front of it.

Andrew's phone rang. "Pop loved those books," Allegra said. "They meant something to him."

"Pop is dead. Fuck him."

He grimaced because he realized that he was yelling above all the other noise in the bus. The woman holding the cat food shook her head at him. Andrew turned away and dropped his eyes. The child pushed over to Andrew. She looked at him and smiled. He didn't smile back. She didn't ask him if he thought her dress was pretty.

Andrew returned his attention back to the phone conversation with his sister. "Melanie took Chrissy and the savings. Allegra, she took everything from me."

Months ago, Andrew returned home after Union Shop training. The second floor neighbor sat on the stoop and mumbled, "Sorry, man." Melanie hadn't left a note explaining the vacant apartment.

"And now you're taking what's left of Pop," Allegra replied.

"I'm hiring an investigator."

Allegra got quiet for a moment. A phlegmy cough came out of the phone earpiece. "I got really sick today."

"It's the chemo treatments."

"This felt different. I passed out when I went looking through the closet for the box of comics."

The bus stopped and more people piled in. A man

pointed out a travel agency advertisement to another woman. Chrissy really loved those beach pictures.

"I'll be back, soon."

"How soon?"

"Allegra, I need the money."

She sighed. Usually, disagreements with his sister ended in yelling. Not now. He told her about the comic shop looking for older books. She didn't seem to care. Andrew said the shop owner might give a good price. Allegra replied that's great with a sigh. He wouldn't risk heating up the conversation and decided not tell her every-thing. No one else had contacted him about the comics. Allegra didn't need to know everything.

"I'll buy take-out on the way home," Andrew said.

"Just make sure you have bus fare to get back home."

"You're hungry, aren't you?"

She didn't say much else, only that she would see him when he got back. "Yeah, later," he told her and hung up.

The bus stopped near the corner of Lawrence and Lincoln. Andrew's shoulders carved a path out, box in front while raising a tight-lipped smile. The dark haired girl, hands pressed against a window, stared back at him as the bus doors hissed closed. Her eyes reminded him of Chris-sy's, his daughter's memory haunting him as the vehicle lumbered out of sight.

On Lincoln Avenue, a shop bearing bright lettering displayed neatly stacked bags of floral and spicy Ethiopian coffee. Behind another window, so polished clean and reflective that it seemed a diamond, organic citrus soaps from Hawaii mixed scents with the Swedish bakery next door. Two blonds passed by in high-heels and deserved a second look. They both laughed and Andrew smiled.

The comic shop squatted at the far end of the block. On

the window of the comic shop stood a muscled hero in faded blue tights, exclaiming 'POW!' in bold yellow and black letters. A decal of a pink anime bunny girl with half a vinyl ear opened her arms in a suggestive welcome at the door.

Andrew had read the comic pricing guide several times. He had memorized all of the sell prices. He was ready.

Inside, a burnt orange carpet covered the floor. The shelving had seen better times, most likely having been purchased years ago. Only one customer leafed through books, his belly pressed against a gondola and holding a hard cover anthology to his pimply face. At the back of the store, an old man wearing a blue guayabera leaned on a cracked Formica counter. He watched news on a Sony tube television and chewed on the stem of a dark red birch wood pipe.

"You responded to my post," Andrew said, interrupting the weather report.

The old man clamped down on the pipe stem and grinned. "I respond to many."

"You said you were interested in older books."

"Depends."

Andrew dropped the box of Pop's comics on the counter. "I have an *Eerie Comics. Issue Number One.*"

"Oh, yes. You said nothing about the conditions of books in your reply. No pictures. Didn't even mention the grades," the old man said.

The pimply-faced customer looked away from the anthology and nodded an agreement. Andrew wasn't discouraged. He reached into the box and pulled one of the comics out. He held it up. The old man said nothing. Andrew took out another.

"You don't know anything about comic collecting, do you son?" the old man said.

He reached into the box with surprising quickness. Then he grabbed a stack, leafed through them, and then divided them up into smaller stacks on the counter. He repeated the process several times, sometimes shaking his head. Then he paused over the *Eerie Comics, Issue Number One*.

"Four hundred is the best I can do," the old man finally said.

Four hundred barely paid the investigator to find his missing wife and daughter. And Chrissy also deserved a trip to the beach. "Overstreet values all of them at five thousand or more."

The old man clenched down tighter on the pipe and grinned. "Then I suggest reposting them on Craig's List."

"I've seen auctions selling old books for more than a million."

The old man laughed. "First Superman, sure. It's made a mark on popular culture and continues to impress today. What do you offer? Funny animals and Mutt and Jeff. It's all low grade, son."

Andrew pointed at the *Eerie Comics, Issue Number One* which had been set aside from the rest. "That one is supposed to be rare."

The old man held the book up. "Soiling on front and back covers, extensive creasing and stress lines all along the spine. It's low grade."

On the cover of the soiled book, a red-eyed ghoul loomed over a curvy woman bound in ropes. One night, Pop had smashed a lamp against the wall and Andrew hid behind some boxes stored in the basement. He reveled in the book as he read it under a dim lamp. In his mind, Pop had transformed into the ghoul and Andrew imagined defeating the monster to protect Allegra and Ma. That book was special.

"Fine. I'll keep it and you can buy the rest."

"It's the only reason I'm interested in this collection."

"Okay. Just the Eerie then. Four hundred." Andrew held out his hand for a handshake. The old man pulled the pipe out of his mouth and rested it against his chin. He said one hundred and fifty for just the Eerie. That wouldn't even pay the investigator. "Now, you're ripping me off."

The customer mumbled something about amateurs and put the anthology back to his face.

"This isn't a flea market, son. This is modern art and history we're dealing with," the old man said. "The Eerie might sit on my shelf for months. I can discount the others to move them, if I'm lucky."

"Seven hundred?"

"My favorite show comes on in a minute. I don't like to be bothered when it's on."

Andrew remembered lugging the books on the crowded bus. He didn't want to have to repeat that. And then there was Chrissy. God, how he missed his daughter.

"Okay. Four hundred for all of them."

The old man popped the pipe back in his mouth and grinned. He scribbled out a receipt.

At least some money filled Andrew's wallet again. But it may not be enough. He cursed his bad luck at a corner sandwich shop, purchasing cheap greasy burgers and lukewarm fries.

When he brought the meal back to her apartment, Allegra didn't ask him any questions. She sat quietly and didn't look at the food. He watched a piece of lint hover over her wisp hair before it flitted away from the yellow incandescent light to hide in shadows. She didn't notice. A few papers littered the kitchen counter. Dust collected around window frames, on a small unused corner table and between the central air register vents high up on the wall. She didn't seem to notice anything.

Her burger leaned to one side, drippings spotting the crinkled foil wrap. "You should eat. It'll get cold," Andrew said.

"Maybe later."

Two years ago, she had turned men's heads. Now, dark rings circled two pale eyes that sank back in a head that posted on a thread-like neck. Skinny arms terminated at withered hands. A scratched gold band clung to the knuckle of her ring finger.

Allegra looked over and dropped her hands under the tabletop.

Andrew took a large bite of his burger, wiped away the grease and looked up at the ceiling. He decided to change the subject. "She drinks like Pop did. I don't trust her with Chrissy."

Allegra pursed her thin lips. "You should have gotten her help."

"I think that's why she ran off. I don't know."

"She never said anything to me."

Andrew stared in disbelief. "I can take care of Chrissy."

"You quit the training program. You can't even take care of yourself."

"I was confused. I'll go to trade school after this is all fixed."

A small bit of light shone in Allegra's eyes. She reached over and touched his arm. "Do you any have fond memories of us? Of you and me?"

Andrew furrowed his brow but he took her hand. It felt

hollow and warm. "Pop always told that stupid story about the trip he had won over the telephone."

Allegra laughed. "Three nights in Budapest. Ma wouldn't go because she knew it was a scam. Pop thought she was cheap. He never got it."

"He always blamed Ma. He told that story hundreds of times."

Allegra dropped her smile. "Even on their anniversary. Wished they hadn't drunk the wine."

The flower bouquet, trampled and scattered on the floor, was still a vivid memory for Andrew. "Ma had a cut and a black eye. I tucked her into my bed that night. I can still remember smelling her dark hair—lavender shampoo."

"You loved her."

He pressed Allegra's hand tighter. For some reason, the memory of the scent of Ma's lavender shampoo bothered him most. "I'm haunted by it. Maybe if I took Chrissy on a trip, things would change. I could move on, too."

Allegra pulled her hand away and rewrapped the burger. She slowly got up and placed the burger inside the refrigerator. She said that she'd eat it later. The cotton nightgown, the only thing she wore, hung like a sack might hang on a scarecrow. She needs to eat. No, she needs hope.

"Allegra, would you like to go to Florida with me and Chrissy?"

Allegra walked toward her bedroom and then stopped. She turned around and cleared her throat, wiping at an eye. "The doctor wants me to go into Hospice."

"What the hell? You're doing the treatments."

Allegra shivered, the quivering slight. "I don't want to be alone with strangers. I'm staying here."

Andrew refused to believe the doctor's diagnosis. The

burger turned inside his stomach. "We'll get a second opinion. Doctors make mistakes all ti—"

"After Don left me, I had a hard time getting over him. I
told him I was sick and thought he might come back."

"The doctor made a mistake. You'll see."

"Nothing changed." Allegra went to bed.

Andrew cleaned up the house but not the way Allegra
could. Not really. He missed little things like water spots.
The burger in the refrigerator dried out and so he tossed it.
He purchased more groceries with Allegra's debit card. He
cooked her meals and wrapped up nearly full plates. She
slept a lot. Sometimes, he browsed trade schools and stared
at the home page for several minutes. He read customer
reviews about self-help and natural cure books. JPEG
oceans cast blue waves on deserted sandy beaches as the
sun sank down into the Gulf Coast horizon.

The house stood dead quiet except for a steady whisper
of air conditioning. The land line rang and startled Andrew.
He jumped up and answered the phone. He tingled all over
and his hands shook.

"She's in Peoria. Living downtown, if you can call it
that. Want the address?" the investigator said.

Finally! He gripped the pen as if trying to clamp it in a
vise to keep it from wandering on the paper. "Sure. I had
almost forgotten." Andrew forced a laugh.

The investigator reported the information discovered in
the special database. Said some local construction equipment company exec paid for her condo. Didn't know if
Melanie still dated the guy. That would cost extra to do
field research - a lot more money - if Andrew wanted to
pursue it further.

"Won't be necessary," Andrew said.

The investigator paused. "She's taken out a restraining order."

The restraining order branded Andrew's fate. He had no money. The cogs of court machines would just grind him into dust, scattered in the shifting winds of justice.

It was like a punch to the gut. That exec talked her into it. Andrew was sure of it. "She stole all the money I had. You should look into my checking and savings account history. Her account, too."

"That would pretext me into a jail cell. Maybe I could talk to people in Peoria. It's safer that way."

More money, more talk and maybe a payed-for privilege to see Chrissy once a month if he was lucky. This needed action. "How do I make your final payment?"

"I'll mail you a bill. But you might reconsider. I could build a case for you."

Andrew had already made up his mind. "You've helped enough." The investigator started to say something but shut up. "This is bullcrap and you know it," Andrew said.

"Don't do anything rash. It never ends well." The investigator hung up.

The comic book money didn't amount to much. But it was enough for a round trip bus ticket and a one way ticket back to Chicago for Chrissy. He promised himself to return immediately and look after Allegra. Andrew took out another three hundred dollars from her account at the Greyhound depot's ATM. He had wanted to tell her about it but she was sleeping when he left the apartment that morning. That was at nine a.m., a vial of Dexamethasone and the phone placed next to her.

Andrew brooded alone in the back of the bus. Each time his visit played out in his mind, it got better. Melanie always agreed with him in the end and confessed regrets.

Chrissy came back to Chicago, Allegra delighted to see her. Then the three of them took that beach trip to Florida.

At four p.m., Andrew arrived at the Adams Street depot in Peoria. Allegra had never called his cell phone. An attendant warned passengers to take all belongings. People scattered out the depot exit. He tried calling Allegra after he stepped out onto the sidewalk. She didn't answer. He tried to recall his plans, couldn't remember them and decided to pick up some flowers. He could only think of Chrissy as he absent-mindedly paid for a small bouquet of roses. Then he unfolded a crumpled, perspiration-soaked printing of a Google map. Melanie's condo was only several blocks away.

The condominium complex's front desk attendant chatted on the phone. He looked at Andrew who suddenly felt like a third grader caught making too much noise in the classroom. But the attendant looked at the roses and waved him in. He took the elevator up to the fourth floor which felt like a vacuum. It was quiet, like a fancy hotel kind of quiet. Smooth, curved wall sconces sat high on nickel bases. They lined up in laser sight precision. Andrew's lumbering footsteps disrupted the quiet as he approached Melanie's door. The numbers four-one-three were engraved in a heavy wood door.

He took a breath and knocked.

Chrissy peeked out, her dark eyes peering up. She smiled and then quickly dropped it. "Mommy's not here."

His Chrissy was taller than he remembered and even more beautiful. She wore a dress he had never seen on her, the hemline too high and the neckline too low. "I brought you pretty flowers."

"Mommy's friend gave her flowers."

He could leave, now, and take his prize and run. But part of him wanted to know why Melanie changed. Months of eating meals alone and unexplained rejection needed answers. He might stay a minute and then escape before Melanie returned. Andrew held out his hand and Chrissy guided him inside.

Several empty bottles of chardonnay rested by the kitchen sink full of dirtied glasses and snack plates. A greeting card, magnetized to the refrigerator, said that dreams always come true. Empty shopping bags were crammed together inside a stainless steel trash can.

Melanie smiled in a plastic picture frame, cheek to cheek with a man twenty years older than her. Back in high school, Andrew's friends called her Asian hot. She still looked pretty good, only now she wore lots more makeup.

"Mommy left you alone?"

Chrissy pointed out the vase on the living room table. "She went to the midget store."

Having raised a child, Andrew had learned how to decipher toddler talk. He wondered where she had picked up the word midget. It wasn't a nice word but it felt odd to correct her.

"You mean the mini-mart?"

Chrissy nodded.

He plucked a rose from the bouquet he carried in the other hand and placed it inside the vase. He smiled sadly to himself, knowing that the rose was a temporary pleasure which would wither and die as time passed. A flower's beauty never lasts.

Andrew turned to Chrissy. "Would you like to see the ocean?"

"You didn't put all of the flowers inside the vase."

"Let's go find Mommy. We can talk about Florida." He said they were all going to take a bus ride to the beach.

Chrissy's brow furrowed. She pulled back as Andrew

grabbed her hand. Keys jingled and the front door opened, Melanie standing inside the door frame. She dropped a plastic bag, two full wine bottles clanking together as they hit the hardwood floor. She gasped.

He held the rose bouquet out to her. Andrew flushed. He wasn't sure what to say to Melanie who's face had paled in shock.

"I missed Chrissy. You didn't even tell me where you took her."

Melanie threw her purse on the kitchen counter. She pulled things out, scattering lipstick, receipts and a wallet. A bottle of bright red nail polish rolled off the granite surface and oozed on the tile.

Melanie held a phone in her hand. "I took out a restraining order on you. I'm calling the police."

Andrew plodded forward. She grabbed a wine glass and threw it at Andrew's protective hands. It smashed apart in tiny slivers and crunched under his boots. Chrissy started wailing.

"Get out," Melanie screamed at him.

"She's my child, too. You had no fucking right to take her, whore." Andrew couldn't hear Chrissy, anymore. It was like being in a tunnel, Melanie standing at the end of it. He remembered Pop smashing the lamp and hurting Ma. Anger raged in him. His hands moved up and down several times. "Not even a fucking note."

Melanie's phone smashed to the floor, the display cracked. She struggled to sit up. Andrew eyed the trampled bouquet lying around her. He thought of the *Eerie Comics, Issue Number One.* He thought of the red-eyed ghoul that loomed over the curvy woman on the cover. Pop's ghost wasn't exorcised.

Chrissy's screaming broke the dream-like state. "You hurt mommy," she said.

Andrew picked her up and she kicked and snotted herself. Melanie's hand wavered as she held the phone in front of her face. Her jaw seemed to hang loose. White light glimmered on thin tears that rolled from her eyes. The phone clicked. Andrew wanted to pick Melanie off the floor, too, and ask her if she was okay. He wanted to tell her that he was sorry. He really wanted to. But he left the apartment with Chrissy pinned between his arms.

He took three flights of stairs down and left out the back door. No one noticed him and the crying child—at least, he didn't think so. The hike back to the bus depot was a blur. He dropped Chrissy in a pleather seat and thought he might puke.

Chrissy rocked in her seat and whimpered. Some people whispered. Andrew stared at himself two rows of seats back, holding a comic book and hunkered down as if hiding in the chair. No. No, it was some red-headed, ten-year-old drooling monster who stared at him, mouth open. Don't fucking judge me, Andrew thought. He had a second urge to puke.

He fumbled around with his phone's keypad and Allegra's voicemail said leave a message. He called again. "Where are you?" She's hundreds of miles away, he thought. Hundreds. "Wake up. I have Chrissy." The phone beeped and terminated the call.

Piercing the outside dusk air, two strobing red lights appeared in front of the depot glass doors. A cop, then another, strode in and loomed at the entrance. They looked around.

Andrew put his arm around Chrissy. At least she could tell him how glad she was to see him, to say she had missed her Pop. Chrissy stopped rocking and muttered something about broken dolls. It didn't make sense. He kissed the top of her head and smelled her dark hair – lavender shampoo, like Ma used to wear.

"Pop loves you," he said.

YESTERDAY NEVER, TOMORROW, AND TODAY

MENHIR-X, a circumbinary planet circling two rapid stars, travelled a dangerous path. The P-type planet maintained a just-barely distance of twice each sun's separation. Any closer, the celestial orbit would destabilize and a hot sun would swallow the unfortunate world where the introverted Allohms resided.

The yellowish humanoids had always been aware of this possible apocalyptic demise. Translated into the human tongue, the cataclysmic end sounded like *Dead Day*. Instead of fearing this future, the Allohms chose to focus their thoughts on the small pleasures gained from exchanging a rare xenon gas for raw sugar with the Far Edge trade union. The trade union dared to venture so far out into their part of the Laniakea supercluster, using indentured farms to continue the flow of goods. And the worn-down indentured farmers, criminal types, sweated over genetically modified cane fields on the planet. They struggled to pay off never-ending debts to a faraway Earth society and to a thankless organization. And they never enjoyed a single nanosecond in their current worried states of existence.

The high blood-red suns constantly sweated out moisture from Jax Kepner's sugarcane plot of land. Irrigation spray guns avoided his hardening soil. Billets strained to push dry stalks upward toward a punishing sky. By afternoon, a stilted rainfall teased the dying plants and promptly gave up on the small crop. The sugarcane slumped. A slow wind exhaled a long sigh.

Jax cut another handful of the thin grass. The machete blade quickly sliced through hollow, empty rods. He kicked at the pathetic yield, imagining Dol Ray grinning and knowing that the trade-union debt was piling up. He worried that Delna may starve this season. And the farmer wondered if a paradise waited somewhere else.

If Jax didn't pay a small amount on his loan this season, the trade union could sell his debt and sugarcane field to Dol Ray. Unfortunately, Dol didn't forgive obligations and he raised interest rates so high that the loan principal could never be paid. Jax needed a loan to pay for irrigation fees before his entire crop died. The farmer had asked the trade union but the trade union refused. His account was in arrears. So Jax would have to ask the only person he knew for a loan—Dol Ray. And Dol not only wanted his plot of land but he also seemed interested in Delna.

A four-wheeled transport growled up a nearby path, making its way over. Dol Ray stopped close and got off the machine.

"Beautiful day," Dol said.

"Too hot," Jax replied.

"Every day's a new grace."

"For some."

"Temperance, my friend. I have respect for all."

Dol crushed cane stalks under his boot and spit. He pulled a cigar enclosed in a glass tube from a jacket pocket and grinned at Jax.

"To honor our new deal?" Dol said. He held out the tobacco stick, a bent Earth Dominican that somehow had been damaged in shipping.

Jax snatched it from Dol's meaty hand. "Gone in a puff of smoke."

"At least the water flows again—for now."

"A debt will be paid."

Then Jax watched Dol wheel away. The farmer decided not to tell Delna about the loan. He would make it work.

———

Large rock surrounded Jax's shack walls, hiding its poly-plastic exterior on three sides. It was an eyesore less solid than the landscape itself. When Jax knocked at the front door, Delna hesitated before opening it. She offered him a brief smile as the farmer ran his soiled fingers through his hair. He glanced inside before entering. A *sayur nganten* roiled over an unchecked flame.

"The crop...it's OK?" Delna asked.

"You'll eat well this season. I may have to buy you a new dress."

Delna rubbed her belly. "I could use more clothes."

Jax eyed her young, slight figure. Dol Ray's loan might afford only a small dress for her. He avoided his wife's eyes. "Size petite, right?"

Delna studied his worn face as if his creases counted out the failures that slowly broke his body down. "Why would I ever need a new dress? This one fits me."

"Is there something you need to say?"

"No." Then she took a deep breath. "Yes. An Allohm wandered around outside. Poor creature. He looked sick."

Jax disliked the Allohms even more than the other traders he dealt with. The Far Edge union locked in a monopoly for the stated purpose of controlling sugar trades for xenon gas. At least he understood their motivation. But the Allohms were secret. They disclosed little to the farmers and maintained a mostly silent cabal. And some aliens' sugar addictions could devour entire crops in days. He walked over to a cabinet where he stored a projectile gun to keep away vermin.

Delna suddenly looked worried. "No one should get hurt," she said.

"I'm looking out for us. You want to eat, don't you?"

Jax's eyes tunneled onto the unlocked prison shackles also hanging in the cabinet—heavy, black steel that burdened a man's legs and arms. He kept them as a reminder of his criminal past and as a symbol of hope. But more and more, the possibility of ever working off his criminal sentence was dying off like the sugar cane withering on his small plot of land. His face flushed and his eyes grew hard. He snatched the manacles out of the closet and held them up for Delna.

"Six years' hard labor. This farm is my chance. Ours." His voice was tense and gruff.

Delna cringed away from his looming shadow. She protectively wrapped her small arms around her belly. Tears welled up in her eyes. She said nothing.

He suddenly regretted frightening her. "I'll search for the alien in the morning," Jax said, his voice softening. He went to bed without dinner.

Two early suns rose over Jax's sugarcane field, their rays revealing stems that struggled to grow into full stalks. Each stalk reached up toward the dawn sky, potential to become more than dead, useless fiber. He heard the irrigation pipes once again gurgled to life and the farmer felt hope. But he couldn't allow a trespass. With the projectile gun in hand, he crept forward through just barely green stalks to find the Allohm.

The farmer had decided to kill the alien on sight. He would make up a story and tell Delna that the Allohm must have left the farm. That part probably wasn't true because a lone Allohm was most likely an outcast or about to die. It would still be nearby. And the Far Edge trade union wouldn't care about one lone alien. They fiercely protected their financial interests and so the board of governors would probably ignore the incident if ever reported.

Jax puzzled over some nearby crushed sugarcane. His wary eyes followed a trail that paused and then shuffled off to the center of the field. The farmer followed it, his projectile gun growing heavy as he hesitated before a small clearing. His hand quivered over the gun's trigger. The steel barrel wandered, searching for somewhere to point.

"No today," the Allohm said.

Jax saw the alien weakly pointing at the gun and it seemed to smile. The thin, yellow alien lay on its back, sucking at the air. Half-chewed stalks of sugarcane surrounded the creature. Bile covered its cracked lips and sunken chest. Blue eyes blinked, wet with tears.

"Yesterday never," the Allohm said, half to Jax and half to the morning suns. "No more tomorrow. No today."

The farmer cocked his head and spotted tiny manacles

that swallowed the creature's skinny wrists and neck. Jax suddenly felt sympathy for the sick alien. He remembered when he too wore manacles that held him chained to a wall. His father had visited him in prison. Then he spit on Jax and told him that he wished that his son was dead. "The fear of the Lord is to hate evil. Pride and arrogance and the evil way and the froward mouth do I hate," his father had said. Then he told him that he regretted visiting his son, calling it, "A moment of weakness." Jax could only reply, "A debt will be paid." He never saw his father again.

Jax lowered his gun. He swallowed hard.

"A gun is not the right way," he said.

The Allohm wept pleas, repeating the words *No tomorrow* and *No today* and muttering other words that the farmer didn't understand. It pointed at the gun as if begging for Jax to shoot. Finally, the alien vomited and passed out.

Jax scooped the alien up in his arms. The featherweight creature was no heavier than a dried cane stalk.

———

"Did you?" Delna said.

"I put the Allohm in the mill," Jax said.

His wife's eyes brightened. "I'll make extra soup. You can feed the Allohm tomorrow."

Jax looked at his pitiful kitchen which was barely stocked with food. "I had a moment of weakness."

"You talk as if it is an animal," Delna said.

He dropped into a chair and lay the projectile gun on the table. He fingered the trigger guard. "The thing might be contagious. You might breathe in its sickness."

"I won't go near it. And I'm sure you're fine too."

"I should have killed it. The trade union is the law this

far out from Earth. They don't recognize smugglers and aliens as being protected."

Delna jammed her cooking spoon into the simmering pot. "Then what am I to you?"

Jax said nothing. Delna was a Penuranian, another alien race that coexisted with humans. He had spoken too rashly.

Her eyes softened. "The Allohms are pacifists. Dol and other trade-union members have enslaved them."

"The creatures are fatalists. They willingly do this to their own kind."

"Feed the poor creature."

Jax continued to play with the gun's trigger guard. He tapped his foot and fidgeted. "Why am I helping that alien?" He thought out loud. "I'm indentured. The trade union barely even recognizes me. I'm barely human."

"Please. For me," Delna said.

"If this farm fails, I will not become a thing that would die for sugar."

━━

Jax watched his mill chopper shred the month's haul of sugarcane. Bagasse fueled a boiler furnace that was designed for larger loads. The machine easily worked through the small yield, a single roller quickly squeezing and crushing the fibrous plant. By late afternoon, a pump piston *tsk-tsk-tsked* while a downturned hose pulled cane juice away to be thickened into syrup.

The sugarcane yield would be too small to service Dol's new debt. As the two suns set outside the mill, Jax ignited carbon rods and looked around the mechanized work area. The homemade arc lamp burned too bright, outshining any last hope within the farmer's mind.

Before prison release, Menhir-X had offered freedom. "We'll finally have control of our futures," Jax had told Delna. "If it is your dream, then it is my dream," Delna had said. But bringing his wife here was wrong. She remained shackled to his false promise.

Delna, nightmares are dreams too.

The chopper continued to churn. Jax could hear the scrawny Allohm making noise above the machine's din. Lying on a provided cot, it thrashed and screamed for more cold sugar soup. Its swollen face, neck and belly made the creature look like a leech. Jax glared at it.

The Allohm quieted and pointed at the aluminum ceiling. "No today," it said.

"I'll never pay off my debts. I'm imprisoned forever. You did this to me," Jax said.

He knocked a soup bowl onto the dirt floor. His shadow loomed over the creature. The alien's eyes grew wide as it stared back.

"Dead day?" it said.

Jax wrapped his hands around a neck that felt like string in his calloused fingers. The farmer squeezed. Gurgles coughed out but the alien didn't resist. Instead, the Allohm wrapped its long arms around Jax as if in a lover's embrace.

The alien's spaghetti arms were far stronger than the farmer could have imagined. They pulled him close, almost nose to nose. The creature's body grew hot to the touch. Jax squeezed its throat harder and the Allohm's red eyes rolled far back in their sockets.

"Let me go, dammit," Jax said.

"Yes-s-s-s-s," the Allohm said, a hiss rising from its mouth.

A brief smell of rotting meat filled Jax's nose and a gas invaded his throat and lungs. He choked. Throttling the

Allohm's neck, he thrashed the melon-shaped head several times against the metal cot rail until the alien finally released him. The Allohm lay motionless except for its belly swelling and collapsing like a ventilator bag. A hiss streamed from its open mouth.

Panting and numb, Jax sat over the alien. The farmer leaned in and sniffed, detecting no more odors. He contemplated further suffocating the creature to make sure the alien couldn't recover. His eyes searched the mill for some way to dispose of its body.

Suddenly, the overhead lamp crackled. Electricity burst into a bright blue arc between the carbon rod tips. Jax shielded his eyes as flecks of hot, black material sputtered down onto his hand. He jumped up and shook off the burning flecks. As the Allohm's belly collapsed again and its throat hissed out some kind of gas, the lamp strobed. The alien's body seemed to dance and freeze with the pulsing light. Jax struggled to escape the mill, temporarily blinded by the bright phenomenon.

As he stumbled to the door, Jax realized that the Allohm's dead body was producing the same xenon gas that the Far Edge trade union shipped back to Earth.

—

"Why shouldn't it be xenon gas?" Dol Ray said.

His eyes rapidly blinked as he watched the gas inside the glass cigar tube change color. He stopped the portable gas sampler's igniter and repositioned the tube. Dol started the machine up again for the seventh time. The test result was the same—blue.

"I'll pay on the loan to you in xenon. The gas is more valuable than the sugar," Jax said.

Dol laughed and shook his head. "What do you know about the xenon trade?"

"Bring me shipping Vacutainers and—"

"I don't care if you worked in a laboratory back on Earth. You couldn't possibly supply me enough gas to make it worth my time."

"I need a small, commercial fractionating column."

Dol grinned. "What was her name—your assistant at that lab?"

Jax pushed his boot stiffly into the dirt. Neck muscles corded. "Your loan would be paid off in weeks."

"They never did find her body, did they?" Dol said.

"If you won't help me, someone else will."

Dol's nostrils flared as he looked around. He stepped forward but Jax stopped him by holding him back at arm's length. Dol lost his usual calm and collectedness, his face turning a bright shade of red that matched a prison-uniform red. That color was chosen so that guards could quickly spot someone attempting to escape. Now, it seemed that Dol couldn't hide what he was truly feeling.

"Where's my missing Allohm?" Dol blurted out, spittle flying from his mouth.

Jax smiled. He shoved Dol Ray back and picked up his projectile gun. For once, he felt like he had the advantage.

"Prove it's dead."

Dol swore several times. His face flushed. "Animal! You'll be back in chains for attempted murder. No, it will be murder, you ungrateful piece of shit!"

"You trick the Allohms, don't you," Jax said.

"They sign an agreement, idiot. A virus is killing them."

"That we manufacture on Earth. They ingest it through the sugarcane, don't they?"

"Give me my property! Give me back my Allohm!"

"No cadaver to claim so the gas isn't yours, Dol."

"A debt will be paid, allright. The trade union governors will grant me a search of your farm. I'll be back."

Weeks before Dol Ray would be killed, Jax danced to music in his head while Dol's transport kicked up dirt and wheeled quickly away. The dirt struck Jax but he was too high on his momentary victory. The two Menhir-X suns seemed to pinch together in the sky. One beamed down bright rays that embraced the farmer. But the rush passed. The other star seemed to clutch at his neck and made his sweating skin tremble. He raised a fist. A nausea suddenly gripped his gut. Sugar haunted his mind.

"Dead day!" Jax yelled out at the sky.

———

Inside the shack, a cooking rod struggled to burn hotter. A small red flame hesitated as air reacted with the carbon-based fuel. But two puffs from Delna's warm lips spirited the hydrocarbon gas to life. The sugar soup began to bubble.

Delna's thoughts distracted her as she cooked. Since Jax's second meeting with Dol a few weeks ago, he had become sick and she worried. His skin was cracking and his chest was sinking. He constantly craved sayur nganten, an Asian Earth recipe that she'd picked up before leaving for Menhir-X.

And Jax felt like a stranger now. She had tried to talk to him about his condition but he had become angry. Ever since he had discovered the Allohm in the cane crop, he had withdrawn from her and only glared when she asked questions. He had barely talked about Dol. Delna had grown so worried over his current mental state that she didn't dare mention her pregnancy. She was a Penuranian and her race remained loyal to their partners until death. She could never leave him. She would have to find another way to make Jax talk to her.

The soup pot's lid popped up and settled back.

Delna absent-mindedly stirred the meal. Her mother, Deena, had cooked meals for Jax before her disappearance. When Deena had met Jax, excitement radiated from her mother's eyes. A bond quickly formed. Deena never left Jax even when he sometimes hurt her. And then one day she disappeared. The police on Earth never found her. Jax swore to both the investigator and to her that he was innocent of any wrongdoing. She believed her stepfather, Jax, but the police didn't. All alone, Delna waited for Jax's release from prison. When he was released to be indentured, he swore to take care of her and then married her. He now did the best he could for them.

The cooking flame sputtered. Delna checked the fuel rod. She stirred the meal again. Her thoughts wandered. She would find a way to talk with Jax.

Jax needed to sell xenon gas soon. The Allohm's body that he hid in the mill decayed more quickly now. The alien's limbs began to shrivel and the creature's mechanical breathing was slowing. Its xenon gas output was dwindling.

Unfortunately, the several containers of gas the farmer had managed to collect would not be enough to pay off his debts. Jax had asked around and the only person—if you could call him that—interested in trading for xenon was the smuggler, Click-Click. Jax would have to sell his small supply to the smuggler so that he could round up the necessary equipment. That equipment could collect a lot more xenon, hopefully before the Allohm stopped producing it altogether. Then Jax could destroy the carcass and be free of Dol Ray and his debt.

Jax entered Click-Click's salvage yard, a cover operation for his real business. His downcast eyes picked out gaps through piles of scrapped transports and other forgotten vehicles. Ahead, an impact crusher smashed an older-model toad rocket into a flat disk. Junker spiders quickly stripped off excess metal like someone picking meat off a chicken bone. A yard worker stomped one of the metal-eating insects under his boot as he quickly pulled the pancaked material away from two large hammers. When he saw Jax approach, he made a toothless grin and pointed at a small office just ahead.

Jax entered a dimly lit room. The pentachromat sat behind a desk. Click-Click looked more reptilian than humanoid, an elliptical head resting on a scaly neck and two nasal pits instead of nostrils. His black eyes gazed back at Jax, his crusted lids clicking several times.

"My eyes see better than most in the dark. You're not unnerved?" Click-Click asked.

"No."

"I can also see infrared light. Most traders don't know that."

Jax glanced down at his muddied boots. His pants were torn and frayed from repeated wearings and long toil in the cane fields. He dressed nothing like a trader who could afford to always wear new and clean clothing.

"You're making a joke at my expense?" Jax asked.

Click-Click changed the subject. "How many sealed Vacutainers of gas did you bring?"

The farmer reached into his carrying bag and counted out ten random-sized containers. Click-Click picked one up, studied the translucent covered bowl and tossed it back onto the desk.

"Such a lucrative venture," Click-Click said.

"I need better equipment."

Jax coughed several times. Thick phlegm jumped into his throat. He swallowed hard and gasped several times before his body calmed. His condition seemed to be worsening.

"Time seems to be working against you," Click-Click said.

Jax didn't like the smuggler being so personal with him. "What are you talking about?"

Click-Click leaned back in his seat. His black eyes worked over Jax. *Click. Click.* But he said nothing.

"I'll bring you more gas than what's here," Jax said.

"As I've told you, I can see infrared. There's an aura around you that others cannot see. It's like a soft, yellow life-light that's dying. And in your core being is something more. Something like a red flame consumes your head and your mind. There are two lights, two of you. So who am I dealing with?"

Jax didn't understand what Click-Click meant by *two of you*. But if it meant that the smuggler might help him, he would go along with it. "I'm the part that wants to be free of Dol Ray. Free of my farm."

"I can help you."

"You can get me the gas collecting equipment?"

"No, something else." Click-Click reached into a desk drawer and pulled out a contract. He pushed the paper at Jax. "Read this. I can tell that you are an educated human. Reading shouldn't an issue for you unlike some of the rogues I deal with. If you decide to go ahead with this agreement, there is a signatory line for your beneficiary. Take your time."

Jax looked over the agreement. Where the word *Allohm* appeared in the document, it was crossed out and replaced with *human*. There was a promise to be given unlimited sugar in exchange for the signatory's body upon death. Jax found himself craving sugar more and more and this appealed to him. And what Jax now understood about the genetically modified sugar, habitually eating it meant that death wasn't far off for the Allohms. But did it affect humans the same way? Jax didn't know.

He tapped the pen in his hand on the desktop.

Click-Click cocked his head. "This red flame I see...it's burned for some time inside you. It consumes your life-light. It has a shade of transgression. It is who you really are," Click-Click said.

"You seem to be blaming me for something. I've served my time in prison. I didn't deserve it. The xenon gas would finally unshackle me."

"You wouldn't have time to enjoy your freedom. Besides, I won't make deals with the other you."

———

Jax, I'm pregnant, Delna thought.

She watched Jax's labored breathing but couldn't say the words aloud as she lay in bed beside him. Tender-looking welts crept across his back. He shivered. She tenderly reached out and touched his burning skin. If she showed concern, Delna thought that her husband might open up and talk with her.

"I'm awake," Jax said.

"I was worried about you."

Jax seemed to struggle to sit up in the bed. He turned to her and licked his cracked lips. "I'm thirsty. Make me sugar soup."

"A third pot?"

Jax didn't wait. He rolled over and dropped to the floor, slowly pushing himself up. Then he trudged over to the cooking table and grabbed a cleaver. Delna pulled the blankets closer to her in a protective gesture.

"Dawn comes. Two suns burn bright every day. But I'm always cold," Jax said.

He wasn't making sense. And with the cleaver in his hand, it seemed best if she got out of the shack until he became more rational.

"I'll have to get more water from the storage tank," she said.

Jax's glassy eyes looked like crystal orbs used by vision-seeking fortune-tellers, clouded and unfocused. He grinned and raised the cleaver in his hand. Delna pushed her back up against the wall, trying to put as much distance between herself and the man now before her.

"Don't worry. This is not for you. If my body grows worse, I'll cut off my own sickness," he said.

She cautiously got out of the bed. Slowly, she reached toward him. "A fever is making you talk like that."

Jax dropped the large knife. It made a heavy thud on the dirt floor.

"A sickness burns inside me," he said.

"We'll get a doctor for you."

"There is no tomorrow. Don't bother."

"Have hope. There is always another tomorrow," she said.

"Yesterday never was. I've been imprisoned and who I

was has been wiped away. Now, I'm indentured. There is no tomorrow for those who don't exist."

"There could be more. What if there is more?"

"I'll get the water, Delna. Go back to bed."

Tears welled up in Delna's eyes. She couldn't work up the courage to tell him that she was pregnant. In his current mental state, maybe it was for the best. She fought the tears as she fought with herself. He wouldn't see her cry.

Jax left the shack without saying another word. She felt a relief wash over her. He had become a stranger. Jax seemed like another person altogether.

<hr />

Dol Ray hunkered down at about two hundred meters away from Jax's shack. He watched the place through a pair of night vizos and waited. The farmer should soon be leaving to work his sugarcane field. Well, whatever was left of it. It would soon be his, anyway.

A speckled cane beetle crawled up Dol's arm. The insect was an import from Earth, living off of sugar plants' roots and leaves. They could destroy entire crops in months, even weeks. The pests were no different than the Earth prisoners who rotted out a civilization if left unchecked. Jax had been a convicted murderer and deserved less than he was already given. Dol crushed the cane beetle and wiped its guts off into the dirt, smiling.

So why did the trade union side with Jax when he reported his grievance to board of governors? They dismissed the matter.

"Only one Allohm?" they had said.

"And what's to stop him from abducting more?" Dol had replied.

The board saw no evidence of a trend and closed the case.

But Dol wasn't through with Jax yet. He adjusted the night vizos settings and peered through them again.

The alien's body must be in the shack, he thought. Then he spit on the remains of the dead cane beetle.

The shack door opened and Jax stumbled out. The farmer seemed to have trouble walking. Maybe he was sick. Maybe he'd die in the fields. Dol smiled again. He watched until Jax was out of sight.

Dol got up. He coughed up thick phlegm and spit. Waiting for the farmer to leave had made him thirsty. Maybe there was water inside. Or better yet, maybe there was sugar.

———

Jax's watery eyes gazed upon the two suns rising in the morning sky. Warming rays searched his cracked lips for the words that he so badly wanted to say. He needed to say them.

He should finally proclaim the truth for what he had done to Delna's mother. He held his arms wide open as if to offer the celestial bodies restitution for being alive. "Forgive me for what I've done," he thought. But his admission did not spill out from his lips. The Menhir-X stars must wait longer for the long-hidden secret to be spoken from the farmer.

In the distance, a Cranker warbled. *The right thing. The right thing. The right thing to do.*

Jax pulled the wrinkled contract from his pocket. He reread it.

Beneficiary to receive all ongoing xenon sale proceeds minus 10 percent...

The black text blurred. Jax wanted her to be taken care of. It was the least he could do for her. He dropped the contract onto the dirt. He kicked red gravel and small stone over the stapled sheets of paper. His boot flattened the agreement and stamped a heel imprint. A dog-eared corner poked out.

Finally, he spoke out loud to no one else but himself. "If I sign this, you will know that this was not my fault. None of it. You've shackled me in your dirt. Swallowed us all with your pride and froward mouths. But I die free."

The warbling Cranker hushed. Not even the wind blew. For a moment, the planet seemed to have fallen in total silence.

The ashen-faced man cornered Delna. His clammy hands grabbed her shoulders, shoving her back against the shack's wall. He rattled her small frame and she momentarily lost her breath.

"Where is it? Where's my Allohm?" he shouted.

Delna couldn't look into his eyes. A cold fire seemed to burn inside them.

"I never told him," she said.

"Told who? Tell him what?" The man pressed his bulk against her belly. Life inside compressed. Something tiny, something hidden, shivered and retreated.

"You can't have him," she said.

The man grinned. He licked her face. He grabbed her crotch.

"You're alien. A Penuranian, right? An animal doesn't decide what I take," he said.

Delna's legs turned to water. The man forced her body up. Maybe seconds passed. Maybe minutes. Something like hot steel entered her.

"I'm pregnant," she said.

He said nothing, grunting and ramming hard against her. Ache filled Delna's chest and stomach and loins. She felt a small seed of life inside her quiver and burst. Something flowed down her legs.

She was crying. She shouldn't show this man. He kept ramming.

She had never told Jax about the baby.

━━

Jax entered the shack. Dol Ray's naked ass clenched as he rutted Delna's limp body. His dirty hands pinned her. Jax wasn't surprised to see him like this—that's what really was inside that man's heart.

The farmer decided on the cleaver lying on the table and strode over. *A debt will be paid.* He grasped the surprised Dol's hair, pulled back and slammed the blade into the rapist's neck. Blood sprayed and Dol squealed.

Several more quick chops to the arms. The steel flashed bright, looking like two suns merging into one calm moment that shone light on what hid inside the dark. Jax butchered both hands before pushing the carcass off his wife.

And then, a final silence.

He studied Delna, her arms sprawled out like a butterfly's wings. Red life leaked from between her legs. Jax saw her with new eyes. She had given too much. He had missed a precious moment. But yesterday was never.

Jax sat and pulled Delna onto his folded legs. She looked like her mother. He slipped the grimy contract from his pocket. He read it to her and she said nothing. She would never speak again. Then he caressed her bloodied hair and cheek. Jax saw his secret reflected in her dark irises. He felt a terrible guilt. Jax wished for freedom.

His head bowed. His lips parted.

"I killed her. I killed Deena," he said.

⸻

"Is the gas collection chamber comfortable?" Click-Click asked.

"What about Delna? You'll take care of her as agreed, right?" Jax said.

Click-Click blinked. *Click. Click.* "She's beyond any help I can offer her."

"I mean, she could have been sick too. Maybe she contracted the Allohm illness."

Click-Click sighed. "I have only two gas producers. Dol is the other."

"How do you know that she didn't get it?"

"She was Penuranian. Their race is nearly immune to any airborne disease. They have the ability to endure. That is their strength."

Jax frowned but he said nothing of his doubts.

"Humans worry too much. I'll give her a proper rest," Click-Click said.

"I can't afford burial services."

"You and Dol will more than pay for costs. Now sleep."

Jax relaxed and lay back on the chamber's soft pillow. "I'm tired," he said.

"In dreams we find desire."

"This is the right thing to do, isn't it? I mean, for her."

Click-Click smiled. It was the only time Jax had seen him do that. "The red flame inside your core has diminished. A life-light glows white inside you."

Click-Click operated something. The chamber's translucent cover closed. A minute later, Jax closed his eyes and he remembered his farm and looking one last time at the two suns above before finally deciding to sign the agreement. He thought of Delna's limp body and how he had carried her all the way back to the salvage yard. But then he could remember no more. Time was losing its meaning.

Soon he would sleep a final sleep.

━━

Was it a dream? In the vacuum of black space, he watched two stars consume a lifeless planet. The two celestial bodies seemed to compete for the planet's mass, their gaseous forms growing larger until they merged and both swallowed the orb. But the planet seemed to have no regrets for what the stars had done. All three were now one.

And soon, there would be peace.

JUMP TRAINS AND SIMULTANEITY

THE CHICAGO VI Jump Station is a lively place. All those butter-and-egg men in a rush to go somewhere. The newspaper vendors barking out the headliners of stuff I don't understand or want to know about. Coffee shops slinging fresh ground bean and sizzled bacon breakfast plates. All day, they're ringing up sales from other people who got money to spare. Ka-ching! Ka-ching! Ka-ching!

I bet it's busy just like any jump station at any space city. I could probably visit the cities Chicago II, III, or IV, then make tracks for New York XVI somewhere in the Nebulous Rim at the far edge of the Oberon Galaxy. And at each city's station, I'd probably see more butter-and-egg-men in fancy suits, more newspaper vendors and more coffee shops.

And then there would be me. A thirteen-year-old boy who carries around a box of colored shoe polishes. It's funny. Even if I could afford a ticket to ride a jump train, I probably wouldn't feel like I belong to any of those places anyway.

"Ain't it exciting, Susie? Another jump train's coming in soon," I says.

I still can't help getting worked up. A jump train arrival, that experience always makes me feel...it makes me feel like I might one day find a home. Except I don't know where home is.

Susie is getting herself ready. She hitches up the garters on her long legs. Then straightens out the cigarette packs on a tray that hang from her slender neck by a red strap. She does all that while popping her chewing gum.

"Yeah? Well, you better keep your eyes on those shoes before the polish dries, shoeshine boy."

My brush starts working fast over my customer's oxfords. A deep, warm smell tells me I'm heating up the polish just right. With enough speed and friction, I'll make them shine like new copper pennies.

"That's why I like you, Susie. You keep me honest."

"You better hope I don't get rich selling cigarettes, Bobby-boy."

"You'd miss me."

She just smirks, giving me the high hat before strutting on. From my crouched point of view, all I can see going is a black saloon skirt and those beautiful movin' uprights.

The customer pays, and I do a quick cloth rub which earns me a tip. The dropped coins rattle a nearby tin cup. My dog, a wrinkly basset hound named Mister Pleats, gives a half-hearted wag of thanks before closing his eyes again.

It's 10am. The station energy systems are about fully charged up. The jump train is coming real soon.

I once asked Tom how they work—he's one of three station conductors. Jump trains are faster-than-light machines. So at both the Departing and Arriving Stations, they have powerful computers and energy systems. Both computers are syncopated—or synchronized or synco-some-thing—to mash out some numbers for what Tom called, "An agreed upon singular coordinate in time and space."

"Yeah, what's so great about that?" I says.

"Because it's the numbers that shape the same energy field at both stations. The numbers create two places in space that a jump train exists in simultaneously," Tom says.

A Joe like me, that kind of thing makes my mouth drop.

"Oh, it gets even better," Tom says, thumbs tucked into his vest pockets.

"How's that?" I says.

"It's the computer on the jump train that has to finally resolve the differences between the two locations *actual* coordinates. That's how a train arrives."

I can't say I understood it all. But the idea that I could be in two places at once makes me wonder if I'm not really sitting on my dead Mother's lap. She's rockin' me to sleep as she says that me and Mister Pleats' life is gonna' turn out just swell.

It's 10:02 on the big station clock, and the station energy systems are ready to go. You can almost sense it, like the air's gone thick and heavy-like. Even all the butter-and-egg men know it 'cause they're grinning at the station tracks like some Joe who ain't never seen a Christmas tree.

The place goes stone silent. Even if you tried to speak, no words seem to come out of your mouth. I'm smearing a dab of black paste onto a cloth, but I don't feel like I'm really movin'. Maybe I'm not. I can see the train flickering. A ghost machine jumps into several places on the track. Finally, it turns solid and stands quietly in place.

"10:02am. Arrival from Philadelphia Seven," Tom yells out over the crowd.

Lots of people are getting off. All kinds of suits. Grandparents meeting up with their families. Some scrubs coming out here for the University inside the city.

I'm looking around for a couple of shoe customers, calling out, "Shine your shoes! Shoe's shined here!" as loud as I can. Mister Pleats musters up a yelp or two to help out.

Then I see him comin' right at me. He's grinning, his black eyes shining under a pile of oiled hair. There's a buttoned double-breasted, grey suit hanging on his tall frame, and the patterned green lines that run up and down don't seem to want to be there. And he's swinging a gold pocket watch chain like he owns the place.

Hanging on his right arm is a real tomato. Wavy brown hair down to her creamy shoulders, she's all baby blues and cherry red lips that seem like they want to taste inside your soul.

"If I can see the reflection of a Methane pulse drive in those boots, there's an extra tip in it for you," the strange man says to me. He casually rests his boot on my box's stand.

The tomato pinches his cheek with long, slender fingers. "Silly, you know there's no such thing."

"And that's what they said about humans."

I hop to it, pretending not to listen to those two bumping gums. I quickly start working any dirt and mud off the strange man's boots, my second brush primed to make those boots glow, if that's what it takes.

I look over to see Mister Pleats in the tomato's arms. He's belly up to her like a baby and pawing playfully. He practically oozes when she scratches his chin and tells him that he's the cutest specimen she's ever seen.

"I found him when he was just a puppy. Nobody wanted him. I gave him a bite of my ham sandwich, and we've been friends since," I says.

"Do you have any other friends?" the strange man says.

"Nope. Just me and Mister Pleats."

The strange man studies me. I try not to notice.

"No family? No one else in this city?" he says.

"I sleep under a tarp near the loading bay, if you must know mister. Say, you ain't a cinder dick are you?"

"I'm sorry—a what?"

"A copper. They work the station undercover."

"Do I dress like one?"

I glance around. I see Freckles and a few other of Charlie Hands' street boys loitering nearby. They act like they're just talking, but I know better. They're watching me.

You see, they first wanted me to join their gang because I don't have any family. Said they'd look after me if I gave them a cut of my shoeshines. But I know what always happens to them. They eventually wind up in the hoosegow or get the final kiss off. I told them to take a walk. So now they're wanting to muscle me out of the Station.

"I ain't a stool pigeon, mister."

The strange man thumbs back at Freckles without even turning around, like he's got eyes in the back of his head. Freckles seems to notice.

"You know, you don't have to be afraid of those guys if you don't want to be," the strange man says.

"I said I ain't no stool pigeon."

"No indeed. Just a little mouse in a never-ending maze."

I don't like what he says, but I keep my mouth shut. The polish on the second boot gets so worked up, that even I'm impressed by the rich, black color. I finish up by quickly buffing it out.

The strange man smiles at me and unfolds a bill—it's a whole sawbuck! No one's ever paid me that much for a shine. Then he shoves a business card in my hand and winks.

"I could use an apprentice. And maybe you could use a new career."

The tomato puts Mister Pleats down, and the two stroll off, arm in arm. The strange man is still swinging his pocket watch chain in the other hand.

I look over the business card as they walk away. It's all white except for three words in gold lettering: *Theodore Rattletrap, Xenoarchaeologist.*

When I look up, Freckles is looking at me with this nasty grin, nodding like he knows something I don't.

I didn't think I had seen the last of Freckles, and I was right.

It's One pm. I buy myself a bag lunch over at Danny's Coffee Shop and something else for Mister Pleats. He wags his tail at me, and we both sit down somewhere out of the way on the walkway to eat. Danny can really pack a nice lunch, but his costs more because he's in the busiest part of the station. But after buying the two lunches and a cup of soda, I still have enough cash to finally buy Mister Pleats a small bed for him to sleep on at night.

I've finished my ham sandwich and about to bite into an apple when I see Freckles. He's casually walking over to me, hands in his overalls and whistling. He's alone, just trying to look like he's on the level, but he's as real as a greasy sourdough twenty.

Freckles earned his nickname because he's got so many of them that they practically cover him in one big blot. He's got red hair and little pink-rimmed eyes that bulge out. And his upturned nose and buckteeth make him look like a rabbit—a mean rabbit.

"Bobby-boy, slip me five." Freckles holds his hand out to me, but I just ignore him.

"I told you I'm not joining."

Freckles oozes up and puts his arm around me. He smells like salami and onions, a walking pile of stinky cold cut.

"Look, we're pals, so I'll be straight up with you. I saw that guy give you the sawbuck, so I'm gonna' cut you a deal. You give me the rest of the money, and I'll tell the boys to leave you alone for a whole month. What do you say?"

"I spent it all."

"You know it's just sitting in your pocket. I followed you around."

"Then you must know I bought a train ticket to Scram City, population you."

Freckles just laughs and pulls his arm around me tighter. It's starting to hurt. I try squirming out of his grip, but he's got me locked down.

"Aww, nuts!" I say.

"What was that, Bobby-boy?"

"Nuts!"

"I guess I'm just too nice. And I was trying to be friendly."

He's practically crushing me now. His smile turns downward into a leer. He's about to do something, just not sure if it's a punch to the gut or if he's got a knife.

I do the only thing I can think of. I reach up and smash the apple in his face. Chunks of red and white splatter everywhere.

Freckles lets go of me. He's cursing and wiping his eyes.

Finally, he looks at me, red faced. A very angry rabbit now. I think he's gonna' charge. I brace myself, when Mister

Pleats comes to my rescue. He clamps down on Freckles ankle, and the greaseball lets out a yowl.

"Get him off! Get him off!"

He's hopping about and trying to shake Mister Pleats off at the same time. With his lanky arms flapping about, Freckles is doing a discombobulated Charleston dance. Other people take notice, and they slow down to point and laugh. He looks ridiculous, and I can't help but laugh too. But I kind of feel bad for him, too.

"Mister Pleats, come here boy."

Mister Pleats lets go, wags his tail at me, and waddles over. I give him a scratch on the head.

"You're gonna' give me that money, Bobby-boy. And pay extra."

I look down at Freckle's pant leg, which is torn and tattered where he got bit. He's got teeth marks and small puncture wounds with only a little bit of blood. But he'd be all right.

"Tell Charlie Hands hello for me," I says.

Freckle is limping away. His face is still red, still the mean rabbit. "I know where you sleep, Bobby-boy."

At 3pm, the city dog catcher took Mister Pleats away. I felt like the Chicago Trade Building had just collapsed on my head.

The dog catcher wouldn't say who called about Mister Pleats, but he couldn't allow a dog with no license to be on the streets.

"It's a matter of protecting the public health," he says and rubs at his bristly mustache.

Then he snatches up Mister Pleats like he was a wild

bobcat or something, shovels him into the back of his hover truck, and drives off.

The only thing I can do is flatfoot it out to the Pound on West Madison Street and Monroe. So I hide my shoeshine box beneath the tarp I sleep under, and hope I can get Mister Pleats out of the hoosegow.

The Pound is about fifteen blocks away. I'm running past people—some who are yelling at me—"Watch where you're going, buddy."—but I keep on rushing. Several more street crossings, a cut through an alley, and I get there at about a quarter to four. Fortunately, the place doesn't close until six.

It's an ugly, squat building. Sad red brick that's faded by too much dirt and time, only one small window facing out, and a heavy front door that's rusting orange at the hinges. When I enter, it's not much better. The overhead light above the front desk paints the room phlegm yellow. It smells stale in here, like hardly anyone ever comes here. There's a receptionist, her short blond hair hanging down near her eyes as she works a file over her nails. It's a rough, scratchy sound—krrrrruck, krrrrruck. She doesn't even bother to look at me when the door chime announces my arrival.

I've got about eight-fifty in my pocket, and it better be enough.

"Hi," I says.

She just keeps filing her nails. I raise my voice.

"I'm here to pick up Mister Pleats. How much is it? I ain't got all day."

The receptionist still doesn't look at me. "I don't know any Mister Pleats."

"The dog catcher picked him up a couple of hours ago."

She huffs through her nose, puts down the file, and picks up a clipboard.

"A basset hound?"

I get excited. "That's him."

I pull out my money from my pocket, a wad of crumpled bills and some change.

"It's thirty-five, kid."

"What? That ain't right."

"Twenty-five for the impound fee. Ten for a new license. I don't make the rules."

She goes back to her nails. Krrrrruck. Krrrrruck.

My mind is spinning faster than a loop-the-loop. I'd be lucky to make a couple bucks in a day, but I still got to pay for food and stuff. What if it took a month to save the thirty-five? Two months?

"What happens to Mister Pleats if I take too long to get you the dough?"

"You don't want to know, kid."

Just then, the door chime announces someone else behind me. The receptionist jerks up straight in her chair, drops the file, straightens out her hair, and smiles. Yeah, she actually cracks a smile.

"Hello little mouse," a man says.

I turn to see Theodore Rattletrap and his tomato standing there. Same pile of oiled hair, same double-breasted suit, and that gold watch chain he likes to swing around. The receptionist is making whoopee-eyes at him, totally ignoring the tomato.

Rattletrap turns to her. "I was looking for a basset hound. I hear that they're an amazing specimen of what you call 'dogs.'"

The receptionist still can't take her eyes off him. "You are so lucky. One just came in. I'd be happy to show you."

"Thank you. You are the loveliest creature.'

She lets out a strained laugh that sounds like a tommy gun—ha-uh-ha-uh-ha. Then she scoops up a keycard. Rattletrap isn't even looking at me, so I'm about to say something. But the receptionist opens the door that leads back to kennel before I can get a word out. I tag along.

The dog cages are stacked two high and run along both the left and right. A lot of them have mutts inside, and they perk up when we walk by, hoping we're going to notice them.

When we get toward the end of the row, the tomato lets out a squeal of delight. That's when I see Mister Pleats at the back wall. At first he's looking kind of sad, his chin flopped down on his front paws. But he sits up, wags his tail, and gives out a deep-throated bark to let me know he's okay.

The Tomato runs her slender finger across Rattetrap's chin. "Can I have him, Teddy? He's so cute."

"This is the one. We'll take him," Rattletrap says.

The receptionist doesn't even mention the thirty-five, probably thinking Rattletrap is loaded with dough or something. She says she's going to get some paperwork and that she'll be right back.

"I'm already missing you," Rattletrap says.

The receptionist's mouth drops and she goes all goo-goo like. Then she kind of fumbles backward as she makes her way out, all the time Rattletrap is making cutesy waving gestures at her.

"Rattletrap, what are you trying to do to Mister Pleats?"

"He's my dog now, little mouse. Maybe I'll change his name."

I'm getting mad, and I can feel my legs and arms shaking. I feel like I want to cry, and I'm wiping at my eyes so I don't look like a baby.

"You're going to xeno...xenogist him, aren't you?"

Rattletrap laughs.

"I'm a xenoarchaeologist, not some human taxidermist. Do you even know what a xenoarchaeologist is?"

The tears are starting to flow now, and I can't stop them, big blobs of wet. I still remember the first day I gave Mister Pleats a bite of my ham sandwich. I shake my head.

"I study alien life forms. Like you. And Mister Pleats. I find your kind totally fascinating. But I promise you that I mean you no harm."

Rattletrap isn't making any sense. There's space cities all over the Oberon Galaxy. Jump trains coming and going from the Chicago VI Station all the time. And I've never seen little green men getting off a train, antennas poking out of their round heads as they chirp out strange words like excited birds.

"There's no such things as aliens, mister."

Rattletrap smiles.

"That's what we've said about you. Our councils thought you were a mythical creature until humans began spreading further out amongst the stars."

"You're just saying that stuff because you think I'm some dumb kid."

"I have no reason to lie."

The receptionist returns with some paperwork. She hands it to Rattletrap with another tommy gun laugh. Then she opens Mister Pleats cage, imprints his license number on one of his ears, and scans it to make sure it takes.

"He's all yours, Mister..."

"Rattletrap. Theodore Rattletrap."

"That's such a nice name. Can I call you Teddy?"

"You can call me most anything you want, just don't call me naughty."

Again, the tommy gun laugh—ha-uh-ha-uh-ha.

"I'll be sure to remember it so I can update your paperwork."

The Tomato squeals again as she takes Mister Pleats in her arms. He's pawing at her playfully, not even bothering to look at me. I start crying again.

"Mister Pleats, don't you miss your pal?" I says.

"You. Move along. Don't bother these nice people," the receptionist says.

Rattletrap and the Tomato are walking out of the kennel, Mister Pleats in the Tomato's arms. I don't know what to say or do. Then Rattletrap turns back to me.

"You still have my card, don't you little mouse?"

"Yes," I manage to blubber out.

"Then come work for me. Be my apprentice."

"Will you give me back Mister Pleats?"

Rattletrap doesn't say anything as he's about to leave with my dog.

"Where do I find you, mister? Where do I find you?"

"You will. You just will," Rattletrap calls back.

I'm sitting on a bench, back at the station, and the place just isn't the same. At 9pm, I'm usually packing up my shoeshine box, counting my money, and then I go see if Danny's got any left overs for me and Mister Pleats. But I'm just sitting there on that bench, alone, not even bothering to go over Danny's. I watch the night sweepers pushing away garbage with their bristled brooms. I feel no better than a crumb that gets swept away into a bag. A real crumb.

Susie must have finished her shift because she doesn't have the cigarette tray strapped around her neck. She's walking my way, but I don't even bother to look at her gartered legs. I don't feel like talking.

"Hey Bobby-boy. Hey, I'm talkin' to you."

"Yeah?"

She pops her chewing gum.

"Some friends of yours were looking for you. They said they got something for you."

I sit straight up. The only person who'd be looking for me is Freckles. He wants revenge for when I smashed that apple in his face. Made him look like a twit in front of a bunch of strangers. And some of Charlie Hands' street boys would make sure that I wouldn't be smashing a second apple. My night is about to get worse. Much worse.

"Geez. You should have told him to take a long walk on a short pier."

Susie puts her hands on her hips. "Bobby, don't be rude with me."

"Sorry. I'm just a little glum."

"What's a shoeshine kid got to be glum about?"

That makes me pretty mad. I want to yell at her.

"Yeah, what do you know? Nothin', that's what. You know nothin'."

"Geez, Bobby, you'd think you'd lost your best friend or something." Then she walks off in a huff, like I'm the one insulting her.

I want to say more, but I spy out Freckles searching around an empty ticket station further down. He's out here at the station's closing time because he knows that no one is going to be around to help me.

I've got to find some place to hide. I can't go back to Loading 'cause Freckles has already told me that he knows I sleep there. The only place I can think of is cargo storage. It's several levels high with stairs and elevators, and I might be able to slip into one of the units to hide behind stacked boxes.

As quietly as I can, I sneak off toward the back end of the station.

I have to creep alongside the hovering tracks because there's less light here. Just to my left is the open space of where the jump trains appear. Living in a city that exists literally in space, you eventually come to a place where the concrete stops and a deep plunge into cold vacuum happens. The only thing between everyone who lives in Chicago VI and a quick death is some sort of energy shield that protects us all. But that hasn't stopped a few crumb-bums from taking their own lives by taking a leap over some guard railing. That's not going to be me.

I can see the first set of stairs leading up to storage. My feet are clanking on the steel steps. Below, I can hear someone say that they hear something. I grab another cold handrail and continue on.

The first unit's door is locked. I jiggle at it, trying to not make any noise. There's a window, but it won't slide open. I can see boxes stacked inside. If I were to break the window, someone would hear that for sure. I go up more flights.

Two more units and still no luck. This situation is throwing me a curve. It's when I get to the fourth level one that I finally get a break. The window is cracked open because someone forgot to close it. I pull myself up and flop over to the other side. I bang my arm up a little as I land, but that's nothing compared to what Freckles will do to me if he catches me.

Then I lock the window closed from the inside and hope for the best.

It's dusty in here, small bits of stuff floating all around tied rolls marked *Cotton Batting* and some sort of insulation.

Maybe that's why someone opened the window. It makes me want to cough, but I cover my mouth when I hear clanking footsteps coming up.

"Bobby-boy, you up here?"

It's Freckles, and he's just a level below me. Someone plays at the unit's door, testing it. Then several footsteps come up to where I'm at. I slink down in a couple of rolls of cotton.

"Bobby, I found your shoeshine box."

They test the door which doesn't budge. I can see someone peeking into the window, their beady eyes scanning around. I try to get even lower when my nose starts to twitch. I want to sneeze.

"Your shoeshine box is in little itty-bitty pieces, all over the station."

Some of the boys laugh. I'm desperately fighting back the sneeze. My eyes are starting to water.

"You got nothing left, Bobby-boy. So come out."

Freckles gets quiet for a moment, listening. I'm pinching my nose, holding back the sneeze. I don't know how much more of this I can take. Fortunately, he gets tired of not hearing anything and decides to move on.

I'm holding my breath to stop myself from exploding out of my nose and I'm starting to get a headache. A minute goes by. I take a few cautious breaths. Then a few more minutes pass. Finally, the urge to sneeze passes.

I must have waited about an hour. I don't hear Freckles and the boys anymore. I sneak a peak out the window. Only empty stairs. I start to cough, getting all this dust out of my lungs—it's almost like a spasm. Then I calm myself. I listen. Nothing. No one noticed.

I really want to get out of this dust box, so I open the window again and crawl out. I land with a thud on steel platform. I hold my breath, but I still don't hear anything. Maybe Freckles got tired of searching for me. I don't think it's true. If there's any quality I can pin on him besides being mean, it's that he's really stubborn.

I look around. Then down. The coast is clear.

My luck seems to have changed for the better.

Going slower, supporting my weight on the handrails, the steel steps clank is muffled as I make my way back down. No one shouts out. Third level. Second level. Almost back on the station platform, when murmurs carry somewhere from behind me, the storage units three rows down.

So much for luck. I'll have to make my way back along the station tracks, get to the main entrance, and escape into the city.

I'm creeping along the hovering tracks, again, but this time in reverse. There's columns every ten feet, so I get to another one, press myself against it, and scan ahead for trouble. I'm moving pretty slow. It's better to be cautious.

It's when I get to the thirteenth column—yeah, lucky number thirteen—when I freeze. Ahead, a group of Charlie Hands' boys are loitering in a group, smoking cigarettes, and telling dirty jokes. They don't see me. The murmuring that I heard earlier is coming from behind, and it's getting closer. I'm trapped. My odds of just sneaking by the boys without being seen aren't good. I'm thinking about making a run past them and hoping for the best.

"Psst. Little mouse. Over here."

Goosebumps are crawling up my arm and neck. It's definitely Rattletrap's voice. But I don't see anyone.

"The tracks. I want you to jump," Rattletrap says.

"You some kind of genius? I'll fall and die."

"No you won't. I promise."

Suddenly, Rattletrap's face appears in mid-air over the

tracks. He's grinning at me. I almost yell out like I've just seen a ghost, but manage to control myself.

"You don't have much time. Jump the guard rail now."

Then his grinning face disappears again.

The murmurs are getting closer. I don't have much time. Rattletrap is right.

I make a break for the guard rail. My breath is sucked in. I will all the strength in my legs that I can manage.

I run right at the rail which is about three feet high, plant my hands, and vault over.

My eyes are closed. If I'm going to fall into space, I don't want to see it.

Someone yells out, "Hey, did you see that?"

"Yeah, I think someone's over there," someone else says.

I'm waiting to free fall. But I don't.

I can feel solid floor underneath my feet. My shoes shuffle on something that might be a knit rug of some kind as I regain my balance. I hear the soft tick of a nearby clock and a throat clearing. Odors of old paper, cedar and leather are filling my nose. The smells and sounds reminds me of the downtown library for some reason. It's where I sometimes go to hide away from my troubles and get lost in an adventure book. It's a place I can feel safe for a bit.

When I open my eyes, I'm standing in a strange room that seems to hover in space. Books cover one wall from top to bottom. Yellowed charts and diagrams, hundreds of them, cover another wall painted red. Pinned collages of unreadable figures and sketches are everywhere. There's two lounge chairs with a small table between them, the legs made of sculpted metal to look like lions.

Rattletrap is sitting on one of the lounge chairs and the Tomato is in another. She has Mister Pleats on her lap. As soon as I sees him, he wags his tail and barks.

"Isn't the control of simultaneity a marvel?" Rattletrap says.

I shake my head. I have no idea what he's talking about.

"Where are we?"

Rattletrap is studying his pocket watch, the protective flap open. "We're in a different inertial frame of reference. A room within another space and time. As far as your friends out there are concerned, we don't exist. Very complex stuff."

I turn and see Freckles and the boys scratching their head just several feet away. But they can't see me.

"So, am I trapped in here or something?"

"On the contrary. The galaxy has now opened up to you."

"I can travel without a jump train?"

"Little mouse, you do ask a lot of questions. I'll explain a little, for a little is all I still know about humans. After your great wars on Earth, humans thought it best to span out through various galaxies. Spreads out the risk of another incident, I suppose. It's also why your leaders limit your access to technology. Only approved operators are allowed the limited secrets humans possess. Can't have everyone learning too much, doing too much. That goes for jump trains, too."

The Tomato gets up and brings Mister Pleats over to me. He's wiggling with excitement and practically jumps into my arms.

"Thank you. I've missed him. But I still don't understand any of this."

"Let's take a ride," Rattletrap says.

He does something on his pocket watch. Suddenly we're standing in a jump train car. There's only one other person here, a man reading a newspaper. The headlines are dated for yesterday. He doesn't see us.

Then we appear in another car. Or maybe it's another jump train because the windows have different colored curtains. There's a family here, a father, mother, and a boy. The father is smoking a pipe. The warm cherry tobacco smell makes me think that this is how all father's smell. The boy is reading a comic book, and his mother is stroking his wavy hair. I want to be in that boy's place, letting his mother comfort me, telling me that I don't have to shine shoes anymore.

"I feel like I'm home," I says.

"In a galaxy so vast, what really is home?"

And now we jump again. I'm surrounded by stars and darkness. It seems to go on forever. I suddenly feel tiny, insignificant. Freckles is far, far away. I don't even care anymore. There is so much more out here than shoe shine boxes and a jump train station.

"What do you think of all of this?" Rattletrap says.

"Like I could find a family some day."

Rattletrap smiles at me. He puts his hand on my shoulder.

I'm still taking in all the stars that surround me. Small ones, bright ones, blue ones. Thousands of them. And further on, thousands more. I feel good inside, just like I ate the best ham sandwich in all of Chicago VI.

"It's only your imagination that will limit you, little mouse."

"I want to be your apprentice. I want to be a Xeno...Xeno..."

Rattletrap smiles again. "You have much to learn before I can call you anything."

The stars all seem to say my name, an invitation of twinkling wonders. There must be some place out there for me. It's like a happy dream.

Mister Pleats gives me a warm, wet lick.

I hug him close. For once, I feel like I could belong to something else. I could find it. Maybe I ain't such a crumb, after all.

AFTERWORD

Fiction writers are motivated to write a good story. Or at least, they wish to write something not yet read before. If this wasn't true, most wouldn't publish their work with the hope of an audience turning the pages of their book. You may think that there are exceptions to this such as writers of metafiction. The book *If on a Winter's Night a Traveler* by Italo Calvino comes to mind. It's a frame story that intentionally draws attention to the fact that the reader is trying to read a book titled, *If on a Winter's Night a Traveler*. Most readers are probably looking for an escape or for a story setup that builds to a satisfying ending for a character, myself included. I relished Calvino's experimental book as much as I might enjoy flipping through the pages of a high school chemistry text. But even so, Calvino does have a captivated fanbase and to each their own.

My point is that there is still an audience for interesting works of fiction. Stephen King's works are partly the reason I'm inspired to write fiction in the first place. *The Stand*, *The Shining* and *The Eyes of the Dragon* managed to satisfy my early bibliophilic appetite. Later, I devoured Orson Scott Card's *Ender's Game* and Patrick Rothfuss' *The Name of the Wind*. And I'm still hungry for more books.

As a writer, I'm certainly no Stephen King. And my audience is even smaller than Italo Calvino's. I'm okay with that and grateful that you've actually made it this far into *Spectrum*. It means that you've at least enjoyed some of the stories within these pages. If you did enjoy some of the stories, then I managed to do something right. Perhaps, I applied the fiction formula correctly.

A story has a formula and it's a rather basic one—a person plus a struggle equals story. But the formula is not quite as simple as it first appears. The author soon discovers complications as he or she begins constructing the scenes of characters interacting with other characters. There's the matter of ordering causally related events so that the reader understands why the characters do the things that they do. And finally, the story should have an acceptable structure. When the author types out the last page of manuscript, combines the pages into a bound novel or a collection of shorts and publishes the work for the world to consider, it's only then that the author discovers if an audience agrees that the simple formula was applied well. And the reader proves this by using a lesser mechanical determination—the reader continues to turn the pages of the book until the story finishes.

I'm waxing poetic. But I'm only explaining the mechanics of a story—person plus struggle equals story— because I'm writing this Afterword. And as a reader, you're probably curious to know why I wrote some of the stories in Spectrum. Let's start with the short, "Three Nights in Budapest," a story I wrote back in 2014.

"Three Nights in Budapest," is my earliest attempt at a character story. Andrew is unhappy with his life and he struggles to change things. As the story goes on, the reader begins to suspect that part of the problem may be Andrew. In our own cultural clichés, a person like Andrew is seen as a villain and rightly so. But it's too often that we read stories where the victim is the one who finally makes the change in life. These stories risk becoming clichés of clichés. Being one of my first stories, I wanted to be different. I began asking questions of the characters. Is the victim truly a saint? Probably not because we are human, after all. Is there good inside Andrew? He does have a motivation and it is relatable. I feel that the story events unfold in a way that we can begin to see why he does the things he does even if the results aren't for the better. My goal to write something different *and interesting* was hopefully achieved.

Stories like "Winter Sleep," "The Big Crash," "Good-bye, Sweet Mercury" and "AA for Happy the Mouse" are more experimental. When I asked an editor to read "CRDL," he told me it was gratuitous violence and refused to further critique it. I admit that it is a disturbing story but the editor missed the point. The story is a metaphor for what can happen when cynicism turns into something much darker. The metaphor *is* the character. Each of the characters in the story represent a piece of the darker nature of this metaphor. And the story poses a question in the title itself, "What does the acronym CRDL actually mean?" When the story question is answered, the reader may begin to see that the over-arching character, the metaphor, is harming itself and not willing to stop the pain. But is there ever really an answer to such questions? Maybe not. Humans truly can be unusual and unpredictable.

My favorite types of stories have a world-shattering event take place and someone must address it before further chaos breaks out. J.R. Tolkien's *The Lord of the Rings* is a great example. Sauron has returned to dominate Middle Earth and it's up to Frodo Baggins to toss the One Ring into the fiery Cracks of Doom. The books kept me up into the early morning hours and caused self-inflicted grogginess during middle school class periods. But such threats can happen in sci-fi too. In "Edge of Twilight," aliens are making their way to Earth by ingesting one terraformed planet after another. Still being somewhat experimental for a short(er) story, I don't always write the story from Kelvin's point of view. By changing characters, I feel that the reader gets a better understanding of what's going on. And I still manage to stay within the story structure because Kelvin does manage to save the day at the very end.

"Jump Trains and Simultaneity" comes closest to being a milieu story. Bobby hasn't actually explored any place just yet because he's still stuck at the train station. But he doesn't consider the location home and the ending hints at some-thing more. To be honest, I feel like there is much more story waiting for this character. Perhaps the concept of simultaneity will provide a framework that leads to an ongoing sci-fi series. Maybe Bobby and Mister Pleats will continue to roam through the universe in search of some place where he can finally kick his feet up and be content.

But even if there is an underlying formula for some or all of the stories in this book, there is one thing I can never write into the pages—the reader's application or interpreta-tion of themes. This is where the book truly becomes unpre-dictable. Like the characters in this book, you experience the world in your own way. And those experiences shape the way you interpret events in these stories. Does Markey VI in "The Sound of Blue" truly experience what it means to be human? And what was the apocalyptic event that destroyed civilizations? Those are questions that I don't answer. Only you can resolve them.

ABOUT THE AUTHOR

Michael's most recent story, "The Sound of Blue" won Silver Honorable Mention from Writers of the Future. This has fueled his passion for writing fiction.

He lives in Ohio with his wife, three dogs and two cats. He writes because his cat hates him. You can find out what he's up to at www.authormichaelduda.com.

facebook.com/MDudaAuthor
twitter.com/MDuda_author

The Sound of Blue: Four Science Fiction Stories